My Movie Memoir
Screenplay Novel

(and other disjointed storytelling techniques)

for my family,
who allowed me to tell our story

My Movie Memoir Screenplay Novel

(and other disjointed storytelling techniques)

starring **Betts Keating**

RELEVANT PAGES PRESS

RELEVANT PAGES PRESS

Published by Relevant Pages Press, Charleston, South Carolina.

Publisher can be contacted at www.relevantpagespress.com
or relevantpagespress@gmail.com.

Song lyrics for *You're Still God*, from the album *Air* (2008), used by permission
from Margaret Becker. All rights reserved.

Cover design and interior layout by Betts Keating Design.
Author photo by Anna McSwain.

ISBN-10: 0692587926
ISBN-13: 978-0692587928

Printed in the United States of America.

CONTENTS

Mountains tremble
when you least expect
I am shaking, I'm a mess, but
You're still God
You're still God

~ Margaret Becker

THE PREVIEWS

"So, I wrote this book" is something I never thought I would ever hear myself say. Honestly, I'm the last person who thought I would ever be writing a book. Even now, as I'm writing this book I'm resistant to the idea of… writing this book. I'm reluctant to share a piece of myself; on paper or in any other type of permanent documentation. I'm actually a very private person. I know, how can I say that? When the pages of this book filled with stories all about me actually make that statement a lie? But it's true.

I have a group of dear friends, sisters really, that I know from my college days. Even after all these years we still get together once a year for a "girls weekend." I look forward to spending time with these ladies all year long. Somehow, we have figured out a way to keep the bubble of those friendships safe, even while the world around us has tried to make it burst.

One year, as a gesture of gratitude to our host, one of my friends put together a beaded charm bracelet. You know the kind with the sentimental beads and charms that somehow all go together and represent all the different events of your life? Yes, those. Anyway, my friend put together a bracelet with random beads and a set of charms - one charm for each friend in our group. My charm was a puzzle piece. Everyone, including me, enjoyed a giggle over my friend's perfectly placed insight. She nailed it.

I know, I could have been insulted, but I wasn't. I was relieved to discover it's not only me that finds me confusing.

Even though I don't mean to be mysterious, I suppose in some ways, I have enjoyed the fact that other people see me as a puzzle. I grudgingly admit I am prone to keep people guessing. "Open" is not a word people usually use to describe me. Usually, it's something more like "challenging." I don't always make it easy for friends to be part of my life. Even those who know me well might find themselves scratching their heads when I do something completely out of character. Like how I have spent my whole life being shy, self-conscious, and private and yet here I am writing an extremely personal book all about me. Yeah, I think it's weird too.

However, there are times in life when life itself intervenes and forces you to do something you would otherwise think impossible. That's what happened to me. Life intervened and gave me a story.

I'm a big fan of stories. I love to read, I'm a total TV junkie, and I love to watch movies (probably why I ended up marrying an actor). Sure, it is a form of escapism and not at the top of the list of intellectual endeavors, but I'm totally addicted. I can't resist it. Even if the book/show/movie is terrible, I still have to read/ watch view it. And I most definitely need to see how it ends. I can't let it go. I have to experience the whole story. That is, of course, as long as that story is about someone else. As long as all those extremely personal details are not my extremely personal details. As long as that story is not about me. Write a book about myself? No thank you.

As I contemplated the thought of putting anything down on paper I was bombarded on all sides with little messages that I was on the right track. Over and over again I kept hearing the message... speak, tell, share.

That was the year the Starbucks holiday campaign was "Stories are gifts. Share." Every time I saw a cup of coffee, there it was, seemingly screaming out at me: Time to share.

My husband wore a t-shirt that year with the words "Every story deserves to be told..." written across the back. Every time I saw it, the message was clear: Time to tell your story.

Finally, I was drawn over and over to a Bible verse in 2 Corinthians 4, that says, "It is written: 'I believe therefore I have spoken'. With that same spirit of faith we also believe and therefore speak." It's tough to deny it when it's right there in front of you in black and white, in the Bible. How was I supposed to argue with that? Newsflash: I couldn't.

I chose a slightly disjointed way to tell this story so don't get thrown by it. Technically, it's a memoir. It's the story of some events that happened to me during a particularly tough time in my life. The stuff happened, I survived it. That's the story.

Sometimes, it may also seem like a work of fiction. I wish it were, but it's not. While I did take some creative license in the way I told the story, the events that take place are actually true. The people and places are real, not figments of my imagination. I was, however, relying on my memory for guidance, so I can't completely confirm the reliability of my source.

Sometimes this book may also seem like a movie. I couldn't help it. When I tried to find a comfortable way to tell my story (as if spilling your guts for all the world to see is ever comfortable), my memoir kept getting interrupted by movie scenes playing in my head. I found myself anxiously watching to see what would happen next, as if I had switched on some kind of internal DVD. Stepping "out" of my own life to watch from the audience gave me the freedom to tell the story of what I saw, rather than try to describe what I felt. The distance was a necessary tool. I used it liberally and with absolutely no discretion.

I couldn't ignore the memoir that struggled to be written like a work of fiction. I also couldn't ignore the movie scenes that struggled to be written like a book. That's why sometimes the story is a book, but also sometimes a movie, and also sometimes a memoir.

It's a puzzle. It just is.

I invite you to share in these moments of my life with the hope that you will recognize something of yourself in this story. During my long, tough, sad season I felt lost, discouraged, and misunderstood. Even though I was surrounded by people who tried to love me through it (for example the group of friends I mentioned above), I still felt lonely and sometimes even abandoned. It is my hope that by reading this book you will discover that you aren't.

Enjoy the show.

If you are one of those people who normally skips the previews, you might want to consider making an exception in this case. Thanks.

CHAPTER ONE
I LOVE NYC

The lights in the theater have dimmed. The previews are complete. You just finished eating your fifth or maybe sixth handful of popcorn. You are nicely settled into your chair. A drink in the cup holder next to you. One foot propped up on your seat. Arms wrapped around your leg. Chin resting on your knee. You're all set. You're ready to watch a good book... wait a minute, I mean read a good movie... wait a minute, I mean read and watch a story unfold. This is the beginning...

OPEN: EXTERIOR NEW YORK CITY/
EARLY AFTERNOON/HUDSON RIVER

MUSIC: something stereotypically New York
(jazzy with big horns)

We follow a helicopter shot moving quickly across water at a dizzying speed. The afternoon sun glimmers off the water of the Hudson River.

CONTINUE along the Hudson River until the steel girders at the bottom of a large gray bridge

(George Washington Bridge) come into view.

CAMERA MOVES up the steel structure of the bridge all the way to the top of the tall towers holding the suspension cables.

CONTINUE into the sky, staying focused on the bridge, until from above we see four lanes packed full of cars slowly inching across the long expanse.

CAMERA pauses briefly.

CAMERA begins a slow decent toward the cars until finally it focuses on a tiny, yellow moving van working its way slowly across the bridge.

Hold on VAN.

VAN exits bridge and drives south along the Hudson River.

CUT TO: from van's passenger point of view (POV), CAMERA looks out the window of van. New York in all its glory passes by.

VAN finally stops in front of a New York brownstone on a cross-street on the Upper West Side of New York City.

CUT TO: from street point of view (POV), door of van opens and YOUNG WOMAN tumbles out (only show door).

CLOSE UP: of the young woman's running shoe-clad foot as it touches down onto a NYC sidewalk. (as big as if she were reaching the summit of a mountain, or landing on the moon)

CAMERA moves up to YOUNG WOMAN's face. She stretches, sighs, and smiles contentedly. Driver's side door closes.

YOUNG MAN/HUSBAND circles around from the driver's side of van to stand next to YOUNG WOMAN.

YOUNG WOMAN grabs his hand.

They stand in comfortable unity as the city noise continues around them.

CAMERA circles couple in close up, city noise and chaos blur behind their faces which are full of excitement and anticipation. After full circle, CAMERA STOPS on YOUNG WOMAN. She looks up to sky, closes her eyes and breathes deep.

                    VOICE-OVER/YOUNG WOMAN
                          (sigh)
                         Home.

YOUNG WOMAN looks at HUSBAND and he smiles at her in understanding, as if he is able to read her mind. They are united in their feeling. This is home.

FADE TO NEXT SCENE

OPEN: EXTERIOR UPPER WEST SIDE BROWNSTONE
SAME DAY

MUSIC: Cheery and full of adventure

CAMERA follows couple through unpacking montage.

YOUNG WOMAN and HUSBAND playfully carry boxes,
chatting, joking, excited.

We see them enter and exit through a garden
gate that leads down a flight of three stairs
to a small court yard. They pass by two large
windows covered with ornate iron grill work.
They enter through another iron gate located
under the steps to the above ground entrance,
go through the front door, down a small hallway
and then hang a right into a one-room, studio
apartment. The light from the large windows
make the studio sunny and inviting which is good
because the room is tiny. Only big enough for a
futon and a table. The kitchen is the size of a
closet. The bathroom is only slightly larger. (@
200 square feet total)

Finally, they put everything into place. It
doesn't take long, they didn't bring a lot of
stuff with them. When they are done they plop
onto the futon satisfied. Happy. Done.

HUSBAND picks up pile of take-out menus and
shows them to YOUNG WOMAN. She points to one.
He picks up phone to order take-out.

YOUNG WOMAN leans back against futon and smiles.

FADE TO BLACK

Everything came into perfect focus the moment I poured myself out of that tiny yellow moving van and placed my foot onto that NYC sidewalk. The agony of sitting for so long in a cramped, uncomfortable truck cab totally evaporated. I could not comprehend it, but finally I was home.

My husband and I had taken the circuitous route from where we lived in the south to our new home in the big city. We made stops at both of our childhood homes in North Carolina and Georgia in order to drop off the last of the belongings we would be leaving behind. We had sold or given away almost everything we owned, including our car. I didn't mind. I was not one to collect clutter.

There is a story from my childhood my family loves to tell about me and my trusty bag of "tangs." That's what I called the pillowcase full of my belongings I took with me... everywhere. To the best of my recollection, my bag included a ceramic statue of a young girl holding a cat, a couple of books, a blanket, my stuffed animal Piglet (my favorite) and a hairbrush. All very vital to my survival as far as I knew. Apparently, even then I was a girl on the move. I was on my way... to somewhere else... and I didn't need a lot of belongings to drag along behind me. See? I was already a New Yorker.

From the moment my husband and I arrived, everything about New York City was immediately familiar to me, except I'd never been there before. In some strange way, I felt like I was connected to roots growing beneath my feet. I felt solid, grounded, and secure with no explanation for why. As far as I know, no one in my family had ever lived in NY. As far as I know, my family never even passed through Ellis Island. Yet, there I was, completely comfortable in unfamiliar surroundings.

Concrete was everywhere. On the ground, on the buildings, and even on the window sills. Everywhere. Somehow I found all of that cold hard concrete comforting instead of numbing. Buildings rose up from what used to be dirt, but the soil had long been buried by, you guessed it, more concrete. Solid, steady, cold, boring, gray concrete. I know it's weird, but I thought it was beautiful.

The only evidence of something green was the urban friendly trees arranged strategically up and down both sides of the narrow one-way street. If someone had a ruler, they could have measured the exact distance between each one. They lined up perfectly. Thank goodness, because I would have hated to pull out my jack hammer in order to replant the one that was out of place (that's a silent high five to all over-achieving perfectionists - you know you were lining up those trees too). I couldn't help but wonder how these trees were able to grow in what was no longer earth? How did they find a way to sprout in an area smaller than a flower bed? The nutrients they needed were buried deep down, under all that concrete. They had strong roots.

I knew a little something about strong roots. I had some myself. I came to this place from a tiny, TINY town nestled high in the mountains of western North Carolina. It was a one-stop-light affair with minimum amounts of concrete and an overabundance of trees. It was very scenic and all of those mountains and trees satisfied my childhood love for climbing, but it couldn't hold my attention forever. I was a girl with a pillowcase. I was on the move.

I attended the only school available to attend. One town. One school. The entire student enrollment was a total of 400 students, K-12. My best friend's mom was the entire high school math department, my dad was the science. My graduating class was a whopping 33 students. Like I said, tiny.

In the winter, it was a sleepy little town with a population of around 2,000. In the summer, it was a booming metropolis of ten times that size. People loved to spend their summers there. The more outsiders learned how great a summer in a remote town in the mountains could be, the more my town grew. It now has three stop lights. *Three!*

Over time it changed from a sleepy little remote mountain town into a highly desired resort community. This created a uniquely unbalanced coexistence. It became a place where farms backed up to golf courses, where electricians and carpenters found work building multi-million dollar homes, and where the locals kept the town going so the visitors could vacation.

I was one of those locals. I grew up on one of those farms. I actually got up at five a.m. and milked cows. I planted gardens, gathered wood, and collected eggs. I have the hen-pecked scars to prove it. I spent more time in a barn shoveling more piles of barn animal material than I ever care to remember. Yes, it was as smelly as it sounds.

My family planted themselves into the soil of that town and dug in deep with hard work and endurance. The land we lived on was hearty. The work we did to maintain it made us tough. My grandparents lived less than a quarter of a mile down the dirt road. My aunt and uncle another quarter. I grew up surrounded by other aunts, uncles, cousins and family friends. Roots.

I don't get it either. How did someone like me end up somewhere like New York? How did a tree lined street surrounded by tall buildings made out of concrete appear as gorgeous to me as a mountain vista? How did I find this hard, gray place beautiful? I don't know. The irony was at the same time perplexing and comforting. Suddenly I knew why I always felt like I didn't fit in, like something in me was missing. I may have been raised a farm girl, but in that moment I discovered I was a city dweller at heart.

Really? Me? Are you sure?

Yes, me.

ENTER: BETTS KEATING - THE STAR OF THE SHOW
Character Bio/Background Info
23 years old. Brown hair. Brown eyes. Married.

Raised on a farm. Tough, hard working, very disciplined. Will fall over in exhaustion before giving up on something that needs to get done. Believes any problem can be solved with enough hard work.

Athletic. Very competitive. Played volleyball, basketball, softball and ran track in high school (yes, all of them) and played volleyball in college. In NY, played club volleyball, basketball and roller hockey for fun. Loves to run. No, really, really loves to run. Good student.

Not worldly but smart... okay, okay NERDY. Liked doing homework. Loves to read. Creative. Artistic. Crafty. Likes to write poetry.

Majored in Communications in college, but in a fit of over-zealous, over-achiever-ism minored in Journalism, Creative Writing, Art, and Photography (yes, all of them). Settled on a career in graphic design.

Independent. Why ask someone for help when you can do it better yourself?

Has integrity. Honest. Will chase down someone who drops a dollar rather than keep it for herself.

Socially awkward. Shy. Private. Modest. Prefers to sit in the back of the room or in the corner. Doesn't like large social gatherings. Feels awkward making superficial small talk.

Finds it hard to express what she is thinking and feeling. Often wears a mask to hide emotions. Believes in stoicism but has an alter ego she refers to as her "inner two-year-old." All that stoicism has to leak out somewhere.

Sarcastic with a dry sense of humor. Sometimes uses humor as defense mechanism.

Healthy. Eats well. Doesn't like to take medicine. Doesn't drink (much). Doesn't do drugs (except for the occasional prescription kind). Doesn't like going to doctors.

Adventurous but not dangerous. Loves to climb - trees, mountains, playground equipment - has been known to swing from barn rafters. Has enjoyed many a day gazing down at a plummeting waterfall, or out at a mountain view, or looking down from the tallest tree branch. Does not have a death wish, but enjoys testing her strength.

Brave but not rebellious. Obedient but not rigid. Able to see the shades of gray between the black and white.

Doesn't like labels, stereotypes or generalizations. Feels strongly it's not nice to call people (any group of people) names.

Has faith. Believed in God at an early age and takes her faith seriously but is not obnoxious about it (well at least not all the time). Perfectly okay giving other people the space they need to come to their own conclusions. Has an inner voice she listens to - her spiritual compass (not the same voice as her bratty inner two-year-old).

Got all that? Confused? Me too. Even I would find it annoyingly hard to be my friend (thanks to those of you who became my friend anyway. You know who you are...).

I wanted to be all the things that made me *me*, but I didn't want to stick out, or draw attention to myself. Like a chameleon, I tried to blend. Unfortunately, that left me in a place where I felt like I was a little bit of everything but nothing specific. I often felt like I was a little too nerdy to totally fit in with the jocks, a little too creative for the brains, a little too athletic for the artists and a little too goody, goody for everyone. It felt like I fit in everywhere and nowhere at the same time. Bummer.

It didn't help that I was uncontrollably shy and extremely self-conscious. I hated to be in front of crowds (still do). I did not like to talk about myself (still don't). That is until those times when I *had* to. Then I would put on my mask and step in front of the crowd and "perform" as needed. Even though my voice was cracking and my knees were shaking, I would do what was needed rather than be labeled "difficult."

By contrast, if a friend took the time to look past my defenses, the dam would break. Usually, I was a blubbering idiot when I would try to talk about even the simplest of things. My insides would flow out uncontrollably like snot after a good cry. No matter how hard I tried, I couldn't seem to find a balance between being completely closed off and uncontrollable verbal diarrhea. How many friends like that would you like to have? None? Yeah, I get that.

Even though I felt a bit lonely at times, I did have friends, classmates, teammates, siblings, cousins, etc. Some of those people I consider my friends to this day. I grew up in a small town. There's an automatic connection in that fact that binds us all to each other forever. It never goes away.

Still, I felt cut off from the world around me. Managing a farm is hard work. It rarely left room for trips, or sleepovers or parties, or outings. The responsible thing, the right thing, was to be home to make sure all the things that needed to get done… got done. This gave me a fantastic work ethic, but was a real hindrance to my social life.

My major escape was on the playing field. As long as I could shoot, spike, catch or run, my awkward shyness didn't apply. As a special bonus, I was excused from farm chores when (and *only* when) I had practice. I found I absolutely preferred the challenge of athletic endeavors over the stench of animals. I mean, who wouldn't?

My need to go unnoticed showed up in other places too. Once, when a friend teased me about the way I pronounced the word "light," it stuck with me. I realized people have a funny thing called accents attached to their voices. Since I didn't want to be labeled based on how I talked, I spent the next couple of years listening to national news broadcasts and mimicking the sounds I heard. With my stubborn will and unswerving determination, I taught myself how to speak without a discernible dialect. Once again, like a chameleon I changed my stripes. I applied this technique often. It worked.

The down side to all the "sacrifice your own feelings and desires for the sake of anonymity" philosophy, is it taught me to set aside my emotions for the sake of pragmatism. Since I was an over-achieving perfectionist, I took that concept and expanded it into a major life practice. I rarely showed on the outside exactly how I was feeling on the inside, particularly in regards to my emotions. I was really good at stuffing those down into oblivion. This is not always a bad thing. It did have its perks.

For example, when I was around 9 or 10 years old, one of the bulls on our farm got loose and my dad and I were the only ones around that day who could "corral" him back into his pen. He was running around willy nilly fully enjoying his freedom… until he decided I looked like a fun toy to throw around. Suddenly he charged at me. Yes, I almost peed my pants.

"STAND STILL!" my dad, who was all the way on the other side of the field, yelled.

What? Stand still? Even though a bull was racing, full speed, right at me? Are you kidding? *Why in the world would I agree to do that?!*

But I did.

I believed my dad knew what he was talking about. He had experience. I was just a kid. Besides, my dad spoke with a parental kind of firmness that makes a child say "Yes sir!"

I obeyed. I stood still.

From where I stood, my dad appeared to know exactly what he was doing. Little did I know he is also good at setting aside fear for the sake of action. He was too far away from me to save me. He was no match for a charging bull. All he could do was yell for me to stand still. I'm sure it was equally agonizing for him to watch as it was for me to experience. Well, maybe not quite....

While my ability to stay still while a wild animal charged toward me was probably 80% frozen fear, and 10% blind childlike obedience, the other 10% was the part of me I like to call the rational big picture girl. That girl could set aside fear and panic and get results. That girl could realize that standing still was the better course of action. She knew that if I ran I would be prey. She knew standing still would make the bull lose interest. I had never actually proven this fact, but I stood still anyway. I knew it was the right thing to do. I had faith.

The bull stopped inches from me. I'll never forget the way his nostrils flared as he stared me down. He dared me to run, dared me to play his game. I didn't. He eventually became so bored by my lack of engagement that he turned around and calmly walked back towards the barn. He met my dad halfway and had become so docile my dad easily led him back into his pen. There was no use running around willy nilly anymore. It was no longer any fun.

I internalized this moment. It defined me. Overcoming my emotional reaction to fear had saved my life. Point taken.

It can be a good thing to be emotionally detached so that an action can be completed. Often times, it can save you from immeasurable pain. It's certainly handy when dealing with wild animals. It's just not good to stay this stoic all the time. That was the balance I was missing.

All that inner turmoil had to go somewhere and so enters my inner two-year-old. She often said in my head what I was incapable of saying out loud. She was (and sometimes still is) simmering just below the surface, waiting for the right moment to pitch an ungodly fit. Sometimes she is seething with burning anger. Even now, she is still a little bit angry at the bull for charging me in the first place. *What had I ever done to him?*

She cries for me on the inside when I can't quite figure out how to cry on the outside. She's able to love big, hug huge, and roll around in the mess without being concerned about what people might think. Unfortunately, allowing a spoiled two-year-old to be your inner alter ego means at some point she has to grow up.

I wasn't sure how to turn all of that disjointed variety into a grown up. I never could quite find a place to land. Until I moved to New York. Even overly spiritual, creative, athletic, nerdy, independent, goody-two-shoes introverts fit in NY. In fact, maybe New York is the ONLY place an overly spiritual, creative, athletic, nerdy, independent, goody-two-shoes introvert would ever fit. All I know is I did. I fit. I had found my place in the world. Finally.

In New York, I had an entire world open up to me and I couldn't wait to go out and explore. Every neighborhood was like its own little town and every day I discovered somewhere new. I had never heard so many different languages or been exposed to so many different cultures. The buildings were tall, the museums were fascinating, the food was delicious, and the avenues were bursting with constant activity. I saw New York through rose colored glasses, so even the smells didn't bother me. Well, at least not all of the time. I thought the constant noise was soothing.

I loved how I could be in the middle of a large crowd and yet feel like no one was invading my space. I could stand next to someone on the elevator and share a ride without once crossing into the invisible line between us. I could be smushed like a sardine in a subway car and still feel like I had space. I found myself so perfectly at peace with urban anonymity. It was liberating for a small town girl who was private but who had spent her life in a place where everyone knew everything about her, *all the time*. Some people have to prepare themselves for that urban kind of lifestyle. I found it perfectly natural.

I soaked in every second. I remember every moment of it. I loved it. It was my home. No matter how hard I try, I have never really been able to leave it behind. The city seeped into my soul and will forever be a part of me.

I know not everyone in the world is supposed to move to NYC, but I do wish this moment was a more common experience. I was given a unique opportunity. I got to go home here on earth. I had no idea how crucial it was going to be for me - to be here, in this city, in this time. I needed this chance to find this home because I needed this chance to find me. The real me. Somewhere buried deep down inside was the woman I needed to become. I just had to find her.

Grab your popcorn, it's time to go back to the movie...

OPEN: EXTERIOR/INTERIOR NEW YORK CITY
MULTIPLE CAMERA SHOTS

MUSIC: continue jazzy feel, quintessential NY

CAMERA follows YOUNG WOMAN in a montage of short clips enjoying all NYC has to offer. She hits all of her favorite places.

Her favorite diner, her favorite coffee shop, her favorite lunch spot, bookstore, museum.

We see her standing in front of amazing paintings, sculptures and giant Egyptian statues at the Metropolitan Museum of Art. Later she walks through the cherry trees that line the street behind it.

She walks in front of the Museum of Natural History, strolls through Strawberry Fields, roller blades through Central Park, sits in front of the Plaza.

She sits on the steps of the Bethesda Fountain, visits the statue of Hans Christian Anderson and watches the toy boats.

She walks down the city streets, smiling, almost skipping. There are people in her way, but she doesn't care. She skirts around them with the graceful agility of an athlete. She is purposeful but gracious, unafraid to let someone else go first.

She squeezes between the hordes to get on the subway and chuckles to herself at the amount of jockeying going on between the masses.

She goes to work at the ad agency smiling. She comes home smiling. She's not worried about getting where she wants to go, she's enjoying the ride.

She stands at the windows at the top of the World Trade Center and soaks in the skyline. The memories of climbing to the tops of trees, the tops of mountains, the top of anything in her childhood come back to her and this comfort shows on her face.

Being up high is natural for her. It gives her perspective. It helps her to be able to see. The sun sets and the lights of the big city turn on.

                    VOICE-OVER/YOUNG WOMAN
                       (contented sigh)
                          Magic.

FADE TO BLACK

CHAPTER TWO

GUY IN WEIRD SHIRT
AND PINK BATHROOMS

OPEN: INTERIOR/SMALL NYC APARTMENT - DAY

Different apartment from opening scene, an upgrade. Now a small one-bedroom instead of a studio.

TITLE: Five Years Later

CAMERA moves across a hardwood floor and slowly rises to show the entire room of a small living area in a NYC apartment (living area because there is no division between living room, entry way, dining room and kitchen).

It has a small hallway with a bathroom that is as small as a hall closet. It also has a separate bedroom. About 450 square feet including bedroom and bath.

As the camera rises, we see a cheap green futon

and a beige, boring area rug and an "eclectic" decorating style. This is the home of a young married couple living as two artists in NYC. It's homey, but cheap.

CAMERA pans to the left to a small door that opens into a bathroom. Door is opened halfway giving partial view. Inside we see YOUNG WOMAN standing at the bathroom sink. The tiny space is tiled in an obnoxiously bright bubble gum pink with matching pink bath and sink.

The young woman is staring down at the sink with shock on her face and in her body language. The camera stays on this moment as if we just pushed the pause button.

                    VOICE-OVER/YOUNG WOMAN
                         (whisper)
                          Uh oh.

HOLD on YOUNG WOMAN. After a beat...

                       YOUNG WOMAN
                      Uhhhh, HONEY!
              You should come look at this!

HUSBAND comes running from kitchen/dining/living area.

                         HUSBAND
                      Look at what?

YOUNG WOMAN holds pee stick up to face camera.

                    YOUNG WOMAN
                      This.

CUT TO: Close up of stick. It has a HUGE neon plus sign. (emphasize moment like winning the jackpot on a pinball machine)

BACK TO: shot of both.

He looks at her. She looks at him.
They can't decide whether or not to be happy.

FADE TO: Black Screen

TITLE: PREGNANT pause.

FADE BACK TO: shot of both.

                  YOUNG WOMAN/HUSBAND
                     (together)
                 We're having a baby.

FADE TO BLACK

  I entered into motherhood reluctantly. I had waited several years into my happy marriage to even approach the subject of children or family. I was so happy with our life in NY, that I didn't want to rush into anything more. I was content but probably more accurately, I was complacent. I guess my biological clock started ticking because, at some point, my husband and I gave the idea of having a baby a try.

After about 18 months of "leaving it up to nature" with no results, I began to think maybe a family wasn't in the mix for us.

My husband and I had been married for five years. I was about to be 29 and he was almost 33. Since we couldn't seem to get the pregnancy thing to work, we decided to put our plans for a family on hold. We decided now would be a good time for my husband to go to grad school.

The plan was for him to get his masters through a three year program, get a job, and THEN start a family. It sounds almost dreamy, doesn't it? So full of hope were we, all set with our "plans." As we all know, plans get... um... interrupted....

My husband (he's an actor, remember?) enrolled in grad school in September. He had decided to obtain a Masters of Fine Arts in Acting with the goal of someday being able to teach. Don't assume the adage "those who can't do, teach" is always true because in this case, it was not. This was supposed to be the back-up plan. The preparation move for the inevitable later. It made sense... on paper.

At this time in our marriage, I was the main bread winner. I had a good steady flow of gigs as a freelance graphic designer, and I loved my work. I had been supporting us financially for years, so my husband could work odd jobs and continue to audition and perform. This system worked great for both of us. I loved the stability, and he needed the freedom.

However, we knew the winds of change were coming. Trying to get pregnant and failing had given me new insight. Balancing a career that involved non-stop deadlines with motherhood was something I did not want to do. I made a choice. I continued working to bring home the bacon, and my husband went to grad school. We agreed, the sacrifice of the now would be a huge payoff later. So how did we end up in a pink bathroom staring at a pregnancy test? Well, if you've got a moment I'll be happy to tell you. Time for a flashback.

We have one of those super cute "how did you meet?" stories. The kind that can make your teeth hurt. It is a story that is uniquely ours and so, we tell it occasionally, and remember how crazy it is we got married at all. I mean I just told you how much I like to be alone, right? Well, he changed all that for me. Without him, I would probably still be all closed up and private. Without him, I never would have moved to NYC. And yes, obviously, without him, I never would have been standing in a tacky pink bathroom staring at a pregnancy test.

As we have already established, my husband is an actor. In a twist of fate, it is because of this career choice that we met. I grew up in a small town, but it was a small town with a theater. When I was younger, the summer theater season was a well- known, popular attraction. So much so that they collaborated with a nearby university and offered something similar to a internship to theater students who were willing to spend a summer in a small mountain resort town. I don't think anyone begged the students to participate. Even though, I don't really connect with where I grew up, it really is a "lovely" place.

One summer, I was home from college and working the multiple summer jobs I always worked throughout my entire stay in this tiny town. Again, the town is nice. It's me who's got the issues.

This particular summer, I was working in the early morning making chocolates for a local gourmet candy and ice cream shop. After I delivered all of those chocolate covered goodies, I headed over to the recreation center where I was a day-camp counselor for five and six year olds. In the afternoon, I spent a few hours in the gym working through my off-season workout for my college volleyball team. Finally, I went back to the ice cream shop to work through the late afternoon and evening as a cashier.

It was a pretty grueling schedule, but I never noticed. I was young and working my way through college. That history of descending from strong, hard working mountain stock showed up, yes, but in a good way. Besides, that's what locals do, remember? They work hard so the tourists can vacation.

Occasionally, my boss at the ice cream shop would arrange to stay open late so the actors from the theater could come over after their show. Which they did, often.

It was a cool, summer night in the mountains with a sky full of stars and a cool breeze rustling through the trees. Perfect conditions really, except I hadn't been outside to enjoy a single moment of it since I came in to work the evening shift around 6:00 pm.

I gotta say, most of the time, I didn't mind working until 11:00 or so at night. However, I had been up working since six that morning, so I was looking forward to some well-earned sleep. It was this exhaustion that allowed me to let my guard down when my future husband walked in.

He had previously been reluctant to join in with the ice cream brigade but on that night, he decided to participate. He walked in the door and in an instant I realized my life was never going to be the same. I took one look at him and I knew, he was either going to be the love of my life or he was going to break my heart into a million pieces.

It was a pretty uncomfortably romantic place to be for a pretty unromantic realist. I even had goosebumps. I did not like this, not one bit, and yet I couldn't stop the call of my heart. *Play it cool girl, just play it cool.*

"Can I take your order?" I said through my well established exterior facade (sometimes the ability to smush down your emotions comes in handy).

"Uh, yeah. I'll take a chocolate milkshake," he said.

"What?!?" his friend standing next to him said. "I don't think you get how this place works! You can put anything you want into your ice cream. Chocolate, caramel turtles, fruit, nuts... anything!"

"Oh, I can have anything I want?" my future husband answered. "Great. I'll take a chocolate milkshake."

So the love of my life is a little bit stubborn. Adorable, but stubborn and a little, okay, okay, a *lot* cocky.

Hmmm..... nope, don't care. Still so cute.

As I finished writing the ticket for his order, I quietly said, "Sir, I need your name."

That's what you do in cute little gourmet ice cream shops in small resort towns. You actually write down and call people's names when their order is ready. It's very quaint. The tourists love it.

Unfortunately, the love of my life was also rambunctiously loud and too busy laughing with his friends to hear my shy voice. He completely ignored me.

Again I said, "Sir, I need your name."

Again he ignored me. Sigh.

One more time, "SIR, I NEED YOUR NAME!" (translation: Hey! Look at me! Notice me! Please?) Nothing. Completely ignored. *What's a girl gotta do to get a name out of this guy?*

That's when his friend said, "Just write down 'guy in weird shirt' and we will all know who you mean."

"Guy in weird shirt" was wearing a very dated tie-dye tee in a multitude of colors. A one of a kind really. He was wearing it with striped shorts for Pete's sake! And still, I thought he was cute. Go figure. I played along and wrote down "guy in weird shirt" on the ticket because regardless of how many times my stomach was doing a flip-flop, I still had a sense of humor.

My boss at the time also played along because when the infamous chocolate milkshake was ready, he promptly called out, "Guy in weird shirt your milkshake is ready.... guy in weird shirt?"

Oh, boy. *Everyone* thought that was *so* funny. Every single one of his friends laughed hysterically, and pointed at him saying, "Ha, ha, ha! That's for Thomas!"

Oh, his name is *Thomas*. Got it.

And finally, that's when he looked at me.

Take another bite of popcorn, it's time to go back to the movie...

OPEN: INTERIOR/QUAINT ICE CREAM SHOP

Has light pink walls with purple trim, full of candy, chocolates, fresh waffle cones and happy noise

CAMERA focuses on face of young man as he looks at young woman for the first time.

CAMERA toggles back and forth between two.

> VOICE-OVER/HE SAYS
> (pleasant surprise)
> Hey, when did you get here?

> VOICE-OVER/SHE SAYS
> (smug)
> What do you mean?
> I've been here the whole time.

> VOICE-OVER/HE SAYS
> (confident smile)
> Hi.

```
                    VOICE-OVER/SHE SAYS
                        (nervous)
                          Hi.
```

MUSIC: heavy on the violins, sappy and romantic

CUT TO: Shot of both facing each other. There is an obvious instant connection.

MUSIC: shifts to something jaunty, full of sunshine and happiness. Young man turns away and leaves with friends. Young woman smiles to herself as she starts to wipe down the counter in preparation for closing the shop.

And romantic interlude is complete.

FADE TO BLACK

Remember, when I said I had faith? Remember I said I take my faith seriously? I should back up a little bit and give you some background.

When I was 13 years old, I heard a woman speak at a women's conference I attended with my mother. I'm sure the speaker said a lot of good things, but there was only one thing I heard that stuck with me. She said she used to spend time in prayer over her future mate. She went on to tell the story of how God had answered her prayers, but I barely listened to that part. I wasn't concerned about God actually answering the prayer. I knew He would. What I found curious was the idea that I could pray for someone, even before I met them. Somehow this idea made sense to a young, somewhat prudish, overly spiritual 13-year-old. So I did it too. I started praying.

Even though I wasn't much of a romantic, I did see the value in believing in "the one." It wasn't out of a sense of having a beautiful, "Disneyesque" moment with my one true love, but out of a need to be free from the drama of dating. I found all the ups, downs and sideways craziness of "dating" to be tiresome and a waste of time (rational-big-picture-girl strikes again).

I wanted to by-pass all of that and cut to the chase. I prayed I wouldn't waste my time with all the wrong kinds of boys. I also prayed I would know the right guy for me the moment I met him. That's how I knew that this guy, with his loud voice and his even louder shirt was *the* guy. I had prayed I would know him the moment I saw him, and I did. However, I was not completely at peace with this information.

We had come to this romantic interlude from two different worlds. Me, a long time woman of Evangelical faith and He, a loosely affiliated Catholic in the middle of practicing a lot of nothing in particular. I was clueless about a lot of things, and he was way too knowledgeable about more things than I ever want to think about. It wasn't at all darkness meets light. He was far from degenerate, and I was far from perfect. It was more like sheltered, naive and oblivious meets open, worldly and extremely tolerant.

It does not make sense how we found each other. It does not make sense why he decided to waste his time with a goody-two-shoes like me. It makes a "little" sense why I was attracted to him. I'm afraid I followed the cliché of a good girl crush on a boy rough around the edges. I was surprised by this revelation. I did not expect to fall in love with someone so far outside my comfort zone. I didn't expect to fall in love at all, not like this.

Unfortunately, we did not have a fairy tale version of a courtship. We had a lot of "kinks" to work out. My husband, who is now a man of faith, was not a man of faith at the time I met him. I did my best to use that as an excuse to get rid of him. In fact, I gave him a bit of religious overload. I fully expected him to call me a Bible thumping psycho (he probably did more than once), and run for the hills. But, even that didn't scare him. People often say I saved him, because knowing me caused him to question his faith. But, really we saved each other.

It was easier for him to fall in love than it was for me. I was buttoned up inside and overly cautious about sharing my heart. He walked around with his arms open just waiting for someone to hug. I liked to keep things simple and quiet. He has never entered a room without fanfare and noise. I wanted everything to measure up into a nice little pattern. He was messy. He even jumped into my mess feet first and rolled around in it a little like it was a party. He wasn't scared, not even for a moment. I was terrified.

He is the one who said he "loved" me first. He was the one who "wooed" me, even when I made it incredibly difficult for him to do so. The flip side of that equation is I required a commitment he wasn't ready to give. He didn't go away, but he didn't change his current lifestyle either. I may have wanted him to choose me over all other things, but he wasn't ready for that, not yet.

Sometimes, he made those choices out of sheer exasperation because of how hard I made it for him to pursue me. Sometimes, he made those choices because it felt better to do what he knew than to wait for someone like me to come around. Some might say this was a form of betrayal, on both of our parts. Maybe to some extent it was. In truth, we both struggled with just how much we were willing to compromise. It was a hard line for both of us to cross. While we loved each other very much, we couldn't figure out how to be together.

I could have written him off as unworthy of my time. He could have walked away. But, there was so much more to this love than either of us knew. Even though we both felt the space between us was too big to cross, we obviously we chose to figure out a way to cross it. "Obviously" because, as you already know, somehow we ended up together in a tiny, pink, NYC bathroom looking down at a pregnancy test with a neon plus sign. Ready or not, we were about to become a family.

CHAPTER THREE
OUCH

OPEN: NYC APARTMENT/BEDROOM

CAMERA HOLDS on young woman asleep.

SLOW DISSOLVE TO DREAM SEQUENCE
(in woman's imagination - exaggerated)

YOUNG WOMAN standing on the edge of a cliff.
Before her stretches amazing open space. In
the distance she sees a NY city scape blended
together with an expanse of Blue Ridge Mountains
(weird combo of both "homes"). Backdrop contains
gorgeous blue sky with white puffy clouds. It's
breath taking. She is smiling. She stands there
for a while enjoying her view. Her foot slips.
She regains her balance.

> VOICE-OVER/YOUNG WOMAN
> (gasp) That was close.

Suddenly what was once a perfect dream quickly

turns into a nightmare. Her foot slips a second time and this time she can't regain her balance. She starts falling, plummeting down towards the ground at an incredible speed. She is going so fast everything in the background is one giant blur. Her clothes and hair are flying upwards from the force of the wind. Her arms and legs are flailing in all directions reaching out for anything that will stop this ride. She is falling, falling, falling. Suspense builds and builds. Suddenly, she hits the ground with a giant SMACK! It replays over and over again three, four, five times. SMACK! SMACK! SMACK!

CUT TO: View from above as if looking down from sky. Camera moves back slowly in a spiral away from the woman left lifeless on the ground. Body is sprawled in all kinds of weird directions obviously in great pain, but not dead. Oh, no, not dead.

VOICE-OVER/YOUNG WOMAN
Ouch.

After five utopian years in NYC, I hit bottom and I hit it hard. It felt like I had fallen from the top of a cliff. This first obstacle for me, this first measure of brokenness, came at what was supposed to be a time of joy. I was about to give birth to my first child, a daughter. It should have been wonderful. It should have been full of shiny light and angels singing and mother earth opening up her arms to welcome me. It should have been a lot of things, but it wasn't.

From the beginning, this was no easy pregnancy. Right out

of the gate, we were hit with multiple challenges. At eight weeks, even with an internal ultrasound (sonogram), the doctor could not find a heartbeat. She sadly informed me I should expect a miscarriage. I had mixed emotions about this news. I mean after all the timing couldn't have been worse. Just a few paragraphs ago, I was saying to myself, *O crap. I'm pregnant.* But, no, it still hurts. Even a woman as reluctant to be a mother as me did not want to hear she was going to have a miscarriage.

Three weeks later, right on schedule, I started spotting. After speaking to my OB on the phone, I left work to hustle myself over to her office. I completely expected to go through the aforementioned miscarriage. After waiting through all of the excruciating "time" it takes to get from the waiting room to the ultrasound to the actual results, amazingly, the doc said everything looked fine. The baby had a nice strong heartbeat.

WHAT?!? The baby was fine? Are you sure?

Yep, she was sure. Everything was fine.

After my exam, the doc said the words my brain and body both HATE to hear.

"You should slow down and take it easy," she said calmly, as if this is the kind of thing all hyper-active, over-achieving, mountain-born, stubborn athletes want to hear.

"I am not sure what is going on here, but your risk of miscarriage is high," she continued. "If you don't slow down (translation: stop it with the extreme exercise you nit wit!) you could still miscarry."

Uh, oh… here comes the immature inner two-year-old. She was not happy about this.

No, no, no! she screamed as she stomped her foot and clenched her fists.

I wish her anger had changed how this whole situation was going to go down, but it didn't. I was stuck on the bench until

I completed my time in the penalty box. The crowds were still cheering, but not for me.

I didn't know how to slow down. I got really CRANKY if I didn't exercise. There was no way I could comprehend how I was going to stop running, playing volleyball, riding my bike, slapping the hockey puck around, rollerblading to work, etc., etc. How was someone like me supposed to respond to something like this? Not very well I'm afraid. Not very well at all. *Sigh.*

Thankfully, soon after this visit I became extremely nauseous. This was a good sign as far as pregnancies go, but as anyone who has ever thrown up uncontrollably can tell you, it's not a pleasant experience. I could eat nothing but baked potatoes. *Hooray for starch!*

My second trimester took a small up turn. I was still participating in the extreme sport of nausea, but feeling better and finally able to eat something other than a plain boring spud. I was able to add cheese on top of my previously plain potato. It felt like a gourmet meal.

My third trimester took the normal turn downward. I had become extremely tired, uncomfortable, fat, and freaked out about my impending delivery while still trying to work, ride the subway and figure out what to eat.

Take a quick gulp from your giant soda, we're going back to the movie.

OPEN: INTERIOR/EXTERIOR NYC
MULTIPLE CAMERA SHOTS

SCENE 1: Pregnancy montage where we see multiple trips to the doctor... and to the bathroom.

SCENE 2: Ordering take-out and then not being able to eat it...

SCENE 3: outgrowing fashionable clothes and having to settle for old t-shirts...

SCENE 4: multiple moments of trying to figure out how to live in NY where everything is so small compared to a stomach that is growing so big. End montage with YOUNG WOMAN back in pink bathroom. She tries to squeeze into the small space and struggles to figure out whether to climb into the bathtub before or after trying to close the door…

FADE TO NEXT SCENE

OPEN: INTERIOR/CROWDED NYC SUBWAY PLATFORM

YOUNG WOMAN with a red face and hair drenched in sweat stands on subway platform. Noise erupts as train arrives.

YOUNG WOMAN steps into an overly crowded subway car. She glances around desperate for a place to sit. She glances at the young male athlete, he ignores her and stays buried into his music player and headphones (this was a long time ago so not an iPod).

She glances at the stock broker reading a paper. Nope, nothing.

Awkwardly she makes eye contact with the dark skinned young man wearing jeans down around his knees, a bandanna around his head and a plethora of gold around his neck and on his teeth. He, unlike the other multitude of people on the train, hops up right away, pushes aside the passengers between him and YOUNG WOMAN and gently muscles her through to the now empty seat. Small town white girl smiles in thanks to the dark skinned street youth and he smiles back. Two human beings made a connection.

                    VOICE-OVER/YOUNG WOMAN
                    I do. I love NY.

FADE TO BLACK

Finally, I arrived at my 35 week check up. Since I had survived the pregnancy up to this point, I was feeling pretty good about myself. I even thought, for a brief moment, maybe, just maybe, I was going to get through this thing. I was wrong.

After my examination, the doc says, "You are completely effaced and at four centimeters dilated. I'm going to check to see if you are having contractions."

WHAT?!?! (pause) *WHAT?!?!*

A few tests later and the doctor confirmed, I was in fact having mild contractions. Not the fake Braxton Hicks kind, but the real, get-yourself-ready-here-comes-labor kind. You will never believe what the doc said next. That's right you guessed it.

"You need to go home and take it easy."

AGAIN with the take it easy?!? How could I take it any easier than I already was? Are we talking bed-rest here?

"Stay home from work," the doc said, "light activity, and let's see if we can buy another week before you go into labor."

Okay, so not bed-rest, but close enough.

I had already been scared straight about this whole "you're

pregnant and now you need to actually have the baby thing," so I decided not to take any chances. All I could think is who wants to go into labor in NYC in the middle of summer? With my luck, I would probably be standing in the subway when my water broke. Not a pretty picture.

I did what the doc ordered. I sat around, all day, inside a tiny NYC apartment, in the middle of summer, in a chair parked directly in front of the air conditioning window unit set on high. For respite, I took small walks to the park down the street. I stretched. I rested. I drove myself crazy.

Back to the movie...

OPEN: INTERIOR DOCTOR'S OFFICE

HUSBAND and YOUNG WOMAN (a giant waddling mess of a pregnant woman) walk into a doctor's personal office.

TITLE: Two Weeks Later

DOCTOR
Well, believe it or not...

VOICE-OVER/YOUNG WOMAN
Don't say it

DOCTOR
...there has been no progression.

VOICE-OVER/YOUNG WOMAN
Are you freaking kidding me?!

DOCTOR
So our plan to rest is working.

VOICE-OVER/YOUNG WOMAN
You better get this baby out of me
and you better do it right now!

HUSBAND places hand over YOUNG WOMAN's hand, instinctively calming her down. YOUNG WOMAN breathes.

DOCTOR
(with annoying cheerfulness)
We'll see you back here in one week!

HUSBAND squeezes YOUNG WOMAN's hand harder.
YOUNG WOMAN'S lips form a firm straight line.

FADE TO BLACK

Two weeks later, and there was still no baby. I had been having steadily increasing contractions for two weeks. Those things, those "minor" contractions, hurt. I had a headache and my back was killing me. I couldn't sleep. I couldn't eat. I was GRUMPY.

Five days later, I went back in to the doctor's office for yet another follow-up. After a quick examination, the doctor discovered I had high blood pressure (headaches) and I was starting to look swollen. *Did the doctor just say the word pre-eclampsia? Pre-eclampsia???*

Next thing I knew we were checked into the hospital, and I was being induced. *Was anything about this pregnancy going to go well? Anything???*

Nope. This ride was just beginning.

```
OPEN: INTERIOR/
LARGE NYC HOSPITAL ADMINISTRATION DESK

COUPLE hurriedly checking into a hospital. YOUNG
WOMAN sits down in wheelchair and is rushed to
the delivery room. Sense of urgency.

CUT TO: INTERIOR/DELIVERY ROOM

MULTIPLE CAMERA SHOTS: Mad crazy labor scenes
flash before our eyes. DOCTORS scurry around
bed and spout demands quickly and succinctly.
HUSBAND is running here and there and here and
there again. Everyone is in reaction mode so
whatever comes to mind first, is what is said.
It's mayhem.

PAUSE
```

I'll try to spare you the gory details, because I want to keep this movie/book rated PG. So here are the highlights.

```
UNPAUSE

Labor. Lots of pain. Some moaning. No progression.
Enema. No progression. Water broken. No
progression. Heart rates rise dangerously. Room
fills with medical professionals. Decision made
for epidural.

INTERRUPT MAYHEM with an epidural induced nap.
```

Crickets and elevator music playing in the background.

PAUSE

Best nap I ever had.

UNPAUSE

YOUNG WOMAN wakes up from nap. Starts pushing. Baby is stuck. DOCTOR places a vacuum on the baby's head.

PAUSE

Yes, a vacuum... a tube attached to a suction cup... yes, exactly the way you imagine.

UNPAUSE

Vacuum pops off of the baby's head. More pushing. Vacuum placed on baby's head *again*. Vacuum popped off of baby's head *again*. More pushing.

DOCTOR picks up large pair of scissors and starts cutting.

PAUSE

I know from all of the books I read this is called an episiotomy.

UNPAUSE

Doctor cuts one, two, three, four… seven snips.

PAUSE

What could she possibly have needed to cut seven times?

UNPAUSE

More pushing.

PAUSE

And… nothing, nada, no progression. Somebody better do something soon or I am going to rip this baby out myself.

UNPAUSE

Clock shows: 2:00 AM

DOCTORS coach and encourage YOUNG WOMAN to keep pushing.

                              NURSE
            Come on, Mama. You gotta push harder!

YOUNG WOMAN grabs nurse by the scrubs and screams into her face

                         YOUNG WOMAN
                Shut up! Shut up! SHUT UP!

PAUSE

There was this one nurse who kept yelling at me, "Come on, Mama! Push harder! You've got to give a 110%!"

All I could think is obviously this woman doesn't know me very well. I don't know how NOT to give 110%. It was not in my farm-girl-mountain-stock-athletic-DNA to do something half-way. In my mind, my inner-two-year-old alter ego was thinking of creative ways to pinch, choke or do anything to make her stop yelling at me. Please, just stop yelling.

UNPAUSE

Clock shows: 4:00 AM

Labor mayhem continues.

Doctors working hard but still calm.

YOUNG WOMAN continues to look desperate.

PAUSE

My outer calm collected adult eventually lost all control as well and was thinking of creative ways to cause violence to all individuals involved in this attack on my body. It was all taking way too long. After three weeks plus 14 hours of labor and 4.5 hours of pushing, it was painfully obvious this baby was stuck (translation: *DUH!*).

UNPAUSE

Clock shows 6:45 AM

YOUNG WOMAN is still pushing. Nothing is working.

Desperation fills the room.

Doctors inform YOUNG WOMAN that they are going
to prep for a c-section.

                    YOUNG WOMAN
                    (to doctor)
              Should I stop pushing?!?

                     DOCTOR
              Yes, stop pushing.

                    YOUNG WOMAN
          (in an otherworldly guttural scream)
                    I CAN'T!!!

BABY falls out into DOCTORS arms.
DOCTOR caught off guard and nearly drops baby.

                     DOCTOR
          Oops! OK, OK, I've got her.

BABY held up in triumph by DOCTOR for YOUNG
WOMAN to see. Everyone in room is talking over
each other with joyful exclamations, except for
YOUNG WOMAN, she's an exhausted mess.

DOCTOR cleans up baby and wraps her in a blanket
and places BABY on YOUNG WOMAN's chest.

HOLD on HUSBAND and YOUNG WOMAN as they look
at baby.

                    YOUNG WOMAN/MOMMY
                         (whisper)
              Hello little girl. I'm your MOMMY.

                     HUSBAND/DADDY
                      (at same time)
              (loudly talking over YOUNG WOMAN)
                  Hey, cutie. I'm your DADDY!

After pause MOMMY continues

                         MOMMY
              And your name… your name is Abigail.

FADE TO BLACK

    And... whamo. Baby born.

CHAPTER FOUR
GIVING BIRTH IS SO EASY, ISN'T IT?

OPEN: BLACK SCREEN

TITLE: 10 Hours Later

CAMERA: From behind closed eyelids. We see the blink of light. Small slivers of awareness. Someone is waking up.

Stereotypical hospital noise in background (beeps, intercom announcements, etc.)

CUT TO: view of hospital room from opposite wall. Hospital room has low lighting but is obviously stark and empty. Divider curtain separates one patient from the other, but the additional bed is empty for now.

CAMERA moves closer so we can see our YOUNG WOMAN/MOMMY is a patient lying in a hospital bed. She is groggy and confused, slowly coming awake after a long ordeal and anesthesia. She looks slowly around the room with her eyes. She moves her fingers, yes they work. She rubs her eyes trying to focus. She looks down at her body that is now about ten pounds lighter and rubs her stomach.

Suddenly full of panic, she tries to sit up but she can't. She tries to roll onto her side but she can't. She can't seem to move. The panic is on her face and in her eyes and in her desperate attempt to grasp the nurse call button.

Something is wrong. Terribly wrong.

                    VOICE-OVER/MOMMY
            (soft, almost inaudible sob)
                         Help

FADE TO BLACK

I truly believe there are moments in our lives when God chooses to intervene. He sees a pattern forming, and for better or worse, He chooses to step in and consequently change our point of view. Sometimes, it can happen through a gentle whisper. Sometimes, it is more like a wrecking ball. I'm more familiar with the wrecking ball.

There I was lying in the hospital bed, having just woken up from a 10 hour nap. I was so disoriented at first I couldn't really place where I was. Then it hit me... *where is my baby?!?* There is nothing like the panic of a new mother, is there? It washes over you as if you are drowning before you even have a moment to process reality. I fought my way back to the "surface," popped up from my pillow, swung my legs around to the side of the bed and… nothing happened.

All of that took place in my mind. My brain sent out all of the right signals, but my body did not respond. I could not move my feet or sit up or swing my legs anywhere. I was cheering myself on… *Sit up. Sit up. Sit up, now!*

No dice.

I was disoriented and groggy, but that did not stop me from wanting to demand an immediate viewing of one baby girl Keating. *Where is she? Let me see her now!*

Thankfully, I could still use my arms. I reached out to grasp the call button for the nurse. Ouch, it hurt to even turn my head. *What in the world had happened?!?*

It took quite a while, but a nurse did eventually come to my room. She did eventually go to the nursery, and I did eventually meet one baby girl Keating. It was agony to wait, but finally, they rolled in the little, plastic, newborn travel box and there she was, my daughter. It was a great relief to see her, alive and breathing. I was momentarily distracted by this beautiful bundle. This little girl who was supposed to be a miscarriage looked pretty darn perfect to me.

My husband showed up soon after the nurses. We gave our new daughter plenty of ogling, and then we set her back into her rolling plastic box. We quietly watched our new daughter fall back to sleep, and I finally felt calm enough to sleep some more myself. Later, I was sure I would feel better.

I kept telling myself I had been through a very traumatic labor and delivery. I thought perhaps I was having some kind of delayed recovery. Maybe, I had an adverse reaction to the epidural. Maybe, I was experiencing some kind of temporary paralysis. Maybe, I pinched a nerve. Maybe, I pulled a really, really, really big muscle. Maybe.

Before I went back to sleep, I met my roommate (back when new mothers shared recovery suites). She walked in to the room (without assistance), and held her baby out for me to see (braggart) and acted like nothing at all had even happened (I hate her).

"Giving birth is so easy, isn't it?" she seemed to be screaming at me.

I didn't want to compare, but I couldn't help it. She was so gleeful, so excited, so *happy*. She sort of epitomized what I thought a "normal" delivery experience should be. There was supposed to be some relief at the end of the labor process. The hard part was supposed to be over. Based on her recovery, I fully expected the next time I woke up I would be able to move. I wasn't.

Eight hours later, I found that I still unable to move my feet. I mentioned this problem to the nurses, the doctors, my husband, my roommate, and even the janitor. I attempted to express my concerns to anyone who would listen. I was desperate to figure out what was going on.

Right away, I was treated with a brusqueness that can only come from an impatient nursing staff working under the assumption that every new mother is a diva who will milk the hospital stay for all it is worth. I tried to explain that my situation was unique (*Hello, my legs aren't working!*). Instead of receiving understanding, I was ignored, waved off, and "tisk-tisked."

"Now mama," the nurses said, " you will be just fine. You just need some rest."

Rather than investigate my claims of incapacity, they filled my head to distraction with how to hold my baby, how to breastfeed my baby, how not to fall asleep while holding a newborn, and how to only push the call button in cases of emergency. *Ummm... I think I'm having one of those? Help me? Anyone?*

No one even paused for a second to consider that maybe we needed to go over how to get to the bathroom without assistance? No one thought it was strange that my husband had to carry me back and forth? Nope, they just shuffled me along and treated me as if I was "over reacting." Since I'm the epitome of "under reacting," I knew something big was going on, but I chose to play along because inwardly, I really wanted for them to be right. *Please, oh please, just this once let me be a diva.*

The next morning, a nurse came in to check on me. I had continued to get little to no sympathy from the staff of that (what shall remain nameless) hospital, so I braced myself for more of the same. They continued to treat me like a prima donna first-time mother, and I had tried hard to believe them. I tried to convince my body that this was all in my head, but it didn't do any good. My body didn't believe me.

Thankfully, the flow of the tide was about to change. Finally, all the necessary pieces fell into place when that nurse, by accident really, happened to notice I had placed my ice pack erroneously.

How dare I.

"Mrs. Keating," she said as she looked down on me with patronizing disdain, "you are putting your ice pack in the wrong place. That ice pack is for your episiotomy."

"Well," I said with a barely veiled sarcasm, "that's not where it hurts."

The break in my body was not where it was supposed to be. This *whole* time I had allowed everyone around to treat me like an imbecile because of it. I had trusted that the medical staff knew my body better than me. I was wrong. They didn't. At least I can say this moment of nurse enlightenment resulted in a new and improved response to my situation.

At first she looked at me with raised eyebrows, her surprise vividly showing on her face. As I slowly explained again what was hurting and what wasn't, she began to realize I wasn't kidding around when I said I couldn't move my feet. She began to realize I was not exaggerating, make-believing, or milking it. She called my OB right away, and within minutes I was taken to radiology for an MRI. *Hmph! Told you so!* says smug inner two-year-old.

A few hours later, I was diagnosed with a separated pelvis. A separated what?!? That's right, a separated pelvis.

INSTANT REPLAY

YOUNG WOMAN hits the ground over and over.

SMACK! SMACK! SMACK!

                    VOICE-OVER/MOMMY
                        Ouch.

Apparently, a separated pelvis is an extremely rare thing that occasionally happens to women during childbirth. There are very few cases of it happening these days (thank God!) thanks to the increase in safety of c-sections. Even I was a few short minutes away from avoiding this injury when nature took over.

As I look back, I can see that "whamo… baby born…" was actually a life-threatening event. So life-threatening, my body felt the need to take over and seriously injure itself in order to save both my baby and me. Otherwise, it would have been too late.

Amazing. Miraculous. Painful.

Anyone who has had a separated pelvis will profess that their body is absolutely, irrevocably, without a doubt, completely changed. You really do use your pelvic muscles for EVERYTHING. It is no small statement when all those exercise gurus call this area your core. I'm painfully aware of how every move I made then, and still make today, was based on a very fractured and broken section of my body.

As an athlete, I had a variety of injuries over the years. That knee injury in college? Nothing by comparison. That severely sprained ankle from intra-murals? Chump change. That benign scar tissue I had removed from my wrist? Easy peasy. I had absolutely no idea what it was like to be injured like this.

I was a new mother but I couldn't walk or even sit up by myself. If I couldn't get out of bed. How was I going to feed myself? Bathe myself? Go to the bathroom? More importantly, how was I going to take care of an infant? I was in big, big trouble. *Now what?!?*

We learn early, if you need anything, you ask for help. "Don't be afraid to ask questions. I'm your teacher/parent/coach and I'm here to help." "Someone will be right with you." "We are happy to help." "Please stay on the line and one of our service providers will assist you." "Can I help you?"

Unfortunately, I didn't know how to ask for help, not really. I came from a long line of DIY type of folks. Don't have set of bookshelves? Make one. Need a new roof? Climb up and get to work. Need a present for a friend? Sew one, paint one, create one. Can't find what you need in the store? Figure out how to do it yourself. Just do it yourself.

These are normally great qualities to have. Unfortunately, those skills were going to be useless to me in this situation. I could not manufacture a new piece of cartilage. I could not rush this process. I could not push through and heal faster, better or stronger. I was stuck.

The fact that I was going to have to ask for help was painfully clear and we were desperate. My husband was in the middle of a grad school program that would have been idiotic to quit. He was going to need that degree because our back-up plan had just become our Hail Mary pass in the last 30 seconds of the fourth quarter. Our plans for me to go back to work were equally demolished. I practically needed a full-time nurse, not a full-time job.

We ran through (and quickly out of) possibilities for the kind of person who would be able to interrupt their life in order to help us through this. Apparently people have their own lives to lead. *Who knew?*

Although she wasn't our first choice, the SOS finally went out to my much younger, fresh out of college, baby sister. She was eight years younger than me. By the time I went off to college, she was only 10 years old. I barely knew her, but even I knew inviting a 20-year-old college graduate into this mess was a ridiculous request. I was not at all comfortable asking her to give up her young, carefree life to come and take care of an invalid and an infant. It was awkward. It was uncomfortable. We were practically strangers.

She accepted our invitation, why, I will never know for sure. The promise of living in NYC rent free for a year probably helped. We couldn't pay her, we couldn't give her anything really, only a place to stay and some food. Still, she said she would come. She just had to finish up her summer job first.

She planned to leave the comfort of our small hometown for the bright lights of New York City in about two weeks. Of course that was fine, it was perfect timing really. It meant she would step into our lives about the same time my husband would be starting his next semester of school. Unfortunately, it still left me stuck in a hospital with a separated pelvis, a newborn and a husband who needed to go back to classes. *How was I ever going to be able to do this?*

Back to the movie.

OPEN: INTERIOR/SAME HOSPITAL ROOM

CAMERA stays on MOMMY sitting in hospital bed. She holds the phone to her ear. DADDY standing

next to bed. Infant DAUGHTER next to husband in
rolling box.

                    MOMMY
          Okay. We'll see you in two weeks.
                (hangs up phone)

DADDY squeezes MOMMY's hand and then walks out
of room pushing DAUGHTER back to nursery.

MOMMY left in bed alone. One tear falls down her
cheek. She brushes it away, shakes her shoulders
and raises her chin in resolve. Determination
written on her face.

CAMERA: pulls back slowly

MUSIC: melancholy, but hopeful

FADE TO BLACK

CHAPTER FIVE

THANK GOD YOU'RE HERE

In the human body the pubis symphysis (pubic joint) is normally a firm joint held together by strong fibrous cartilage necessary for keeping the pelvis in place. From this fixed point, the pubic joint acts as a place of stability providing the hips, legs and torso with a wide range of mobility. DIASTASIS SYMPHYSIS PUBIS (separated pelvis) occurs when the two pubic bones are dislocated or pulled apart to a distance too wide for the joint to maintain stability, causing serious injury. Women who have suffered this injury often describe hearing a pop or a snap at the moment the cartilage, of the once firm pubic joint, severs.

(various sources)

OPEN: EXTERIOR NYC UPPER WEST SIDE - DAY

CAMERA HOLDS in front of NYC apartment building on the upper west side. It's well maintained but not the luxury type of pre-war buildings that have doormen and awnings. This is a more common, middle of the road apartment building where you have to open the door by yourself. Two large columns flank the glass front doors. A set of stairs (six) rise from the sidewalk to entrance.

TITLE: Coming Home

An old, well-loved four-door SUV pulls up to the curb. It is full of balloons and flowers and four people. MOMMY, DADDY, DAUGHTER and the friend who owns the car.

CUT TO: MOMMY looking out of car window from backseat. Camera toggles back and forth from the car to the building, the building to the car to establish the distance between the two. It's short, less than 10 yards.

CUT TO: from MOMMY's point of view (exaggerated), she is standing on a mountain side similar to where she grew up and the distance of the walk before her looks like an uncrossable gorge.

CUT BACK TO: MOMMY, her face becomes stricken with panic. The distance is too far. She knows it but she can't change it.

                    VOICE-OVER/MOMMY
                       (whisper)
                         Crap.

The panic quickly gets squashed down into determination. MOMMY braces herself for the task ahead.

MOMMY attempts to exit the car. Painful. She tries to walk. Painful. She hobbles along going nowhere fast. Painful.

Finally DADDY scoops her up and carries her to the building and up the stairs.

> VOICE-OVER/MOMMY
> Ouch... ouch... ouch... ouch...

FADE TO BLACK

I received another large dose of reality when we arrived home. I checked out of the hospital early, because I had lost my ability to tolerate the nursing staff of "that" hospital. I thought being home would be easier and certainly more comfortable. I forgot to consider the actual "getting home" part.

Getting out of the wheelchair at the hospital and into the car was excruciating, but that was nothing compared to "walking" across the sidewalk from our friend's car to our building. Ten yards might as well have been ten miles.

It is truly annoying to figure out how to walk without being able to pick up your feet. I had two separate legs trying to figure out how to work without a tiny piece of cartilage to ground them and give them direction. The piece of material that used to hold my pubic bones together had been severed. Normally, that meant you should not try to walk without assistance. Somehow, I thought that medical advice applied to everyone... but me. All I wanted to do was be able to walk. It was such a small yet insurmountable request.

I do not know why I insisted on being so stubborn. I thought

I could walk the distance by myself. I couldn't. I thought I could make it holding on to someone for support. I couldn't. The only way to get from where I was to where I needed to go was to let go and let someone carry me. Sometimes, you carry yourself and sometimes, even more importantly, you have to let go so someone else can carry you. Literally. Frustrating, but undeniably true.

Back to the movie.

OPEN: INTERIOR APARTMENT

CAMERA pans through same small apartment. It has the same furniture set up as before but now it is cluttered with what seems like endless baby equipment.

MUSIC: cheesy, drums and piano, with humor

MULTIPLE SCENES of MOMMY trying to do various activities and not succeeding. (seen as short clips)

SCENE 1: DAUGHTER crying. MOMMY tries to sit up... can't. DADDY comes to help her sit up. DADDY smiles and then hands her the baby and walks away. MOMMY frowns.

SCENE 2: Baby done eating and needs to be changed. DADDY shows up, takes baby, changes baby and hands baby back to MOMMY. MOMMY holds baby for a short while and then tries to put baby into small basket on the floor... can't. DADDY shows up takes the baby, puts baby down for a nap. Walks away.

MOMMY frowns.

SCENE 3: MOMMY tries to get out of bed alone... can't. DADDY comes back into room. MOMMY gives husband sheepish look as he helps lift her out of bed and carries her to bathroom. When MOMMY is done and still sitting on toilet, she motions to DADDY. He comes back to bathroom to pick her up off toilet and holds her while she washes her hands and then carries her back to bed. Walks away.

MOMMY frowns.

SCENE 4: DAUGHTER crying next to bed. MOMMY nudges DADDY so he will wake up and get the baby. He's fast asleep. MOMMY tries to roll over to reach down and get baby herself... can't. MOMMY punches DADDY again with more vigor. DADDY slowly comes to life and in a stupor reaches down, grabs baby, hands baby to MOMMY and goes back to sleep.

MOMMY looks down at baby and frowns.

> VOICE-OVER/MOMMY
> (Growl of frustration)
> GRRRRRRRR!!!!

CUT TO: CAMERA holds on front door.

TITLE: Two Weeks Later

Doorbell rings. Sister walks in.

                    DADDY
              Welcome to the city!

                    MOMMY
              Happy Birthday!

               VOICE-OVER/MOMMY
              (internal whisper)
            Thank God you're here.

FADE TO BLACK

My husband and I had been doing the new baby dance for two weeks. Wake, feed baby, change baby, stare at baby, take photos of baby sleeping, fall into a stupor of exhaustion, sleep, repeat. It was almost robotic.

Thankfully, our daughter was a pro at being a newborn. She slept, ate and pooped right on schedule from the moment we came home. We could almost set our clock to her. This need for schedule and order may be the only thing that makes my daughter like me. Otherwise, she is very much like her father.

So much of that time was just like any other situation experienced by a majority of new parents, except, we were doing it all with a little extra challenge on the side. My husband also had to help me do, well, everything. I have no words to describe how much I could not function nor how helpless I felt.

My sister arrived in NYC on September 10, 2001. Her birthday. She bounced in with her suitcase and her flip flops and I have never been so happy to see someone in my entire life. She had grown up when I wasn't watching. She was no longer the bratty red-headed pest I remembered. Before me stood a young woman with curly, reddish brown hair and bright blue eyes.

She drove me crazy when we were younger and shared a room. Her stuff was constantly scattered everywhere and she never cleaned (granted she was five, but still!). I was constantly annoyed by her presence (granted I was thirteen, but still!). It was clear we were both going to have to put aside our childish habits because there we were, sharing again. Only this time, it was the extended edition director's cut on redux. I will always treasure this time, this forced community, because it's when that little brat went from stranger, to sister, to friend.

My sister may have been a brat when she was younger, but she grew up into a gracious and loving caregiver. She walked into the middle of our crazy situation and seamlessly became a part of our life. I suppose this surprised me even though we were raised in the same place. We both knew how to look at something before us, accept it, and then do it. We both believed this is just what you do for family. It just is.

As my sister settled in, we began the process of getting her "familiar" with her new, not so desirable, job. We warned her over and over about how much I could not do and how much she would have to do. It was a long list.

Probably one of the best aspects of my sister's personality is her ability to let things roll off her back. She is way better at doing this than me. I get hyper sensitive when my order is disturbed. She just rolls with chaos.

It was not by accident she was the only person who was available to come and live with us. No one else could have done what she did, not even close. She was the ONLY person uniquely qualified for this obscenely crazy moment. She instantly became my husband's best audience (she laughed at all of his jokes) and my daughter's favorite person.

Back to the movie.

OPEN: INTERIOR APARTMENT

TITLE: Next Day

DADDY and SISTER are packing up baby gear and gathering DAUGHTER to go out. DAUGHTER in baby carrier asleep.

MOMMY sitting on futon (uncomfortably), giving out directives. (example: Yes, we should pack extra diapers just in case. Yes, bring extra burp cloths. No, she doesn't need an extra blanket.)

The morning news (NY1) is playing in the background. MOMMY is watching the weather.

A news bulletin interrupts.

> NEWSCASTER ON TELEVISION
> We can now confirm that a plane has made a direct hit into Tower One of the World Trade Center. It is unclear at this time what exactly has happened...
> (fades into background)

CAMERA HOLDS on three adults. They chatter nervously and wait for the news to return. When it does, we see this little family watch in shock as a second plane crashes into tower number two.

CAMERA HOLDS on living room and gently pans back "exiting" the room.

Devastating silence.

FADE TO BLACK

My sister had only been in NYC for one day. She left our small, safe, and rural town and ended up in the middle of a national crisis. What in the world was I thinking? How is it possible I had invited my sweet baby sister to this nightmare?! My mother was never going to forgive me. This was almost as bad as leaving the house wearing dirty underwear.

The whole thing seemed fake, like someone's idea of a horrendous prank. At first, I thought I was watching a movie trailer, or someone's "this too could happen to you" documentary. I wanted to believe those airplanes on the screen were toys and the two towers of the World Trade Center were actually models of the real thing. They weren't. Unfortunately, it was all very, very real.

We were sitting there watching TV while the World Trade Center exploded into mass hysteria. This was one of my favorite "high" places. This was one of my favorite places ever. We went there often, and I always dragged all of our out-of-town guests there. Even now, I haven't fully reconciled that this part of NY is utterly and completely... gone.

I definitely did not process through it at the time it was happening. It was so close to us and yet it was so very far away from where we were, physically and emotionally. We had other things on our minds. September 11th was also my daughter's two-week appointment with her pediatrician. Every new parent has to trek to the doc at the two week marker. It's a rite of passage.

At that point, everyone assumed it was just a freak accident. We had no reason to be afraid. No reason to think that what was happening on the other end of the island was anything more than an unintentional disaster. No deaths had been reported. No injuries. So it made sense that we focused on our task at hand. We gathered ourselves together to go to the doctor anyway.

Even without a terrorist attack mere minutes from our apartment, this task was going to be challenging. Especially when it came to the task of getting me downstairs, into a taxi, out of taxi, into a doctor's office, out of a doctor's office, back into a taxi and back home again. I suppose the good side of squashing down panic into determination is you find yourself able to achieve things that would otherwise be impossible.

We all went to the appointment. I know. Ludicrous. At the time it was important to me for everyone to meet the pediatrician and go through the whole, ugly situation, together. I wanted everyone on team Keating and everyone in the pediatrician's office to be on the same page.

If we had been on an episode of Family Feud I think it would have sounded like…

Introducing! The mom who can't walk (mom gives a small two finger wave)… the busy dad in grad school (dad spins, gives a double finger point and winks at the camera)… the newborn baby (baby doesn't wave)… and the younger sister from po-dunkville (waves exuberantly). These are the Keatings!

Our pediatrician was somewhat tolerant of our situation, but he suggested (in perfect New Yorkese) that we not bring everyone to every appointment. Point taken.

By the time our appointment was over, just a short 30 minutes later, both towers of the World Trade Center had collapsed.

When we stepped out onto the sidewalk from the doctor's office, the first thing that struck me as unusual was how eerily quiet a city that never sleeps had become. Masses of people were walking, almost marching away from what was happening downtown. Thousands of people walking without making a single sound. You couldn't even hear the shuffle of their feet.

The air was thick with a stillness I have never heard again.

The entire city was in this crazy, unbelievable state of shock. So was I. Someone had just attacked and wounded my HOME, but I couldn't process this tragedy. Just like my pelvis, I was completely disconnected from my life. Floating. In desperate need to find a tiny piece of cartilage to hold me together.

My home survived this attack and since she was my muse, I was going to have to survive as well. Life goes on in the big city.

CHAPTER SIX
DIASTASIS SYMPHYSIS PUBIS

OPEN: BLACK SCREEN

NO MUSIC - SILENCE

TITLE: (dictionary definition font and style)
DIASTASIS SYMPHYSIS PUBIS (separated pelvis):
the separation of normally joined pubic bones.

BACK TO BLACK

TITLE:
   Typical advice usually given to women
   with this condition includes avoiding:

   strenuous exercise

   prolonged standing

   vacuum cleaning

   stretching exercises

   and squatting

BACK TO BLACK

TITLE:
    Women are also frequently advised to:

    avoid lifting and carrying

    avoid stepping over things

    avoid twisting movements of the body

    avoid stairs

BACK TO BLACK

TITLE:
    If the pain is very severe, a walker
    will assist with mobility. For more
    extreme cases a wheelchair may be
    considered advisable.

BACK TO BLACK

                    VOICE-OVER/MOMMY
                       Bummer.

FADE TO BLACK

    Forgive me for using such a cold, medical, opening to
this chapter. I know it doesn't quite fit with the concept of
me honestly telling you my story, but I have found I need
to talk about these next memories within the comfort of
spouting facts rather than emotion. That's what I meant when
I said I was distant from my own life. There was a coldness I
applied to these moments. It was my form of survival. It was my
form of denial.

Of course, I wasn't ignoring what was happening less than five miles from our apartment. I knew what was going on down at the south end of Manhattan was bad, very, very bad. I just couldn't do anything about it. Other than watch the news every morning and commiserate with my sister about the insanity of it all, my hands (or rather my pelvis) were tied. Besides, I had a more immediate task to tackle. Yes, I had to heal, but more importantly, I had to watch my baby grow. She was my distraction from the absurdity of my situation.

Oh, the simple joys of life. There is nothing like a baby's first smile, first bath, first everything. Even in the middle of my challenges, this little human was so fascinating. We reacted like numerous other first timers - with an over-inflated view of the beauty of our baby and a non-stop flow of flash photography. Perhaps we had a more infectious need to document all of the good stuff. We were all desperate for the outlet this little girl gave us.

On the other hand, every day, I woke up to the reality of our situation. There were three adults and one baby in a one-bedroom apartment in New York City. Picture it in your head if you can. Three adults and one baby living in space smaller than your dining room. That's right the WHOLE apartment was smaller than your dining room... okay maybe your living room... or maybe even your living room and kitchen combined, but you get what I'm trying to say. It was crowded in this place.

My husband and I shared one small closet and one tall six-drawer dresser. My daughter had one shelf at the bottom of our bookcase. New York taught us a lesson in frugality. If you don't have room for stuff, you live pretty low-key. I kinda loved it. I was the girl with the pillowcase of "tangs" after all.

Let's not forget my sister lived with us too. We had rearranged our living room so we could fit in another six drawer dresser along one wall. Perpendicular from that along the back wall was the green futon. Next to the futon was a small side table with two shelves and a small reading lamp. Everything my sister brought with her fit into these two small pieces of furniture. She slept on the floor on a camping mat. To be fair she actually chose to sleep on a camping mat instead of on the futon. According to her, she was perfectly comfortable. Wow, I really do owe her. Big time.

It was four months before I could get out of bed by myself. I think in order to put that into a perspective I can share, I will talk about this part of my situation in terms of math. I can't remember exactly, but let's pretend I went to the bathroom a minimum of three times a day. That's three times seven days, times four weeks, times four months. If I lost anyone, that's a minimum of 336 times someone had to help me get out of bed and then help me get to the bathroom. And do you think for one moment I could actually make it to the potty (yes, I said *potty*) by myself? No way. Someone had to help me SIT and STAND and sometimes even WIPE. Awkward and uncomfortable? Yes. Borderline humiliating? Definitely.

There were a minimum of 600 meals, snacks and drinks prepared for me by my husband or my sister. That was just to feed me. A newborn infant eats around eight times a day in the first few months. That tapers off a little at some point, but still that was at least 672 times my newborn baby was handed to me to nurse and then taken back to be cared for by someone else. In addition to this, were all the other times someone had to hand me a breast pump, take the breast milk to be stored and subsequently wash the breast pump. My breast pump, with my breast milk. That's just…a little too personal.

My sister made a minimum of 60 sitz baths. Twice a day for 30 days because not only did I have an extreme episiotomy (remember the overzealous cutting during the labor scene?), the darn thing didn't heal correctly. You know what they do when an episiotomy doesn't heal well? Cauterize the wound at the site. The episiotomy wound site. Without pain killers. Since mine was particularly problematic, I got to enjoy that experience three times. That's right, up close and personal. Has anyone else noticed the lack of privacy I had? For someone shy, private and modest, this experience was…. the opposite.

Most of this stuff had to be done by my sister because, at this time, my husband was almost never home. That's what happens when you are enrolled in a very demanding graduate program, you work your butt off to graduate. That left us girls at home to party solo.

I must confess, in order to survive our long boring days of doing nothing, my sister and I watched an inordinate amount of television. Wonderfully brainless, purely-for-entertainment, (scripted) television. Shows like *Northern Exposure*, *Murder She Wrote*, *Judging Amy*, *Law and Order* (the original), *ER* and of course the cream of the crop, *Magnum P.I.*

I'm pretty sure the theme song from *Magnum, P.I.* has forever implanted itself into my daughter's subconscious. Just the sound of horns sounding out the "bah bah be bum" before the start of the rocking guitar solo makes us both smile uncontrollably. Magnum made our days tolerable. Thank you, Tom Selleck. You rock.

Miraculously, here was where the grace of God appeared. In all that time, over the course of about 11 months, we never felt too crowded. Don't get me wrong, we had our moments. It was very testy at times. But overall, we were actually comfortable. On a lot of occasions, we actually had fun. I was disconnected from my situation, numb and in survival mode, but thankfully, occasionally I was still able to laugh. Some situations are hysterically funny, regardless of your circumstances.

One of my favorites was the time my sister went to the

neighborhood health food store to pick up some eucalyptus oil to help us combat our current stuffy noses (we added a couple of drops to a bowl of steaming water as a type of economical humidifier). I thought it was a simple request to ask my sister to go to the neighborhood health store to get some. I was wrong.

Put your cell phones away, we are going back to the movie.

OPEN: EXTERIOR UPPER WEST SIDE NEW YORK

It's fall (October). Blue skies. Colorful leaves. Puffy clouds.

MUSIC: Sunny. Fun.

CAMERA follows SISTER (happy) down city street in residential upper west side. She looks like an out-of-towner, still wearing flip flops, but is also comfortable as she navigates the street.

CUT TO: Front of a small hole-in-the-wall health food store crammed between the coin operated laundromat and the Indian restaurant. A small green and yellow awning shades an open display window full of fresh produce.

Almost in a voyeuristic fashion we watch as SISTER walks to the small shop and reaches to open door. Even though she has lived in NY for a while she has never been in this store before. SISTER walks into front door.

MUSIC: abruptly stops.

SISTER is shocked by the scene before her.

CUT TO: inside of store from SISTER's POV -
tiny aisles between over-crowded shelves full of
crazy looking holistic remedies.

BACK TO: SISTER. Her expression makes it obvious
the place also smells strange, foreign and
downright "stinky." Cautiously she approaches
the counter.

                    STORE OWNER
                     (Korean)
                   Mi I hep you?

                      SISTER
                    (southern)
                 Uhhhmmm… yey-us.
      (pause as she desperately scans the shelves)
       Eye am looking for yew-caw-lyp-tus awl?

                    STORE OWNER
                    Essuse me?

                      SISTER
                 yew-caw-lyp-tus awl?

                    STORE OWNER
                      (pause)
                   You say owell?

                        SISTER
                No, not owell, awl.
        (raises voice and drags out word)
                      Auuwll.

                     STORE OWNER
                So sohee. I no know,
        (mimics her, slow and drawn out)
                      ahhwel.

                        SISTER
                      No, awl.
                  (then louder)
        Awl! Like you wood rub on your skee-yn?

                     STORE OWNER
                       Dees?
                (points to a lotion)

                        SISTER
            Lyeke that but theeener. Awl.

                     STORE OWNER
            Dees? (points to foot spray)

                        SISTER
                  Noooo. Naht thayt.
            It he-yelps with con-gest-jun?

STORE OWNER grabs bottle of herbal cold remedy
and gestures "this?"

                    SISTER
            (with voice of defeat)
Nuuhhh, uuuhhh. Thayts naht eet eeether.

                  STORE OWNER
            So sohee. We no have.
            I no know this ahwel.

                    SISTER
      Waayt I see it. Eets riaght theyer!
        (points to shelf behind counter)
                  STORE OWNER
        Oh, dis? Eu-coy-ip-tus oyell?

                    SISTER
        YEYUS! Yew-caw-lyp-tus awl

STORE OWNER and SISTER smile and become instant
friends.

FADE TO BLACK

Phew! For a minute I thought we were going to have to
survive our stuffy noses without the assistance of our favorite
holistic remedy. Between my sister's southern accent, and the
store clerk's Korean accent, it took at least 20 minutes of
"communication" to finally get the right thing. Thankfully, the
U.N. can rest easy. Even a country girl and a Korean man can get
through a simple retail transaction. Sort of.

Then there was the time we decided to go to a movie. Disney's
Monsters, Inc., had just opened and my sister and I thought it
would be fun to take my daughter to her first movie. You are
probably thinking to yourself, "this isn't going to go well."

You're right. It didn't.

OPEN: EXTERIOR NEW YORK CITY STREET

MUSIC: something with big horns that implies "action." Similar to theme song from *Magnum P.I.*

CAMERA HOLDS on exterior of apartment building with MOMMY and SISTER coming down stairs.

MOMMY hobbles down carefully with obvious pain putting all of her weight on the guard rail (ironically in conflict with music).

MOMMY is wearing unattractive elastic brace around hips on outside of clothing.

SISTER walks down the stairs without any difficulty, wearing the BABY in front facing baby carrier and also carrying a metal walker.

ALL reach sidewalk, rearrange and begin moving toward street corner. It is torturous how slowly they are moving. Again in direct conflict to music.

The city continues to bustle around them. People zoom past them in a blur of speed. Cars honk loudly.

CUT TO: Close up of MOMMY's feet and walker on sidewalk. Emphasize sound of MOMMY's movement. SHUFFLE. SHUFFLE. THUMP. DRAG.

MUSIC screeches to stop

                    VOICE-OVER/MOMMY
                         Ouch

MUSIC starts again
REPEAT: SHUFFLE. SHUFFLE. THUMP. DRAG.
MUSIC screeches to stop

                    VOICE-OVER/MOMMY
                         Ouch.

MUSIC starts again
REPEAT: SHUFFLE. SHUFFLE. THUMP. DRAG.
MUSIC screeches to stop

                    VOICE-OVER/MOMMY
                         Ouch.

FADE TO BLACK

TITLE: 40 Minutes later

FADE IN: CAMERA HOLDS on front of theater.

Fresh as a daisy SISTER stands next to panting,
sweaty MOMMY leaning heavily on walker.

SISTER buys tickets while MOMMY gives sheepish
grin to clerk behind window.

CLERK shakes his head in disbelief. The scene
before him doesn't make sense.

MUSIC begins playing again

MOMMY puts on brave face and continues into the
theater.

CUT TO: MOMMY as she finally makes it to seat
and collapses in giant relief. Sister swoops in
and sits down with perfect ease, even while
carrying BABY.

SISTER

Are you OK?

MOMMY

Fine, fine, yes, I'm fine.

(brush off - obviously lying)

SISTER looks at MOMMY incredulously (one eyebrow
raised). MOMMY's tough-girl facade dissolves
into a slow giggle which quickly turns into loud
laughter. Soon both MOMMY and SISTER are crying
they are laughing so hard.

VOICE-OVER/MOMMY

Me, myself and I, we're idiots.

Laughter continues.

FADE TO BLACK

The movie theater that I so desperately needed to reach was
literally *across the street*, less than 400 yards away, and yet it took
me 40 minutes to get there. It took *40 minutes*. If you ever want

to really challenge yourself, try walking in NYC with a walker when you have the kind of injury that makes it impossible to pick up your feet. Not pretty, but funny in a thank-God-that-is-not-me-train-wreck, sort of way. I'm giving you permission to laugh, I did.

Choosing to go to the movies with a separated pelvis and a four-month-old was absurd. Looking back, I am not sure I will ever be able to defend our decision.

My doctor had given me an ugly elastic hip brace and walker because that was *all* someone who was on bed rest was *supposed* to need. I was *supposed* to be going from my bed to the bathroom and back to my bed. I was not supposed to be crossing streets *or* going to movies. Yep, still living in a bubble of stubborn denial.

And *that* brings us to the story I have begun to refer to as the Wheelchair Situation. One morning, it dawned on me if I had a wheelchair I could actually travel farther, and for sure more comfortably, than I had been able to with the walker. My husband in his overly optimistic way (denial), suggested he borrow a wheelchair (hunk of junk) from the props department of the school where he was getting his masters. Under the guise of theater, I am sure this wheelchair "seemed" functional. In reality, it was anything but.

Back to the movie.

OPEN: EXTERIOR NEW YORK CITY STREET

CAMERA HOLDS on SISTER, MOMMY and BABY leaving apartment. SISTER holding BABY in front carrier and also carrying wheelchair down front steps (with perfect ease).

In ironic conflict to SISTER, MOMMY hobbles down front steps and moves to sit in wheelchair. MOMMY

looks at sister with secret frustration her
mouth presses into a firm straight line.

Once MOMMY is settled, SISTER begins pushing
wheelchair. Wheelchair wobbles, bounces and
shakes.

CUT TO: Close up of wheels on wheelchair. Every
joint is wobbly, pieces of metal shake, rattle
and screws are so loose they almost fall out.

CUT TO: MOMMY shares sarcastic look of annoyance
with camera as she jostles and bounces around
in a ridiculous manner.

                    VOICE-OVER/MOMMY
              (with bounce and shake in voice -
          like a child in a wagon rolling over
                  a brick sidewalk)
              OwwOwwOwwOwwOwwChChChCh

FADE TO BLACK

   Yep, we actually thought it was a good idea to have my sister
carry my daughter while pushing me in a broken down wheel
chair down a fractured city sidewalk. Yes, you heard me. I had
a separated pelvis, and I still thought it was a good idea. I was
bouncing around so much I looked like I was on one of those
old-fashioned, wooden roller coasters... except instead of riding
across tracks, this coaster was being dragged across a cobblestone
street in the middle of an earthquake. At least, that is how I
remember it.
   Please allow me to take a moment here to defend this particular

choice. The wheelchair we chose to use was, in hindsight, a giant mistake. At the time, both my husband and I had this tiny ray of HOPE this was all going to be temporary. We thought we would be borrowing the wheelchair for a short time, and in just a few "days," I would be feeling SO much better I wouldn't need it anymore. *Right?!?* All we wanted to do was make it through the next few months until he graduated from grad school.

In an alternate universe, I would have made the connection between my discomfort and a valid solution to my problem. My otherwise intelligent brain obviously could not connect the dots. The smart thing to do would have been to get my doctor to arrange for me to have a wheelchair instead of a walker. I never even asked my doctor if that was a possibility. My doctor thought I was following his medical advice and staying home, staying in bed, and following the instructions of that long list of things I shouldn't do. I certainly didn't want to fill him in on my idiotic behavior. *That* would have been stupid.

Unfortunately, even with the reality of needing a wheelchair, I continued to believe I could do more than I actually could. I was too proud to admit how wrecked I was about this injury to my body. I was too worried about being a new mom to care. With an overdose of pride, my inner two-year-old and I continued to stupidly insist on independence.

At least 200 times, I was helped down the stairs at the door of our building. At least half of those times, I should have stayed home. Multiple times I tried to go for a "walk," only to realize I had gone too far, and I couldn't make it back home. I don't mean I made it to the end of the street and then realized it; I mean I made it 100 yards and collapsed (a detail my husband was probably glad about because he had to do the carrying). Just making it to the light at the corner was a major accomplishment. I mean from the front door of our building to the corner... and our building was on the corner.

Remember, when I said I was a college athlete? Remember, I said how I loved to run? This was not a bump in the road. It was a boulder. I think that's why I need to give myself a little space from these details. I was so very not okay with the way this injury changed my life.

Honestly, I was thankful for all of that denial, because if I had really thought through all the pieces of this puzzle, I never would have survived those first few months. If my sister had really considered what she was committing to, she never would have moved into a one-bedroom apartment with a married couple and a newborn. If my husband had paused even for a moment, he never would have finished grad school. Without that healthy dose of denial, none of us would have survived this first round of battle and for sure no one would have been around to take care of the baby.

I had a lot of work to do, but I was actually one of the lucky ones. Someday… in a far, far distant land… I would walk again. According to the doctors, eventually the severed cartilage would create enough scar tissue to be deemed "back together." It would never be whole again, but it would… eventually… be functional. At least someday, I would be able to pick up my feet. But, I would never be the athlete I was before. Not even close.

The silver lining? I didn't have to change poopy (yes, I said *poopy*) diapers.

One more piece of math… my sister changed the majority of the diapers my lovely newborn produced. All of you new parents out there, I see you thinking about how that adds up. That is a minimum of eight diapers a day that eventually tapers off to four or five. So let's pick the number six to make it "even". That's six times a day, seven days a week, times four weeks, times six months (because it took another couple of months before I could stand long enough to change a diaper). That's at least 840 diapers my sister changed for a baby who didn't even belong to her. That's a lot of poop. She was a freshly graduated 21 year old who should have been doing any number of things OTHER than taking care of her sister and a newborn. Challenging for her, I know, and for me, it was torture. My inner two-year-old was angry, because I had to sit there, helpless, while I watched my baby sister float down stairs, glide down streets and take care of *my* baby.

Give her back! She's mine! You can't have her! I screamed on the inside, while I smiled and was so incredibly grateful on the outside.

There was no denying it, like all those poopy diapers, this S-T-I-N-K-S, stinks.

CHAPTER SEVEN
SUCCESS?

OPEN: Black Screen

TITLE: (scrolls from bottom of screen)

The human body is generally very resilient. Bones and tissues are capable of healing and regenerating themselves rather efficiently, even when a serious injury is involved. This is not normally the case with cartilage, which heals at a much slower rate than other bodily tissues. (www.wisegeek.com)

BACK TO BLACK

TITLE: Without continual growth and progress, such words as improvement, achievement, and success have no meaning. (Benjamin Franklin)

BACK TO BLACK

Since I couldn't physically take care of my daughter, I made up for it emotionally and verbally, and not always in a good way. I was desperate to find some sort of control. I was not always pleasant to be around during this phase. I had started out so strong. I had stayed positive for the first five months, and I really and truly thought I was going to beat this thing. Unfortunately, when I didn't heal as quickly as I wanted, I felt myself drop back into a gloomy, rotten place. I was cranky frustrated... bratty. This psychotic over-achiever jumped on the crazy train more than once, or even twice. I think I took up permanent residence there for a while. Yet on the outside, I "looked" like all was well.

I desperately needed to find a way to control something, anything. I turned into super sonic, micro-management mommy. From my lofty perch of self-righteousness, I told my sister and my husband how to hold the baby, change the baby, bathe the baby, and dress the baby. I told them what groceries to buy, how to clean the carpet, wash the dishes, where to sit, how to stand, what to wear... I think you get the picture. I could control my surroundings only by making wide proclamations for those in my immediate vicinity to follow. I also wanted them and *only* them to participate.

Out of pure desperation, I wouldn't let anyone but my husband or my sister take care of me or the baby. It was selfish of me, but I couldn't afford the extra burden. If my daughter got off of her schedule and stayed up all night crying, I stayed up all night crying. Not just from new parent sleep deprivation, but from a place of overwhelming physical pain.

No one intended for this to happen. I knew that. But knowing that and living through that were two very different things. Sometimes that "ugly" inner two- year-old came out, and she was not very nice. Not nice at all.

No one really understood the agony of my constant pain. Rightfully so. For sure I never understood this kind of challenge, until I went through it myself. No one in my immediate circle of family or friends had ever experienced this. It really is a rare and unusual situation. I have only met one other person who has dealt with this particular injury. One.

This lack of connection left a large chasm between me and the well-meaning people around me. It was completely unintentional, but lonely nonetheless. There was also a large gap between my desire to be vulnerable and my ability to actually be vulnerable. Perhaps if I had learned how to achieve this balance I might have been a little less psychotic. Maybe.

All around me people kept saying,

"Hey, we just want to be part of the baby's life."

"Hey, we just want to help if we can."

"Hello. Is anybody in there? Let us in!"

I wanted to let them in. I so deeply wanted to, but I didn't have the strength to deal with it. I just couldn't make room for anything *else*. I was paralyzed by the fear that I would never walk normally again. I couldn't make room in my brain to be "nice" to others also. Again, I allowed this inability to be "normal" make me feel like a pariah. I found myself fighting against the "tsk, tsk" of those hospital nurses all over again. Only this time, I was fighting everybody around me, even when I didn't need to.

In order to endure, I became a recluse. While in the early days, I allowed all kinds of visitors to come by and "check up" on us, now I received visitors in small, short doses. That's all the brave-face-wearing I could handle. Anytime I could steer the conversation away from me and over to the glories of my newborn, I definitely did. I kept everything to myself except for an occasional meltdown. I was sarcastic and brusque and sometimes even downright rude. There are a lot of dear friends who more than deserve an apology from me.

My failings in this area motivated me to rely heavily on my faith. I spent an inordinate amount of my time in prayer (*Might as well, right? What else would I do with all that time?!?*). My prayer life was the one place I felt like I could be "real." The one place where I felt like I could sob uncontrollably, scream, kick (mentally), and be utterly "upset" about what I was going through. I did not feel like I had that kind of freedom anywhere else. Unfortunately, since I was never alone, all of this went on in my mind. It was more of a silent form of prayer and confession. Private.

On the outside, I was smiling at my baby, because it certainly wasn't her fault mommy was in such a funk. I was supporting my husband, because it certainly wasn't his fault he was in grad school when all this went down. I was trying to be kind to my baby sister, because for SURE she deserved to be treated well. I was trying, but I was not always successful at walking out this prayer. I lost it on more than one occasion (just ask my sister… she's got lots of stories), but I can only assume, or at least hope, that without this outlet of faith, I would have been worse… so much worse.

Somewhere in the middle of all that… drama… the fighter in me took over. I began to realize I needed goals. Small, obtainable, daily goals that would bring a taste of sanity to my struggle.

Goal #1:   Get out of bed without help. *Check.*

Goal #2:   Go to the bathroom alone. *Check.*

Goal #3:   Walk more than a couple of feet with a walker. *Almost.*

Goal #4:   Make it down the steps in front of our building without assistance. *Maybe next week.*

Goal #5:   Get OUT of a crappy, rattle ridden wheelchair. *Not so fast, crazy lady.*

These goals were realistically achievable, but as is true with all major injuries, recovery takes time. Lots and lots of time.

Unfortunately, I also had a few road blocks in my way I had to hobble around. I already mentioned the episiotomy thing, no need to talk about that again. I mentioned the walker and the wheelchair, but now I faced something new. Sometimes, a serious injury is like a "handy-man special." You repair the roof only to find you have mold in the walls.

At the sixth month mark, I noticed I was still in a lot of pain, not walking well, and I had a large amount of swelling around my injury. It seemed a little excessive to me, even for a separated pelvis. It seemed doubly excessive to me for a healthy athlete who normally heals quickly. In desperation, I consulted an expert.

Before my daughter was born, my husband and I had both had wrist surgery for very minor reasons. (These surgeries were minor. Trust me, they are not part of the bigger story. I promise.) My husband and I both loved the orthopedic surgeon who performed these surgeries. We kind of felt like he was a rock star (he was). We told him our tale of woe over the phone with the idea that he would give us a referral. He not only listened to us, he immediately booked me for an MRI at his office (told you this guy was awesome). He explained that sometimes with a separated pelvis injury, the cartilage does not heal correctly, and a surgeon will have to go back to the injury site and place a metal plate across the pubic bones to help them to go "back together." He went on to explain that this MRI would reveal whether I was one of those people. *No. Please. Just. No.*

Thankfully, the MRI revealed my cartilage was doing its job. Thank God! It was scarring over just like it should, and my pubic bones had made their way back to an "acceptable" distance. Not back to normal... but acceptable. For the rest of my life, I would have hips where I never had hips before. I'm not sure, but maybe that's another silver lining?

Unfortunately, the MRI also revealed "traumatic arthritic swelling" around the injury site. *Huh?* That's right, instead of healing quickly like most young athletes would, I had developed arthritis. Something else "rare" to add to my growing collection of absurdity. Yay, me.

Ultimately, I didn't care what the diagnosis was as long as there was a reason behind my slowness to heal. It was such a relief to hear that, at least in this instance, I was not crazy. It felt good to have an excuse for what had previously felt like failure.

The healing process for arthritic swelling turned out to be pretty easy. First, I was put on a course of anti-inflammatory drugs. That sounds fancier than it was. I took a double dose of an over-the-counter pain reliever twice a day for four weeks. Yes, it was that simple. No, I do not understand how all the pain I was in could be solved by something that small. This seemingly simple solution worked. I started to be able to walk. And move. And carry stuff. I remember these days as a huge turning point for me. I went from completely incapacitated to having a purpose. If I stuck with the demands of my rehab, I was going to get better... finally.

Thank God for orthopedic surgeons who, even though they are rock stars and are incredibly busy, still find the time to treat you more like a friend than a patient. *And* they actually go out of their way to help you heal. Thank God.

Now that I had the pain and swelling thing worked out I needed new goals. I had walked away from the walker (yes!). I had removed myself from the wheelchair (hallelujah!). I had taken off the pelvic brace (it did nothing for my figure anyway), and now it was finally time to move FORWARD.

Yes! Time to make another list.

Goal #1:   Be able to stand long enough to change baby's diaper. *Check.*

Goal #2:   Be able to carry baby around apartment without assistance OR fear of dropping her. *Check.*

Goal #3:   Be able to bounce stroller down front steps of building without dropping stroller or sending baby head first into the concrete sidewalk. *Almost.*

Goal #4:   Be able to walk to the playground and back without stopping traffic on Riverside Drive. *Maybe next week.*

Goal #5:   Walk across Broadway in one light cycle while pushing a stroller and not put baby in mortal danger. *Not so fast, crazy lady.*

It was going to take great effort to survive living in NYC without my sister's help. The truth was she needed to go home, get a job, and move on with her life. The other side of that truth is I could barely make it through the day without her. Not only did I need to be able to walk again, I also needed to take care of a child. I needed to be able to carry her, feed her, change her, bathe her, walk her to the playground and the library. I needed to be able to handle taking her with me on daily errands like grocery shopping or to doctor appointments or to the post office. I was worried I wouldn't be able to care for my baby in this crazy city by myself.

I also needed to learn how to navigate my city again. In NY, when you can't walk, a lot of things seem dangerous (*actually, when you can't walk, move, or carry stuff, EVERYTHING seems dangerous, but I digress...*). My end game was to get to the point where I could cross the light at Broadway in one traffic cycle while pushing a stroller. I know that sounds simple, but it took me five months to achieve.

I couldn't train for this goal in the way I was used to training. Rehab was very different from the kinds of workouts I used to do. I had to start small, very small.

I worked slowly and gently until I could walk around the apartment unassisted. Yes!

Then, I practiced as often as I could stand it, until I could confidently get down the stairs in front of our building without holding on to the railing. Yes!

Then, I figured out how to work the stairs with a stroller in my hands (yes, of course I practiced this task while my sister held the baby! I was crazy, but not irresponsible).

Once a day, I worked until I could walk to the end of the block and back to the apartment by myself (sorry former neighborhood dwellers... yes, that was me perpetually in your way).

After I found I could walk more than a block, I worked steadily until I could cross a one way street on my own (without my husband or sister stopping traffic for me).

After that, it was officially time to tackle walking across Broadway. This psychotic-over-achiever with a two-year-old alter ego did not like doing things more than once. I liked to succeed on the first or maybe the second try. I was not comfortable with how long it took for me to master this task. I do not want to remember how many horns blared at me on my first few attempts.

I do wish, just once, I had enough energy to slam my hand down on the hood of a taxi and yell,

"Hey! I'm (barely) walking here!"

I have always wanted to say that.

Or at the very least, I needed to carry a giant neon sign that said "Separated Pelvis. Please be Patient." I think even New Yorkers would have extended a bit of grace my way if they had only known. If only...

Since I had become so accomplished in my ability to achieve small goals, I broke down the crossing of Broadway task into small steps of achievement.

First, I had to get from my side of Broadway to the median in the middle. This only took a few weeks to master. Yes. Good. Check that off my list.

Second, I had to make it across the "other" side. Thank goodness for that oasis of benches in the middle where I could stop and rest. Sometimes, I could make it across the other side of Broadway without causing a traffic jam… sometimes.

A few weeks later, I was able to make it all of the way across the street, as long as I was unencumbered (insert: not carrying a baby or pushing a stroller), before the light changed. As long as I had the median in the middle to rest, I felt safe. But, that wasn't my goal. NYC was full of large intersections and most of them did not have medians in the middle. Building up enough speed to cross a two-way street in 30 seconds was crucial to my survival.

Back to the movie.

OPEN: EXTERIOR NEW YORK CITY STREET
CORNER OF 106TH AND BROADWAY

CAMERA at street level focused on group of three. SISTER stands next to MOMMY on corner of busy NY intersection.

SISTER might as well have a ray of sunshine shining just on her. She looks strong, healthy, bouncy.

MOMMY on the other hand looks fragile, broken. Her face showing the strain of her workout.

BABY is well bundled in stroller in front of MOMMY, oblivious to all of it.

It's early spring but it's still chilly. Everyone is bundled in coats, hats, gloves and scarves. The sky is gray and there is a small amount of wind blowing, but it is a decent day. Cold but not bitter.

SISTER
You ready?

MOMMY
Not yet. Maybe the next cycle.

Both stand on corner. SISTER bends down to check on DAUGHTER. She's fine.

CAMERA closes in on MOMMY who stares up at traffic light, and whispers while counting the seconds shown on the traffic box as it clicks down 25… 24…. 23….

MOMMY
Okay. Let's get ready.

MOMMY smiles at her daughter and pats her child's head, more for moral support than anything else. Then she steels herself against the chaotic movement of the city, takes a deep breath and looks up.

TRAFFIC BOX: 9… 8… 7… 6…

BACK TO MOMMY

                              MOMMY
                            (whispers)
                          3... 2... 1... go...

MOMMY takes off walking as quickly as she can. Her
face is determined as she forces herself to move
her body forward while pushing the stroller.

SISTER walks slowly next to her "making space"
with her body to keep the crowds and the cars
away. She does this by instinct and actually has
developed a way to do this without making it
obvious to her sister.

The crowd parts to walk around the slow moving
group. They make it halfway to the median in
middle of street. Group pauses to catch their
breath.

TRAFFIC BOX: 18... 17... 16...

Group continues across second half of Broadway.

TRAFFIC BOX: 3... 2... 1...

Group about 2/3 of the way across.
MOMMY has about 10 more steps to safety.

TRAFFIC BOX: orange hand begins blinking...

Group has almost reached other side of street.
TRAFFIC BOX: orange hand blinks... three... two...

one... DON'T WALK.

BACK TO group as we see all three barely step
onto sidewalk before cars take off.

Exaggerate taxis taking off when light turns green
- like the start of the Indy 500 - squealing
tires, etc. Exaggerate closeness of taxi to back
foot of MOMMY as the car "skims" past.

> MOMMY
> (large inhale and exhale)
> Yes!

Gives high-five to SISTER.
Gives high-five to DAUGHTER.

Beads of sweat show from beneath MOMMY's hat.
She smiles with tears running down her face.
Happiness and sadness in the same space.

FADE TO BLACK

I made it. I completed my task. Success. Progress.
Achievement. I wanted to feel like celebrating in wild abandon,
but I didn't. Something was holding me back. I remember this
moment vividly. It is burned in my brain. It felt like a moment of
great victory, but also like a moment of great sadness. It was time.
My sister was going home soon.

CHAPTER EIGHT
HUMILITY AND HUMILIATION CAN SOMETIMES FEEL LIKE THE SAME THING

OPEN: EXTERIOR NY STREET

TITLE: Two Months Later

Weather has changed to blue skies and sunshine.

CAMERA HOLDS on view of street from sidewalk as SISTER puts last piece of luggage in trunk of rental car.

SISTER walks around car to sidewalk where MOMMY and BABY are waiting.

                    SISTER
        Okay, that's it. I guess this is goodbye.

SISTER AND MOMMY hug for an extended time.

Both have tears running down their faces. BABY
doesn't understand so is just awkwardly along
for the ride.

                    MOMMY
            Go. Do something fun.
                  (Pause)
        (Pulls away to look SISTER in the eye)
               Thank you.

SISTER nods. She takes baby, hugs her and
whispers goodbye through her tears. Hands her
back to MOMMY.

                    SISTER
            (wipes away tears)
               OK. Well see ya.

                    MOMMY
            (wipes away tears)
               See ya.

SISTER climbs into car and drives away. MOMMY and
BABY left standing on sidewalk waving goodbye.

FADE TO BLACK

   Sending my sister back home was... difficult. We were
almost a year in to our extended family dynamic when I finally
released her back to her life. Mostly, I was so happy she could
"go" and live her life without the burden of a newborn and an
injured sister. Selfishly, I was worried. It was never going to
be "good" for her to leave, but it was time for me to take back

this piece of my life.

Remember, in the last chapter, when I listed my goals of accomplishments? The boxes I was able to check? I forgot to list how I worked until I could make it to the playground and back unassisted, or how I worked until I could carry groceries and push a stroller, or how I worked until I could bend over to put shoes on, or how I worked until... you get my point. Crossing Broadway was my biggest goal, the goal that made me feel like I could survive in my city again, but I had all these other little goals that also needed to fall into place. Just because I could "walk" again, didn't mean I had full control of my life. That took several more months to really master.

I focused on my daily motherhood tasks, so I wouldn't have a lot of time to focus on anything else. It was helpful to have this sweet little cutie as a distraction. Somehow, those big brown eyes, pudgy cheeks, and adorable dimples made it all seem worth it. Even though my husband's load was slightly lighter during his third year of grad school, he was still busy in a way that left me feeling alone and vulnerable. I think I would have completely melted into a pile of mush if I didn't have a reason to get up everyday. If nothing else, I had to raise this little girl. She needed me.

It was a lot of fun watching her grow. My daughter started communicating early so I remember doing a lot of "talking." Every day. All day. All the time. That girl could really carry on a conversation.

My sister, who, in addition to being a fantastic caregiver was actually trained to be a sign language interpreter, taught my daughter how to sign when she was around four months old. It was one of the best things we ever did. It helped her say what she needed without having to scream to get our attention. Perhaps this helped her start forming words early. Perhaps she would have started talking early anyway. Bottom line, from the moment she was born, she was already smarter than me. I had to work hard to keep up.

At nine months, she pointed out a window and said, "datdide" (outside). After I got over my shock, I told my sister to pack her up and take her to the park.

At twelve months, she was speaking in full sentences. In the fall, after my daughter's first birthday, my sister came back to NY for a visit. Since she was there to help, we decided it would be a good time to visit the Central Park Zoo. It was the first time my daughter had ever seen penguins. She has loved them ever since.

During lunch, my little communicator pushed her plate of fries away and said, "All done. See quack, quack quacks."

We had barely started eating, so I answered her with, "Finish eating first please and then you can get down."

To which she answered, "ALL DONE! QUACK. QUACK. QUACKS!"

Got it. Penguins are more important than greasy sustenance. We quickly packed up our lunch and hustled back over to the penguins. When a toddler knows what she wants that strongly, I have found it's easier to respond right away.

At sixteen months, we would take rides on the bus just so she could look out the window and identify her letters. She was like a little commentator. "Look, Mommy. A! D! C! Dubbawoo!" she proclaimed, much to the dismay of the other passengers.

"She really likes letters." I would say as a lame form of explanation.

That's called preschool for the price of a bus ticket.

By 18 months, she was forming complete ideologies. She yelled at me once because I was trying to put her shoes on and she was... distracted. She was still practically a baby after all. A fact I would often forget.

In my frustration I yelled, "Abigail! Focus!"

"No, Mommy!" she yelled back. "I have to multi-task!"

Ugh.

She loved to go with her daddy to the corner deli and get a "boogulah" (bagel) for her and a cup of coffee for him. She loved to eat at the diner (challah French toast, yum!). She loved the turtle fountain at the playground. She hated the swings.

On the way home from music class, we always had to stop at the tiny health food store (yes the same one that hosted the eucalyptus oil incident) and get a banana. They were always hanging in the window where she could easily see them. Often, I tried to do some strategic stroller maneuvering in order to block her line of sight, but she was too smart for me. She had memorized exactly where that store was located, and if I tried to skip it, she would strongly remind me of her need to stop.

And, because we lived in New York, and mommy had an injury, we often found ourselves inside a taxi. At that time in NY, there were signs on the back seats of all taxis that read, "COMPLAINTS. 1-800-NYC-TAXI." Because we often saw those words, taxi and complaints were two of the first words she ever learned to spell. She would point her little finger at the back seat and say,

"T-A-X-I. Taxi."

I would respond, "That's right. Taxi."

She was learning to read, NYC style.

All of these memories are sweet, but the one I remember most was the winter when my daughter was around 19 months old, and had begun walking longer distances. She no longer wanted to ride in her stroller. It is a particularly special memory, because I was simultaneously learning to walk longer distances too. I can still see it now, the two of us slowly navigating down the city street holding hands. She was my buffer against the speed of the city, my excuse for walking so slowly.

I was so thankful for this for two reasons. One, my daughter took the stigma of injury off of my back, she helped me look "normal." Two, I see now where this injury created an incredible moment of grace for both my daughter and me. Without this burden, I would not have paused to soak in and enjoy everything my daughter paused to enjoy in this great city. No, I would have gone back to my busy, demanding job and my busy demanding life. I would have made her feel like a constant annoyance, a ball and chain around my ankle always making me "late" for something. I would have driven us both crazy. Thankfully, I was (reluctantly) learning a better way.

People often say, it is healthy to find one positive thing to say about an extremely negative situation. "They" say sometimes it can change a very dour perspective into an opportunity for hope. I was not thankful for much about my injury, but for this ONE thing I'm not only thankful, but grateful. My daughter and I got to conquer this together, and I'm so glad I didn't miss it.

Overall, she was a pretty independent little soul, thank goodness. She took it all in stride (*pun intended*) in the way that little people do, particularly little New Yorkers. I found not only did I love this little human sharing my space, I actually liked her... most of the time. She was delightful, but she wasn't perfect.

No matter how badly I was injured, I still insisted on doing all the things "good" parents were supposed to do (psychotic over-achiever strikes again). We went to music class, swim lessons, the playground, and the library. I did my best to get her out and let her experience the city. She needed to do something other than be stuck in the apartment all day. She wasn't the only one. These trips were also part of my "rehab" so it was a perfect opportunity to have our cake and eat it too.

Thankfully, all that rehab was working. I was finally starting to feel better. My legs had more strength. I was able to walk longer, carry things, cook, take showers instead of baths, shave my legs, and just be better. I almost felt normal. However, if I was looking for perfection in my life, I wasn't going to find it here.

As I continued on in my quest for healing, I faced a multitude of other "humbling" situations. Yes, sometimes even more "humbling" than having someone help you go potty. Sometimes, those situations were out of my control and sometimes, I brought them on myself.

It was early spring. My daughter was around 20 months old, and my husband was almost done with grad school. I had made plans to attend his final drama thesis. It was a vague, intense, ancient classic almost no one has ever heard of, but I was looking forward to seeing it anyway. I think I would have gone out to see almost anything at this point. Life had not been kind to my marriage. No matter how much I didn't want to see this particular show, this was going to be a rare opportunity to show my husband some well-deserved support.

It was also a sweet opportunity to go out. New moms, I know you hear me screamin'. You do not have to suffer a separated pelvis in order to feel trapped by your new title of "mother." I had called upon a couple of friends to babysit, and for the first time since my sister had gone home, I was out, on my own, in my city. Ah, the sweet, sweet feeling of freedom.

The lights of the city had just come on, and the sidewalks were actually damp from a recent rain. I didn't even have to rent a rainmaker to make my scene look better for the camera. Nature had already conspired to create it perfectly. In my head, I felt like a million bucks. I was almost rejoicing at this return to the person I used to know. I even wore my favorite pair of boots. I was ready to take on the world. Did I take a breath and savor this moment? No. I did not.

Get comfortable, it's time to go back to the movie.

OPEN: Black Screen

TITLE: Never mess with a New Yorker, no matter what age she is.

FADE TO: EXTERIOR NEW YORK CITY
UPPER WEST SIDE - EARLY EVENING

CAMERA HOLDS on view of city street on Upper West Side of NYC. The lights of the city have just come on. The soft sounds of people sitting outside at the recently opened sidewalk cafés rise up to the sky mingling with the soft spring breeze. The traffic noise is light, muffled, almost nonexistent. The sidewalks are damp from a recent rain.

MOMMY is walking.... slowly... painfully along on the sidewalk. You can tell by her face she thinks she is walking perfectly. In her imagination she is walking in a way that no one can actually tell she is injured. She thinks she is flying down the street. We switch back and forth from reality to her imagination several times to establish the humor of her delusional thought process.

MOMMY notices an elderly woman walking about a half a block ahead. Elderly woman is hunched over, almost into the shape of the letter "C."

From MOMMY's POV CAMERA zooms in on the older woman with the laser intensity of a warrior. TARGET

SCOPE focuses on the back of the older woman.
BEEP. BEEP. BEEP.

ROBOTIC VOICE
Target acquired

And so the race was on.

MUSIC: Inspirational running music (perhaps something like *Chariots of Fire*)

Sidewalk morphs into running track with a looming finish line. PEOPLE at sidewalk cafés become spectators.

CAMERA toggles back and forth from elderly lady to MOMMY who are both now "running" in slow motion as if sprinting in an epic race.

CUT TO: real time to show elderly lady walking down the street with the café patrons ignoring her and everyone on the city sidewalk going about business as usual.

CUT BACK TO: MOMMY who is still sprinting on track with café patrons cheering her on from the "stands" which are really just the sidewalk café barriers. You can even see the names of some of the restaurants as she "runs" by.

Exaggerate both are moving at same slow-motion speed even though MOMMY's imagination makes it seem like they are both sprinting.

Suddenly, MOMMY doubles over in pain and is forced to stop. In her imagination, it's like she blew out a hamstring just like a world-class sprinter might. She grimaces in pain, tries to keep going but can't and falls onto "track." She crashes to the ground with a face of defeat and agony.

ELDERLY WOMAN sprints across the finish line while the crowd at the tables cheers wildly. The SPECTATORS pour onto the sidewalk to congratulate ELDERLY WOMAN encircling her with crazy celebration. They lift her up on their shoulders. She pumps her fist in victory.

SCENE MORPHS back to reality. MUSIC stops. Sounds of city return. Elderly woman walks calmly down city street.

MOMMY stands in the middle of the sidewalk as the city goes on around her. She is doubled over, breathing deeply, with sweat running down her face.

VOICE-OVER/MOMMY
Owwwwwuchhhhhh. Ouch. Ouch.

FADE TO BLACK

My brain simply could not accept the truth that my body was different. My trek from our apartment to the performance space was the distance of about 14 city blocks, about a mile and a half. It was going to be hard enough just to walk that far.

I had just crossed 110th street when I first saw her, and (in my mind at least) challenged her to an injured, limping version of an Olympic race. She was an older woman, probably more accurately referred to as elderly, but I don't want to be "ageist," so we will just call her older. She was completely focused on herself. She had no idea I even existed. I thought to myself, I wonder if I could catch up to her? I mean, surely, by now, I could walk fast enough to pass a c-shaped woman over 80... couldn't I?

Please understand I'm not knocking that determined spirit that allows people to come back from crippling injuries to overwhelming victories. Under other circumstances, I applaud it. Unfortunately, my overcoming a traumatic injury story needed more time. I needed more patience.

Eventually, I would enjoy a multitude of victories over my injury, but in this moment, I had to come to grips with its permanence. Even my boots couldn't give me enough chutzpah to change the reality before me. My life had changed. Forever.

My only solace, as I doubled over in pain and watched that woman completely leave me in a giant cloud of her dust, was she was a New Yorker. I should know better than to pick on a New Yorker, no matter what age she is. From now on, I definitely would have to learn to pick on somebody my own size. Like maybe an over 80-year-old, c-shaped woman from New Jersey.

I made it to the theater. I watched the show. I cheered for my husband. Ultimately, all that effort was a glowing success. My husband was glad I was in the audience.

Even though the show itself was tortuous to watch, it was a good thing I was able to sit down for 2.5 hours straight. Everyone else was probably itching to get up and stretch. Not me. I was resting up for my walk home.

After my big race, things sort of continued on, in a "life keeps moving even if you aren't moving with it" sort of way. I continued to heal. My daughter continued to grow. My husband finished grad school.

Beyond that, everything else became a giant blur that went something like this:

- my husband started looking for a job
- my husband interviewed for a few different jobs
- my husband reluctantly took a job
- my husband graduated
- we moved

I don't know if you noticed, but there is something missing from the list above. There are a lot of "my husbands" on there and no mention of me. I had no input for what happened next to us. I sat back and let life... take over. It was a strange place for me to be, but I didn't have the strength to fight it.

One more thing about that list, I said my husband reluctantly took a job because the job was in teaching not acting. Our Hail Mary pass had reached the end zone, but we weren't doing a victory dance. We were facing the music.

I think, even though he went to school to have the opportunity to teach, he still had hope he wouldn't have to start teaching *so soon*. We both had *hope* our lives were not going to remain so drastically altered. We had *hope* that these transitions were going to get easier. Unfortunately, it was just the beginning of learning how to adapt for us.

This new job was in Boston. In case anyone missed it, Boston is not New York. Suddenly, we were moving away from my place in this world. My home. My city. It felt like adding insult to injury... literally.

It is hard to move under any circumstances. The stoic in me took the punches with a brave face. Again, my pride did not allow me to feel the full measure of the pain of this moment.

Yes, of course, it is right to figure out how to count your

blessings. It is right to try to see the good in the midst of the hard. It is also right to be present in the moment and allow yourself an appropriate sadness for the things in your life that are painful.

For me, I needed to give myself the time to grieve over my pain first, and then, in a healthy way, embrace the task before me. Unfortunately, I had a bad habit of skipping the grief and embracing the denial. I did not overcome these first major blows in a healthy way. I compartmentalized them for later. My husband was not the only one good at acting.

I did, however, allow myself a small moment of grief as I sat in a rental car and looked at my place of residence for the last time. I looked up at our apartment building and I said goodbye to my life in NYC. I said goodbye to the place where my daughter had been born. I said goodbye to the place where I felt like I had been "born" myself. I allowed myself this one moment to shed a few tears, as I drove away from the only place that had ever felt like home.

INSTANT REPLAY

MOMMY hits the ground one, two, three times.

SMACK! SMACK! SMACK!

                    VOICE-OVER/MOMMY
              Ouch. (pause) Ouch.

CHAPTER NINE

THANK YOU, BOSTON FIRE DEPARTMENT

I decided to treat Boston like a fresh start. I had been knocked down, punched around a little, but I dug in my heels and tried to fight back. I did my best to move forward from my move, my injury, my discouragement and my sadness. Everybody likes to pretend. With my mask firmly in place and my smile plastered on my face, I tried to climb back up to the top of the pile, hoping that from up high, I could see better what was coming next. Everything had changed, really changed, and I was determined to figure out how to make that work. I did not always succeed.

We had only been living in Boston for two weeks. I was barely familiar with our new home and I was still in the process of unpacking boxes. Essentially, I knew where the grocery store and the playground were located. Other than that, Boston could have been Paris for all I knew.

We lived in a typical brownstone building in the Boston suburb of Brookline. We were blessed with the reasonable rent of a small apartment in an otherwise expensive neighborhood. When we moved in, we had no idea we had received such a phenomenal deal. We were too busy focusing on our cool new apartment that had two *separate* bedrooms, a *separate* kitchen, a living room completely *unattached* to the kitchen *and* a bathroom that wasn't pink. What in the world were we going to do with all of this space?

We had a front door to our building that opened into a foyer with mailboxes. Beyond that, there was a second door, the actual front door, that required a key to open. Once inside, we had to climb two flights of wooden stairs (with a beautiful hand carved railing, I might add) up to our apartment. From there, we walked into the small foyer we shared with our neighbors across the hall to another "front" door that led into our actual apartment. Is anyone else tired yet? I certainly was.

For convenience, we had a back door that went down three flights of stairs to the basement, and when necessary, out to the back of the building. I suppose it was also an additional exit for safety's sake, similar to fire escapes, but really it was a way to make it easier to take out your trash. That's what I was doing when I accidentally locked my 23 month old daughter in the apartment... alone.

Hopefully, you have some popcorn left, because it's time to go back to the movie.

OPEN: INTERIOR/BROWNSTONE APARTMENT/BOSTON,MA

CAMERA HOLDS on MOMMY as she stands at apartment back door that leads from kitchen to back stairs. She holds small trash bag in her hand. As she starts down stairs she calls back to DAUGHTER who is in other room.

MOMMY
Hey, kiddo I'm going down to take out the trash. I'll be right back.

                    DAUGHTER
            (answers from off camera)
                   OK, Mommy.

CAMERA HOLDS on MOMMY as she very carefully
leaves door partially open so that it is not
wide open but not closed all the way.

CAMERA follows MOMMY as she starts down dimly
lit, narrow, wooden stairs to back of building.
About half way down she passes by an open window.
A soft, summer, New England breeze blows by her
face and hair. She smiles.

MOMMY walks through cluttered, unfinished
basement and continues out back door. Throws
bag into garbage bin. She turns around, walks
back through basement and up the stairs. She
walks by the open window and continues to her
apartment.

CAMERA HOLDS on open window.

CAMERA follows an animated, exaggerated motion
of wind as it blows from the open window up the
stairs, past MOMMY, blowing her clothes and hair
as it goes by. Sound of door slamming echoes
down stairway.

MOMMY stops dead in her tracks.

                VOICE-OVER/MOMMY
              Was that...? Did I...?

PAUSE as reality sets in.

MOMMY
(chants)
Oh no... oh no... oh no... oh no...
oh no... oh no... oh no... oh no... oh no...

She hurries (as fast as she can) up the stairs to her apartment's back door. She frantically grabs door knob and tries to turn it. She cannot open it. In disbelief, she keeps trying in hopes of a different outcome. She lets go of doorknob and starts moving in frantic circles smacking herself on her forehead.

VOICE-OVER/MOMMY
(whisper)
Stupid... stupid... stupid

PAUSE

I told my daughter I would be right back. She, of course, was fine. She was already extremely self-sufficient, after all she is a native New Yorker. I wasn't worried about leaving her. I was only going to be gone a for a few seconds. When I heard the slam of the door, I felt a very intense panic take over my entire body. I felt like I couldn't breathe.

UNPAUSE

CAMERA holds on MOMMY standing outside door on back steps.

MOMMY
Kiddo? Sweet Girl? Can you hear me?
Can you come to the kitchen please?

DAUGHTER
(from other side of door)
Mommy?

MOMMY
(knocks on door lightly)
I'm right here. On the steps.

MOMMY
Can you help MOMMY?
Can you open the door?

DAUGHTER
Okay.

CAMERA close up of doorknob. Doorknob jiggles.

DAUGHTER
I don't know how Mommy.
I can't, Mommy. I can't!

MOMMY
Okay. Okay. Don't worry. Mommy will get help.
Go back to watching TV, okay? I will be right
back. *Right back*. Okay? (pause) Okay?

DAUGHTER
(whimper, but resilient)
Okay, Mommy.

PAUSE

I stood on the back steps desperately trying to explain to my daughter how to open a door. It was an effort in futility. *How is it she knew how to work a remote but I had, in order to keep her "safe," taught her NOT to open doors? Irony... I do not like you...*

I had no building superintendent to contact. I knew NO neighbors. I had no way to call my husband. I had no way to break down the door. I was stuck on the back stairs, and my daughter was stuck inside the apartment. *And* she was crying. It broke what was left of my fragile heart. I was alone, frustrated and scared. I had no idea what to do.

Note: This is the time in the movie when the audience would be screaming at the person on the screen. Everyone read-watching this right now is yelling, "Pry open the door! Didn't you see that metal thing in the basement? Use that! Come on! Use your head!" But, I'm the one IN the movie/book, and I can't hear you. So stop yelling at me.

UNPAUSE

CAMERA holds on MOMMY. She leans on door with forehead and places hand on door (reaching out for her daughter)

> VOICE-OVER/MOMMY
> (whisper)
> Okay.

After pausing for a moment to get her bearings, MOMMY moves into action. CAMERA follows MOMMY as she climbs down narrow stairway, walks through basement and out the back of the building. MOMMY circles around to alley and moves around to front of building. She climbs the front stairs, opens the front door and enters into mailbox vestibule. CAMERA holds on MOMMY's face. She takes a deep breath and reaches out hoping to find the front door has been left open.

CUT TO: hand on door handle. Door is locked. She tugs on door handle a few more times in disbelief. Again, she rests her forehead on the door and tries to figure out what to do next.

                    VOICE-OVER/MOMMY
          (as she bangs her head on the door)
     ...of course the door is locked... safe
            neighborhood... good for kids...
                 safe... safe... safe...

After another brief pause to collect herself, MOMMY moves to action again. She goes outside and looks up and down residential street searching for something... anything... anyone...

Finding nothing, she begins to walk in circles, hand banging on forehead and muttering to herself.

CAMERA circles around MOMMY to show confusion, anxiety

                          MOMMY
          (muttering, sounds crazy, anxious)
       Should I start knocking on doors? Should I
        walk down to the corner and find a phone?

(repeat several times)

PAUSE

I walked outside to find there was no one in sight. No one. I was all alone in a quiet residential neighborhood in the suburbs of a city I didn't know. I did my best to think clearly. Normally in these moments, I'm relatively level headed (remember that whole story about the bull?), but since I was still functioning from a place of trauma and stress, I was operating from somewhere... else...

UNPAUSE

CAMERA still circling around MOMMY who is still pacing and muttering

CUT TO: Woman coming out of building two doors down. MOMMY runs to catch up to WOMAN.

                    MOMMY
                 (overbearing)
           Can I use your cell phone?

WOMAN pulls away from MOMMY as if MOMMY is attacking her. Her face registers fear and confusion.

                    MOMMY
     (still frantic but trying to sound "normal")
           Sorry, no. I'm just... I just...
         I accidentally locked my daughter
        in the apartment. I need to call 911.

Reluctantly, WOMAN hands over her phone. MOMMY
dials 911. She speaks to dispatcher who assures
her the fire department is on its way. Wave of
relief washes over MOMMY. MOMMY hands phone
back to WOMAN.

                    MOMMY
    Thank you. Thank you. Thank you, so much.

MOMMY walks back to her building. WOMAN turns
quickly and walks away, glad to be getting away
from the crazy woman who practically accosted
her and took her phone.

MOMMY goes back to anxiously pacing in front
of building watching for fire department. With
impatience and frustration, she runs around to
back of building, through basement and up the
back stairs. She yells through door.

                    MOMMY
    Kiddo? You still okay? (pause) Kiddo?

CUT TO: DAUGHTER as she walks into kitchen.

Split screen of MOMMY and DAUGHTER on either
side of door.
                   DAUGHTER
                    Mommy?

                    MOMMY
           (with sigh of relief)
    I'm right here. Are you still okay?

                    DAUGHTER
                 Yes. I'm okay.

                     MOMMY
            I called the fire department
            they will be here soon.

                    DAUGHTER
                     Okay.

                     MOMMY
            I'll be right back. Okay?

                    DAUGHTER
                     Okay.

MOMMY pauses again with head resting on door.
Huge sigh. Turns to go back down stairs and out
to front of building.

CUT TO: MOMMY pacing up and down sidewalk looking
for fire truck. It is eerily quiet. MOMMY wrings
hands nervously. Air is heavy with anticipation.

Loud sirens blare in the distance.

MOMMY looks frantically down the street to catch
a glimpse of the fire truck. Sound of sirens grow
louder as fire truck turns down street. Truck
pulls up in front of building and four firemen
jump out.

                          MOMMY
                       (sheepish)
                          Hi.
PAUSE

The fire department arrived with their lights flashing and
sirens screaming. I was mortified by my introduction to the
neighborhood. Thank God the woman with the cell phone had
already gone.

UNPAUSE

                         FIREMAN
                     (with swagger)
            What seems to be the problem?

PAUSE

He might as well have patted me on the head and called
me "little lady," but there was no time for indignation so....

UNPAUSE

                          MOMMY
          My daughter is locked in our apartment...
        on the second floor (points up to building)...
             the front and the back doors are both
             locked... (embarrassed) I can't get in...

CAMERA holds on fireman as they form a circle
"huddle" that includes MOMMY. From center of
circle, CAMERA moves in close up from person to
person as they banter through options.

> FIREMAN #1
>
> So what do you think?

> FIREMAN #2
>
> Use the ladder? Break through the window?

> FIREMAN #3
>
> Break through glass on front door?

> FIREMAN #1
>
> Breakdown back door?

> FIREMAN #2
>
> Call a locksmith?

FIREMAN #4 (leader) rubs chin and takes a moment to think through ideas.

PAUSE

I was frantic to get upstairs and make sure my daughter was safe. Instead, I was standing in the middle of the street with a bunch of firemen running through tactical options. On the outside, I was trying to look calm, sane, competent even. *Sure, I'm fine. Fine. Everything is fine.*

On the inside, I was burning with a need for action. Inside, I was thinking, *Just get your beepity beeping tools and get the beepity beep upstairs and get my daughter. NOW!*

That's when I had my first clear thought. The fog finally lifted. Unfortunately, profanity and clarity sometimes go hand in hand.

UNPAUSE

                    MOMMY
    Do you have something like a crowbar you
     could use to pop open the back door?

                  FIREMAN #4
                    (smug)
    Of course we do. We're the fire department.

PAUSE

   Oh, right. You know what you are doing. I don't. Boy, did I
feel foolish.

UNPAUSE

CAMERA holds on group as LEADER reaches into
truck and grabs crowbar.

CAMERA follows four fireman and MOMMY as they
march in straight line like ducks around to back
of building. MOMMY leads group up back stairs
and stands aside while leader inserts crowbar
between door and door jamb.

CUT TO: close up of door and crowbar. With one
quick pop the door opens.

PAUSE

   All it took was one quick walk up the back stairs with four
firemen, one crowbar jammed into the crack between the door
and the door jamb, and one simple pop of the lock for the door
to open. Why it took four fireman to perform this task, I do not

know. There is a joke in there… somewhere.

I wanted to rush in, scoop up my daughter and forget the whole thing ever happened, but a fireman held me back. I may have been a reluctant participant in the beginning of this mother/daughter relationship, but reluctance was no longer part of my mommy DNA.

UNPAUSE

FIREMAN #4 enters apartment and begins to assess the situation. MOMMY moves forward to follow but FIREMAN #2 puts his hand up to stop her. MOMMY looks at him with a mixture of question and angry determination.

FIREMAN #2

Hold on. Let us check to see
if everything's okay.

MOMMY

(forceful)

I want to see my daughter.

FIREMAN #2

We know. Let us make sure she's alright.

PAUSE

I was furious with them for keeping me away from my daughter, but of course, I knew they were trying to keep us safe. Since they were bigger and stronger than me, I decided to do what they "suggested."

UNPAUSE

                    MOMMY
            (calls out to other room)
        Hey, kiddo it's okay. These men are
            fireman. Mommy is right here.

PAUSE

Calling out to my daughter made me feel a whole lot better and probably meant a whole lot of nothing to her. She wasn't scared, not one little bit.

UNPAUSE

CAMERA holds on group standing awkwardly outside of apartment on back stairs. Time is passing slowly while FIREMAN #4 has gone to check on child. MOMMY fidgets anxiously.

Finally FIREMAN #4 comes around corner holding DAUGHTER in his arms. All is well.

MOMMY pushes past FIREMAN to reach out for DAUGHTER, she hugs her tight with great relief.

                    MOMMY
            Are you really okay?

Daughter nods, yes.

                    MOMMY
            (turns to face FIREMEN)
                (smiling)
            This is my daughter.

```
She turns daughter to face out and gestures
toward FIREMEN


                    MOMMY
             And these guys are the
             Boston Fire Department.


                  FIREMAN #4
                 (with smile)
               Nice to meet you.


FADE TO BLACK
```

The whole thing took about 30 minutes, or as long as one animated Nickelodeon show if you are keeping time like my daughter. Of course to me, it seemed like hours. It bothered me, this new part of myself that couldn't react in a sane way to a difficult situation. I mean, after all, I'm the girl that faced down a bull. What in the world had happened to me? Where was my strength? Where was my resilience? Where was my *faith*?

I had found myself stuck in the middle of major over-reaction to what should have been a simple situation. Unfortunately, I was incapable of simple. There was a chink in my armor, a scar on my body, a bruise on my heart. I was barely surviving from the aches of my first set of punches, so it makes sense I wasn't able to calmly face something new. It makes sense, but it still doesn't make it okay. I was scared, of this new me. I did not like her.

I made several other blunders as I learned to become a Bostonian. For example, never admit you have ever, even for a moment considered cheering for the Yankees. In Boston, you cheer for the Red Sox or nothing. While you are at it, pretend you know how hockey works, who the Patriots are and what cheering for the Celtics means. As sports fans, Bostonians do not mess around. So I swallowed my NYC pride. I blended.

Just like I lost my southern twang when I was younger, I was going to have to learn to speak another new language, almost as if I had moved to a foreign country. I was going to have to stop saying "cawfee" and say "cahfey" instead. I needed to learn how to say "pahck ya cah he-ah" instead of "pack ya cawr he-uh." I needed to understand that the train stops at "Sta-ah Maahkit" not Star Market. My travels have made me fluent in three languages; Southern Twang, New York Yiddish-ese, and now a wicked Bostonian. I held on to NYC as much as I could, but since I didn't want to stick out, I adapted.

We had only moved a short distance north of New York, but suddenly it seemed like we had moved to Siberia. No, of course not literally, Boston does have other seasons besides "cold." Fall is one of its best. It even has a couple of weeks of what some people call summer. My daughter and I used to celebrate when the temperature climbed over 75 degrees, because that meant it was warm enough to go to the pool. It's all relative to what you can tolerate, right? Ultimately, I had to make peace with insanely cold weather and multiple inches of snow. We invested in several new pieces of winter wear and added an extra 15 minutes to our travel time so we could wrap up before we went out. We adjusted.

We didn't have a car so we settled in a neighborhood close to the trains. We paid more in rent for this luxury, but we didn't have to make car payments, or pay for gas, or new tires, or insurance… yep, you get it. Paying a little extra in rent was worth it. Besides, we were used to walking, we were New Yorkers.

We tried to duplicate our life in NY, but that proved to be almost impossible. Everything about Boston was so incredibly *different.*

Physically, our new town required a lot more work to navigate.

We had to learn to walk longer, carry more and climb more stairs. Elevators were an unusual commodity.

There was more distance between train stops. There was more distance between everything.

Instead of crossing the street and walking half a block to the grocery store, we now walked three blocks.

Instead of running downstairs to the laundry next door to our building, we now had to walk four or five blocks... lugging our laundry.

This created a whole new world of "getting around" for me. It added extra challenges to my already compromised body. I wasn't forced to stop functioning altogether, but I did have to re-evaluate my methods. It took some adjusting, but I eventually got to the place where I could navigate our new neighborhood. I'm a chameleon, remember? I blended, I adapted, I adjusted.

The physical challenges added to my life would have been enough to send me over the edge, but this new town challenged my emotional stability too. I was still reeling from, well, all of it. My brain no longer had power over my damaged body. My heart missed NY. I was challenged to find ways to trust this new life was not only God's plan for us, but also His best. I know I was supposed to believe it, but I struggled to actually see it.

Combine all that emotional weight with a husband who was gone a lot (now a professor of theater, as well as a working actor, and was also working as a carpenter for extra money... because, yes, we were still broke), and suddenly I had a recipe for full-blown anxiety.

Rather than face all of these "issues" head on and deal with them, I turned off that part of me and acted like they didn't exist. Occasionally, they continued to show up at inopportune times, but I thought I had them sufficiently suppressed that I could save face with the "outside" world.

Liar, liar pants on fire! says inner-two-year old.

Didn't I learn anything with the whole separated pelvis incident?

Again, I stuffed down the grief and opened the door wide to denial. I may have looked okay on the outside, but inside I was an ugly, hot mess.

After my glorious intro into Boston life, I was lulled into a short "normal" existence. Our life settled into a semi-regular routine. I continued to heal while I stayed home and took care of my two-year-old. My husband spent most of his time at work.

He did what he always does, he jumped in feet first and made it all look so easy. I mean really, he had just moved to Boston and already he had three and sometimes four jobs. He taught classes, directed shows, performed in shows and built scenery on the side. Since I still wasn't in a position to go back to work, the responsibility of taking on extra work to dig us out of our current financial situation rested solely on my husband. It was a heavy burden. He survived by staying busy and somehow found a way to make sweetness out of the sour.

The other side of that equation is that he got to work out his stuff by *going* and *doing*, and I did not. I was stuck at home learning how to walk and locking myself out of apartments.

Yes, I needed him. Yes, I wanted to find a way to let him be part of my pain, but his over-bearing optimism only made me feel more frustrated that I wasn't "happy" too. Unfortunately, as a result of our different views, we developed a new pattern of survival. I pushed him away, so I wouldn't have to face this new "thing" that was settling over my spirit. He stayed busy, because it was easier to give me the space I needed than to force me to talk. It wasn't necessarily the best of the choices before us, but it was all we could manage at the time.

It took me about a year to feel like I really lived in Boston. That's not unusual. Most people say it takes at least that long to fit into somewhere new. Parts of me had even begun to heal. I was finally walking more normally. I could even pull a wagon holding a toddler and groceries all the way from the grocery store to our apartment. I had even made some friends... well... playground acquaintances with potential.

Under other conditions, I probably could have found a better way to "handle" locking myself out of my apartment. I could have found a healthy way to reconcile our move from NYC. I could have figured out a way to share my burdens with the man who crossed a chasm to love me and be with me. Maybe, I could have even seen our move to Boston as an adventure. Unfortunately, even though I was a woman of faith, I was having great difficulty seeing the bigger picture. My world was closing in on me and becoming very, very small. I wish I could say after this I started to get better. I didn't.

CHAPTER TEN
SO MUCH FOR MY PLANS

OPEN: INTERIOR/BOSTON APARTMENT/SMALL BEDROOM

CAMERA holds on sleeping MOMMY.

DISSOLVE TO: Dream Sequence (in MOMMY's head)

CAMERA follows MOMMY as she struggles to climb
up mountain. She reaches a plateau with a view
where she can rest. She stops to take a break.

CUT TO: Camera shows view of MOMMY standing on
edge of mountainside. She is tired, a little
wound weary, but also resilient.

CUT TO: (from MOMMY'S POV) Vast open expanse
of land and air. In the distance mountains
merge with part of New York which also combines
with part of Boston. It's still beautiful but
also looks a little weird. Slightly disjointed.
All the pieces of MOMMY'S life don't quite fit
together.

She takes a deep breath and looks up. The
rest of the "mountain" continues above her.
She is not as high as she was the first time
she had this dream. She has been knocked down
a notch.

Through facial expressions we see she realizes
she cannot continue to the top. So, she resigns
to stay where she is. In this instance, close
enough would have to do.

She is deeply breathing in the moment. Soaking it
in. Her face shows a satisfaction of achievement
for making it this far.

Then, again, her foot slips on a loose stone.
She rights herself.

                    VOICE-OVER/MOMMY
                    That was close.

Her foot slips again. MOMMY gives the camera
a sarcastic look of "here we go again" as she
starts to fall.

Down she goes flying toward the ground. It is a
repeat of the scene we saw earlier in the film.

MOMMY flies through the air falling down towards
the earth. Clothes once again pulling up towards
the sky from the momentum and wind. She falls
and falls and falls. (fall lasts longer than
previous scene in movie)

Just when we are about to lose the audience
from boredom, she smacks the ground. SMACK.
One, two, three more times we watch the moment
of impact play over and over and over. SMACK!
SMACK! SMACK!

CAMERA from above shows repeat of broken MOMMY
lying on the ground in awkward position.

                    VOICE-OVER/MOMMY
                 Ouch. (pause) Ouch.

It wasn't easy, but by that next spring, I slowly started
crawling out from under my grief and sadness. I almost convinced
myself that the worst was over. I had even started to find a piece
of my old positive, can-do attitude. I thought, OK, I *can* do this.
I'm going to be okay. I'm going to survive.

We had lived in Boston for a little over a year and like I said,
things had become almost normal. Physically, I would never be
the obsessive exercise freak that I used to be, but I was coming to
terms with that. My husband was teaching more than he wanted
but he was trying to embrace it. We found a church to attend.
We met some other parents at the playground. We worked hard,
prayed hard, and did our best to find our way back to... well,
whatever we were going to end up being. We weren't sure exactly
what that was going to be, but we had hope that we were going to
eventually get there.

We even started to like parts of living somewhere "other"
than New York. I can't speak for my husband, but I was learning
to *almost* accept this new life I had been given. I had been
bruised, but I was still fighting. Even financially, we were finally
battling out of the hole we had been in from the separated pelvis,
grad school and moving scenario. We saw it on paper once, we

had it in our hands for a brief moment... a credit card statement that had a balance of $0. I wish I had framed it.

My daughter was a few months away from turning three when I felt like I fell off the cliff again. Again, it happened at a time when I *should* have been celebrating life with joy and sunshine. Again, I was staring at a pee stick and a glowing, neon, positive plus sign. In case you missed it, yes, that's right, I was pregnant. Again.

My husband and I were not trying to have another baby. In fact, a separated pelvis is actually one of the best forms of birth control out there. (In case anyone missed that, that's MAJOR points awarded to my husband for his patience. No wonder he stayed so busy at work, right?) We had just begun to discuss if it was even possible for me to carry another baby when once again, life intervened.

Let me take a moment to say that I'm not an idiot. I know how getting pregnant works. I also know what you are supposed to do to avoid pregnancy. Unfortunately, even though we had instituted the necessary precautions, the power of life was too strong. It overcame numerous obstacles and brought life to an impossible situation. I have no explanation for that. It was truly a miracle. I think that's exactly the way God wanted it to be. If it had been left up to me, I never would have considered going through another pregnancy.

But, *(there's always a but, isn't there?)* even before I found out I was pregnant, something in my spirit had started to stir. I felt it deep down inside my heart it was going to somehow be important for my first daughter to have a sibling. The reason I knew to pay attention to that voice is I could tell it came from that place in my heart where my faith grows. Don't ask me how I knew that this was a voice of truth, because I can't explain it, I just knew. And I was FREAKED OUT by it.

It was a tall order for me to take this risk. If *I* had more time to think about it, *I* never would have had a second child. If it had been my choice *I* never would have put my body through a second pregnancy. *I* never would have "decided" to become a mother again. *I* wasn't ready to be a mother the first time around.

What is that definition for courage? Knowing you have to do something that makes you paralyzed with fear, but doing it anyway? Or is that stupidity? Or a little of both? Either way, it was too late for me to figure it out. I was pregnant. That was something I could not and *would not* change.

When I was pregnant with my first child I did not hesitate to tell people. Even before the obligatory three month waiting period was over, I was blurting it out to anyone who cared. I wasn't exactly celebrating, but I was speaking it as truth over and over until I believed it. I needed confirmation it was for real.

With my second pregnancy, I was much more cautious to celebrate. There was no funny movie scene in a bright pink bathroom this time (our new bathroom was a boring white). There were no gleeful exclamations of, "Honey, come look!" No crazy fanfare. It was a softer, more gentle celebration that was laced around the edges with fear and disappointment.

Don't get me wrong, I was happy about the possibility of another cute human being in my life, but I had just started to get my body back. I was finally walking like a normal person again. I was just beginning to make peace with my new life of being a woman, a wife and a mother. I had even entertained the idea of going back to work. I was terrified to face exactly what it meant to sacrifice all the healing I had worked so hard to achieve. *Pregnant? Now?* Well, there go my "plans." Crap.

I found I was uncomfortable talking about my second pregnancy with anyone, even my family. I didn't even want to talk about it with my doctor. I did not get an early sonogram this time around. I did not want to "find out" anything. I wanted to sit and stew with this one for a while. I did allow the doctor to hook up the little speaker to my belly. I did hear the baby's heartbeat. My OB said everything looked and sounded fine and sent me on my way.

I was doubtful. I didn't believe my doctor when she said everything looked good, but I tried desperately to squash those thoughts. I wanted her to be RIGHT. I wanted to write off those doubts lingering around the edges of my mind as over-emotional fears based on a past traumatic experience. I wanted to shake them off. I wanted for them to go away. They didn't.

What I'm trying to say is my mother's intuition felt funny even as early as eight weeks into this second pregnancy. It felt so "funny" that I didn't mention this "feeling" to anyone, not even my husband.

We were standing in our kitchen in our Boston apartment gathering up snacks when I finally spoke the words out loud. We were on our way to our first big sonogram, the one where you actually see the baby and take cool pictures of the hands, the feet, and the profile. Sometimes you can even tell what sex the baby is (if you want to know). Essentially you get to "meet" the little human inside of you for the first time.

We were gearing up for a long day for us and for our three-year-old. I was 20 weeks along and so far everything had been "normal." I had the same nausea and exhaustion I had the first time around, which I took as a good sign. Except for my irrational fears, everything seemed fine, even better than fine, they seemed *good*. Unfortunately, I had held on to my fears for as long as I could stand it.

That was the day I finally said to my husband, "Don't be surprised if this appointment doesn't go well."

My timing was terrible. My husband looked back at me in shock.

"What do you mean?" he said, trying to stay calm.

"I mean, this one feels funny. I'm afraid we might get

bad news."

"Okaaaay. Um... do you need me to do anything?" he said.

He was somewhat used to my weird prophetic proclamations so he didn't ask for any details. He knew I had none to give. I was just going on my "gut."

"No," I said. "Just be ready for it. And pray I'm wrong."

I have no idea what went through his mind.

I didn't ask.

He didn't share.

Unfortunately, this was part of our new normal. We talked to each other all the time without really talking.

We finished gathering our things and headed to the train. We looked like a cute little family out for an fun adventure, except that we weren't.

Let's take a brief intermission. At this point in a movie you, the audience, would be on the edge of your seat. You can tell by the shift in music that the mood of the movie has changed. You might be wondering what is going to happen at the doctor? Is this going to be another tragedy? Or will we get lulled into the moment only to be relieved and maybe slightly perturbed by another storybook ending? I guess I should let you off the hook. I should stop talking about what could happen and just go ahead and tell you what did. Thanks for giving me a moment to collect my thoughts...

The look on the technician's face was all I needed to know that my fears were not unfounded. He did his best to stay stoic, but he failed horribly. It was obvious something was wrong.

He asked for our patience, while he went out to get someone more senior for a second opinion. All we could do is sit there in that sterile, cold observation room and hope the second opinion would prove a mistake had been made. We hoped this younger, less experienced technician simply over-reacted. We hoped there was a glare on the screen, or that the baby was just sitting at a funny angle. We hoped that when the Chief of Ultrasound came in to take a look they would see absolutely nothing was wrong. We hoped.

My husband and I grasped each other's hands and found that even though there was a distance between us, we were still together. Together, we hung on to that desperate hope until the moment the super smart, overly qualified Chief of Ultrasound removed the wand from my stomach.

With grave faces, both technicians told me to sit up as they delivered the bad news. There was no mistake. It was official. Our unborn baby had a major problem with a little organ called the heart.

CHAPTER ELEVEN
OKAY, HERE WE GO

OPEN: EXTERIOR/BOSTON HOSPITAL

CAMERA HOLDS on sign.
SIGN: Boston Children's Hospital.

CUT TO: INTERIOR HOSPITAL
CROWDED EXAMINATION ROOM

BACKGROUND NOISE: Interior hospital sounds muffled-happening outside of room. MOMMY is on an examination table next to a sonogram machine.

DADDY and DAUGHTER sit in chairs next to table.

Two medical experts (one sonogram tech and one pediatric cardiologist) both wearing mint green scrubs stand next to the table. There is nervous chatter from everyone. None of the occupants of this scene are discussing the reason for being in this room. Stuttered, awkward chuckling takes the place of real words.

The tech spreads the jelly onto MOMMY's stomach.

CUT TO: Close up of belly, jelly, sonogram wand
and the technician's hands.

CUT TO: Pediatric cardiologist (DOCTOR) as she
places hand on MOMMY's shoulder

                    DOCTOR
        (with superficial cheerfulness with
          a weak attempt at reassurance)
              Okay, here we go.

FADE TO BLACK

I held it together while the senior technician at the sonogram
imaging center explained that the results of the sonogram were
inconclusive. They could not deny there was definitely something
wrong, they just couldn't tell us what exactly. I held it together
when that same technician told us we were going to be "rushed
over" to a pediatric cardiologist at Children's Hospital Boston. I
even kept it together on the trip from the imaging office to the
hospital, two train stops away. I kept it together on the outside. On
the inside, yep, you guessed it, not so much. At least at this point,
I still had some hope. Ignorance is truly helpful… sometimes.

At the children's hospital we were seen *right away*. No
waiting. I couldn't help but think to myself, *just exactly how
serious does this thing have to be to get bumped to the front of the
line of the seriously serious cases?* Pretty serious. My hope
deteriorated a little.

Again, we were led into a sonogram room. Again, I steeled
myself for what was coming.

My inner two-year-old wanted to stick her fingers in her ears and chant *"Um not whisening!"*

I knew I needed to hear what the pediatric cardiologist was going to say, but there was nothing in me that was okay with this moment. I don't know how I did it, but I climbed up on the examination table. I allowed them to spread the cold jelly over my belly. I let them scan for images of the little human living inside. Bravery? Complacency? Shock.

Back to the movie.

OPEN: INTERIOR CHILDREN'S HOSPITAL BOSTON
CARDIOLOGIST'S OFFICE

TITLE: The Results

FAMILY sitting in small doctor's office. MOMMY, DADDY and DAUGHTER are sitting across a desk from the pediatric cardiologist (DOCTOR) from the sonogram room.

CUT TO: Camera from MOMMY's POV. MOMMY looks at the doctor but the doctor is out of focus, blurry. She hears the doctor talking but it sounds muffled.

The sound switches back and forth from clear to muffled so we hear snatches of a real conversation. Like someone speaking under water or the way it sounds when someone is waking up from being unconscious.

DOCTOR
muffled words... cannot confirm diagnosis...
warped sounds... one of two things...
warped sounds...

MOMMY looks incredulously at DOCTOR. Then to
DADDY, and back at the DOCTOR. It is clear it is
not sinking in. She's lost.

The DOCTOR finally realizes she's lost the mother
and tries again. Slowly the words start to clear.
The muffled sound goes away. MOMMY is slammed
into reality.

DOCTOR
(muffled words slowly clear to…)
can't really see how serious the situation
is yet. The baby is still too small…

INTERRUPT WITH VOICE-OVER/MOMMY
You're darn right too small!

DOCTOR
…for us to know what exactly we are dealing
with. We are looking at one of two things.
With the first condition, we can't be sure
right now whether or not we can do anything.
The second condition requires a lifetime of
multiple surgeries.

INTERRUPT WITH VOICE-OVER/MOMMY
Is there an option number three?

                    DOCTOR
        I can't tell you what to do. I can't
        even recommend that you terminate
            the pregnancy at this point.

        INTERRUPT WITH VOICE-OVER/MOMMY
        Ohhh… so… that's option number three…

                    DOCTOR
        It's just too early to tell. We would
        like for you to come back when you
            are around 28 weeks…

        INTERRUPT WITH VOICE-OVER/MOMMY
            Wait that's TWO MONTHS from now.
        What are we supposed to do until then?

                    DOCTOR
        …at that time we will do another
        ultrasound. Hopefully we will have more
            information for you then.

CAMERA pans over to two very shocked, numb
parents and a clueless three-year-old.

                    MOMMY
        (with a whisper, very soft, very slow)
                    Okay.

                    DADDY
                Thank you.

FAMILY starts to leave the office.

DOCTOR
By the way, it's a girl.

FADE TO BLACK

I didn't cry or cause a scene in the ultrasound room. I didn't cry or totally lose it in the doctor's office when she delivered the gut wrenching if somewhat vague news. I even kept it together when I walked up to the front desk to schedule our return visit in eight weeks. My husband had taken my daughter out into the lobby, and I had gone up to the front desk, alone. I thought getting the information about our future visit was easier than pretending everything was fine out in the lobby. Out there, I had to look "okay" to a three-year-old and a room full of strangers. Here, I only had to function enough to write down a date. Unfortunately, that was the moment I was suddenly overcome with a massive wave of emotion. *Uh, oh… here comes the verbal diarrhea…*

I felt down right idiotic as I helplessly dumped my bucketful of mess on the poor woman behind the desk. Actually, I was behind the desk as well. The nurse had led me into a little room they had set aside for scheduling. For a brief moment, it occurred to me it was strange to have a "private" room to serve this task. Once I started my spiral into a blubbering idiot, it dawned on me this "privacy" was on purpose. It was set aside for parents like me. Parents who had just received tough-to-swallow news. Parents who by default were going to be "emotional" not just because of what they just heard from the doctor, but because they have to come back to hear more. This poor woman's only job was to tell me when I would be coming back. All she wanted to do was shuffle me through the process and get me out the door. I do not envy her job. She, however, showed me great empathy. She obviously had a lot of experience with this sort of thing. *How do you possibly say thank you for something like that?*

I blew my nose, wiped my eyes and tried to pull myself back together. I walked out of the office and stumbled back into the room full of strangers as I frantically looked for my family. I saw them across the room, in the back, where they kept all the toys.

I had to fight hard to bring myself back from shock to normal. Unfortunately, "normal" is what happened anyway. We still had to eat, drink, sleep, and work. I still had a three-year-old who needed her mommy.

I looked at my little girl sitting with her father on the other side of the room, and I remembered how we had already experienced one miracle. *Would we be allowed another one?* I wondered.

I smiled at her, calling on my well-established ability to hide my emotions. It was necessary. I had to pretend, so I could be a mother to the daughter I already had, and temporarily ignore the decisions I would have to make about the daughter yet to come. I walked out of the lobby with my family, a fake smile plastered on my face, and headed home.

OPEN: INTERIOR/HOSPITAL/HALLWAY

CAMERA HOLDS on a broken, heavy hearted DADDY and MOMMY as they walk with a giant weight on their shoulders down a long hospital hallway.

DAUGHTER walks between holding one hand of each parent. It is ironic how bright and cheery the walls of the children's hospital are in contrast to the shadow hanging over this little family.

                    DAUGHTER
        Can we still stop and get a cookie?

DADDY AND MOMMY stoically nod yes.

                  VOICE-OVER/MOMMY
                    (muffled sob)
                      Ouch.

FADE TO BLACK

CHAPTER TWELVE

BATHTUB SPIRITUALITY

I know we made it back to our apartment, because that's where I was the next morning when I woke up. I remember I told our daughter we could stop and get a cookie, but I don't remember actually stopping to get one. I don't remember the process of actually getting back home. I suppose that lack of memory feels better if it comes from an evening of too much wine and too much fun. I wouldn't know. I was a goody-two shoes nerd, remember? But, I would hope that waking up from an evening of fun would feel way better than waking up the way I did that next day.

I have learned to treasure those brief moments in the morning where I'm still a little bit asleep. Those sweet moments of oblivion where I can be blissfully unaware of what yesterday gave me and unconcerned about what today will bring. They are often my brief window into God's view of my life. He sees the perfect peace that I constantly search for. At this time, I particularly cherished that brief cocoon, because when I woke up... I quickly lost sight of it. I wish I could say that I remembered how deep my faith was. I wish I could say I remembered how close I felt to God throughout my entire life. I wish I could, but the truth is I did not. When I woke up, the peace I had cultivated from childhood wafted away like smoke. It was there, deep down inside waiting for me to discover I still had it, but it was ethereal and hard to grasp.

Back to the movie.

OPEN: INTERIOR/BOSTON APARTMENT/BATHROOM

CAMERA holds on hand as it reaches to turn on a shower.

TITLE: The Next Day

Hand turns on the faucet. Sound of water running. Hand pulls the lever for the shower.

CUT TO: Shower head. Water turns on.

MOMMY places face under water spray. Slowly MOMMY's face starts to crumble, just a little at first and then spirals into complete breakdown. She sobs, quietly but with great agony.

She crumples to the floor of the shower (discreetly keeping everything covered of course... this is still a PG film after all). She curls up on the floor of the bathtub and sobs and sobs and sobs with barely any sound.

The agony of her muffled cries is worse than if there was noise. It's grueling to watch.

VOICE-OVER/MOMMY
(gasping)
Help me. Oh God, please, help me.

FADE TO BLACK.

I have often proclaimed that God always talks to me when I'm naked. Of course, there is great metaphor in that statement. It is a fantastic thing to stand naked before God and feel His acceptance of us anyway, but I'm actually being more literal. Sometimes, the only place I have space to actually receive wisdom from that little voice of peace inside my heart is when I'm flying solo in the bathroom. All of you moms out there, I know you know what I mean. The shower is sometimes our inner sanctum. Sometimes, in those moments, I could leave myself vulnerable enough to feel the earth move.

In the movie, this shower scene would take place the next day. But in reality, I was numb and walking in a fog for almost two weeks before this moment. When I had finally stopped crying, I heard myself say to no one in particular, *Okay, I give up.*

I wish I could have said something more "Christianey" like *I surrender. Or I submit my life to you, God.* Or something fancier and more theological. But the truth is, I'm not very theological. In fact, I'm a total loser when it comes to intellectually defining the way I go about things. I tend to follow my gut. I was in no position to pretty it up anyway. I was lying in the bottom of the shower, crying my eyes out so all I could blubber was, *I give up. Help me.*

That's when the peace from down deep inside helped me realize it was a privilege to have this human life growing inside of me. I finally understood I didn't have the *right* to be a mother to this child, but I had been given the *honor* of receiving this life. So, I surrendered my right to be this child's mother. I surrendered my control over her life. I surrendered my control over her health. I realized somehow I had to come to terms with being okay if she died.

How very "Abraham" of me, right? I mean, really, it sounds so self-righteous, even to me, and I was there. How could I say it's okay for God to let my child die? Because, it wasn't okay, not even a little bit. My human brain could not comprehend it, but that is what I said, in the shower, out loud, to the only One able to actually hear the agony in my heart and understand it. That kind of thing does not happen all by itself. That kind of obedient faith required the intervention of a higher power.

In that moment of complete nakedness and complete surrender, I figured out that holding on to this thing I could not control was going to kill me. I knew that the outcome of this pregnancy was out of my hands. In a very strange but comforting way, I found a place in my heart to be thankful for that truth. I found a way to be thankful that something bigger and stronger than me was able to see beyond the pain and agony of my current bathtub breakdown. Because of that, I finally found a small sliver of that peace that I so desperately needed. That peace did not stay with me all the time, but that moment temporarily gave me the strength I needed to know I would give birth to this child, no matter what.

It was with this new found strength that I was finally able to send out an S.O.S. to all the people out there who loved us. My husband and I agreed it was time to call our family and deliver the news. It wasn't easy, but at least in this case we knew it was vital that we *tell* someone *something*.

We phoned our parents, our sisters, our brothers. We sent an email out to friends. We called upon anyone who cared to start hoping and praying with us that this child would actually be born, and even more than that, survive.

In our message, I included a plea for no one to call me to

"talk" about our situation. I asked friends and family to contact me through email only. It was the only way I could speak about what was going on. I was afraid I couldn't say out loud the way I was feeling in my heart. I could not handle my pain *and* the sadness of the person on the other end of the phone. It was just too much. Plus, I had a three-year-old who needed a mommy who could at least pretend to keep it together.

We spent the next two months stumbling through the nebulous haze of waiting until our next appointment. Every day, I woke up and found that my baby was still alive. The only thing I could do with that information was continue to take care of her the best I could until... later. Later, I would have to face it. Analyze it. Try to make some kind of sense out of it. For now, I would have to *wait*. Until my baby grew some more, *if* my baby grew some more, we could not make any decisions.

Three months later, we were given a bit of relief on our return visit. After we endured another set of sonograms with multiple doctors, med students and technicians (having a rare medical case can really draw a crowd), the pediatric cardiologist met with us again. Suddenly, she was very optimistic. I think I remember her exact words were,

"I am 95% sure we are dealing with truncus arteriosis[1] with pulmonary edema. The reason I can't say I'm 100% sure is

---

[1]Truncus arteriosus is a complex congenital heart defect (CHD) in which a single artery arises from the heart. The normal embryonic heart starts with a single great artery which normally divides into two - the aorta which pumps to the body, and the pulmonary artery which pumps to the lungs. Truncus arteriosus results when the single great vessel fails to separate completely and pumps blood to both the body and to the lungs. Having just a single vessel means that both oxygen-rich (red) blood and oxygen-poor (blue) blood are mixing and flowing out the single vessel to the lungs and the body. A greater-than-normal amount of blood flow through the pulmonary arteries to the lungs can cause congestive heart failure and lung damage. Truncus arteriosus is usually diagnosed before birth or soon after a baby's birth. Truncus arteriosus is rare, affecting less than 1 out of every 10,000 babies. The condition makes up one percent of congenital heart defects.

because her aorta is extremely healthy for a baby with truncus. Normally, the aorta has been damaged by all of the extra work it has had to do, but hers looks really good. Better than it should."

Did I mention the power of prayer?

I forgot to explain earlier that after we sent out our SOS to friends and family a massive prayer chain was set in motion. People whom I had never met, and probably will never meet, started praying for this little human. For whatever reason, people were moved by the story of an unborn baby they may never meet. It went viral before there was Facebook. I know it made a difference, because a baby that was essentially looking at a low survival diagnosis and/or a short life expectancy now had a "healthy" aorta. Maybe, at another hospital, they could have come up with a "medical" reason for this, but at the number one pediatric cardiology hospital in the world, the doctors had no explanation. My baby should not have looked so healthy, but she did. She was going to do this thing. She was going to fight. My little unborn human and I, we were going to fight, together.

The battle was not going to be easy. Here are some of the other things the doctor said to us at that visit.

"We may find some other things going on once we get in there, but for now I think we can all assume we are looking at immediate surgery after birth and then repeated surgeries as needed as she grows. Typically, you will be looking at approximately five-eight heart surgeries throughout her lifetime. Maybe more, maybe less."

Look of unrelenting fear on the face of the parents.

"Ultimately, here is what I can tell you (attempt at reassurance). My oldest patient who has managed this type of treatment is now 18 years old. I cannot promise you she will grow to be 40, but I can say it is very likely she will grow to be at least 18."*

Very *likely* in doctor speech means we can't make any promises, but we *think* you have a pretty good chance.

I thought to myself, "Well, I guess that is better than nothing. I'll take it."

The doctor's optimism gave me the ability to find what was left of my hope. There was a small sip at the bottom of the glass now, a tiny trickle, but it was enough. Keeping and giving birth to this baby was the right thing to do.

It was with that hope that we realized this baby would now *arrive*. It was time for us to begin, to prepare, to start, to get ready, to have another baby. Ugh.

It's been 10 years since this moment. That patient is still going strong and so is our daughter (victory dance).

CHAPTER THIRTEEN
SHE'S OKAY?

OPEN: INTERIOR/DELIVERY ROOM/HOSPITAL

MUSIC: something like "Celebrate"
by Cool and the Gang

CAMERA: Enters into labor and delivery room
through double doors from point of view of MOMMY
being rolled into room on hospital bed.

SCENE looks like big party. (exaggerate from
MOMMY's imagination a party with bright lights,
loud music, streamers, someone playing a
saxophone, etc).

MEDICAL STAFF dances around, talking loudly and
blowing off steam. It's Friday. This is the last
case of the week and all of the doctors in the
room are talking about how soon everyone will
be going on vacation.

DOCTOR leans in and in a cheery voice shouts that the c-section is about to start.

MOMMY can barely hear what the doctor said because of all of the revelry happening, so she just nods like she understands.

MOMMY is trying to be in the party mood, but it is obvious she is a bit wary of all the "happiness" surrounding her.

                    DOCTOR
                   (shouts)
          You're going to feel a little
                bit of pressure…

               VOICE-OVER/MOMMY
          (with a gasp as if she had been
             punched in the stomach…)
                That's a little?!?!

CUT TO: Camera from above. All we see is a circle of MEDICAL STAFFS' backs looking down and working on MOMMY's lower abdomen. They almost look like they are dancing as they move, press down, reach for tools, move and press down again. (over-exaggerate as dance moves) Party continues with bright lights, music.

CUT TO: wide shot of delivery room. Doctors continue to move, talk, joke and dance while they perform c-section. MOMMY still responds to every move with winces of pain. Her form of

DANCING in response to doctors movement.
Finally, BABY cries.

DOCTOR holds up BABY in triumph (in MOMMY's
imagination "poppers" go off and confetti fills
the room) then pass BABY around like a trophy
(still dancing) while they perform all of the
post birth necessities.

MUSIC screeches to halt.

CUT TO: "real" hospital room.

CAMERA HOLDS on baby being held next to MOMMY's
head.

                    MOMMY
                 She's okay?

                    DOCTOR
                   (smiles)
        That cry was louder than I expected.

MOMMY looks nervously at doctor.

                    DOCTOR
        Really. She looks good. If I didn't know
           better I would say she's perfect.

                    MOMMY
            (softly, with emotion)
                   Perfect.

FADE TO BLACK ⸻

My second daughter was born on a cold, snowy, February day. It was the complete opposite of the soggy, NYC August I had experienced with the birth of my first daughter. Not only was it freezing cold in the way that only a New England winter can be cold, but we had also experienced a record snowfall. There was at least eighteen inches of snow on the ground.

We don't have many photos of me when I was pregnant with baby number two, but there is one that is burned into my brain. It's a photo of me standing on the sidewalk outside of our apartment after said record breaking snowfall. I was waiting for my older daughter to follow me through the tiny, narrow path that had been painstakingly shoveled out of the snow. It was like a tiny canyon between two rocky cliffs.

I was wearing a BRIGHT pink, puffy, maternity winter coat with a fur trimmed hood. No, this was NOTHING like what I would normally be wearing. In my opinion, it was extremely unattractive. I look back at that photo and think, wow, I look like a giant, pink, carnival style teddy bear. *Sigh.* It was on clearance, and a pregnant girl on a tight budget in the middle of a New England winter can't be too choosy. At least it was warm.

We were on our way to preschool. In Boston, education is never delayed, even by a blizzard. My older daughter loved school. It was a magical place where her active brain and her gregarious conversation skills got used to their full potential. She needed it. I cannot express enough how well my oldest daughter tolerated my lack of ability to be her mom during this time. She was and still is a great kid.

I was standing there in the valley between the two mountains of snow and it was unimaginable how deep it was. It was actually as tall as my stomach. I could almost rest my tummy on top of it like a melon on display at a grocery store. *Tell me again, why did we decide to move to Boston?* Certainly not for the weather.

Anyway, this is the last photo we have of me before my second daughter was born. Approximately five days later, I was in an operating room having a c-section.

My OB and I opted for a c-section for a couple of reasons. I can say the first reason in two words: Separated. Pelvis. The other reason was a little more involved. There are so many unknowns when you combine labor with a serious heart condition. A c-section seemed to make the most sense. Not to mention that recovering from a c-section is much more simple than recovering from a separated pelvis. I'm not very good at math, but even I know ten days in recovery is easier than two years.

We documented almost every minute of the birth and delivery. We have these slightly grotesque photos to prove it. In a weird way, I suppose we wanted to remember and capture everything we could. We had no idea how long any of this would last. We did our best to stay in the moment. We tried to celebrate the birth of a new life and not think about what that life was going to look like long-term.

The pictures are of normal delivery room fodder: parents looking nervous, doctors in scrubs wearing surgical masks, medical equipment, unidentifiable body parts showing… it was a mess. There weren't really any streamers or confetti or bands in the corner playing, but to me, it felt like everyone in the room was in the middle of a giant party, and I wasn't invited.

My daughter came out screaming. Even though she was a girl low on oxygen with a damaged heart and compromised lungs, she refused to enter the world silently. It was the first of many examples that this little girl was not going to do anything the way she was "supposed to."

I am not sure what it is like for other people who have gone through similar situations, but for me it was all of the little, normal things that amazed me. She's got fingers! She's got toes! She's crying!

Suddenly, there she was with fuzzy blond hair, bluish green eyes and a very powerful voice. I have never been so happy to hear a baby cry. Without noticing or even being ready for it, I had become sentimental. I wanted to hang on to *everything*.

They did all of the regular things doctors do in delivery rooms. They cheered. They cut the cord. They held her up in triumph. They cleaned her up. They wrapped her up. And finally, they placed her next to my head to let me see her up close for the first time. It was weird how "normal" it all was. Even now, I cannot wrap my head around it. Here she was, a beautiful, perfect baby girl who was about to endure a crazy, challenging life.

Again, the thing lying under the surface, below the outward appearance, was overwhelming. It lay dormant and hidden under the happiness and the joy. I wanted to stay here in the moment of new birth and forget all about the rest of it. Have you met my good friend, denial? Yep, she's still with us.

The doctors took my baby to Boston Children's Hospital to the Pediatric Cardiology Intensive Care Unit (PCICU), which is not the same thing as the other kind of PICU where a lot of other babies go. This was a special place for babies who had major cardiac issues. They took me to the recovery wing at Brigham and Women's. Two hospitals, close to each other, connected by a bridge, but inevitably separate.

I did not get to choose whether my baby stayed with me or went to the nursery. That choice was made for me. I barely knew her and already she was taken away from me. For a second time, I was denied access to the very thing I was programmed to protect. For a second time, I was forced to deaden a part of myself. I was forced to suck it up, move forward, and keep going, but I felt like a piece of me was missing. I was thankful I had a private room this time. I was not capable of chit chat and pleasantries. I could not sit there empty handed and watch another mother gush over her perfectly healthy baby. I did not have the strength to pretend or to feel anything other than... devastated...

The next day, I woke up and again, I enjoyed those first few moments of sweet oblivion. For a suspended moment, I dismissed the memory that I had a c-section. I turned a blind eye to the fact that I had not seen my baby since her birth the previous day. I by-passed the idea that I had been through this kind of emptiness before, and I was unprepared to go through it again. I forgot that I was about to feel overwhelmed, full of anxiety and scared. Really, really scared. For a few seconds I caught a glimpse of God's presence. Then, I was forced to wake up.

The first realization I had was I was in pain... again. A c-section is less painful than a separated pelvis but not by much, at least not initially. I knew right away the baby-having factory was permanently closed... forever. There would be no more babies coming out of *any* part of my body *ever* again. I felt very confident about this decision. My doctor had talked me out of a tubal ligation. She was worried that due to the tenuous circumstances surrounding our second daughter's life, I might need to hang on to the possibility of another pregnancy. I didn't.

My only concern was preventing even the remote *chance* of another pregnancy. I was terrified to consider even the mere *possibility*. Thankfully, my sweet, extremely understanding husband agreed with me. After watching me suffer through a separated pelvis and a c-section and two pregnancies, it was the least he could do. I say that like he had a choice. Unfortunately for him, he didn't have a "leg" to stand on (comic drum beat). He had no room to even squirm about it. Nope, it was time to step up to the plate and take it like a man.

Thankfully, there would be no more over-the-top fantastic birthing stories for me. No way. I had paid my dues. I had served my term. I had finished my op. I had completed my mission. I turned in my jersey. I quit.

CHAPTER FOURTEEN

PLEASE DON'T MAKE ME BEG

OPEN: INTERIOR/HOSPITAL/PATIENT ROOM
(Introduce GRANDPA AND GRANDMA)

TITLE: Two Days Later

BACKGROUND: hospital sounds

CAMERA HOLDS on MOMMY who is in hospital bed
staring at TV

CUT TO: opening door. DADDY, DAUGHTER #1, and two
adults (in their 50's) walk into MOMMY's room.
MOMMY smiles and greets them. DAUGHTER #1 runs
to hospital bed and begins to climb up to get
to MOMMY. DADDY swoops in and lifts her up onto
the bed. GRANDPA and GRANDMA walk over to hug
their daughter. Casual chatter fills room. After
a moment...

                    MOMMY
Well, would you like to go meet your sister?

>   DAUGHTER #1
>   (reluctance)
>   I guess...

Adults chuckle. Act like this is just another "normal" sibling answer to what should be another "normal" introduction to a new baby.

>   MOMMY
>   (to DADDY)
>   Go ask the nurse for a wheelchair please.

CUT TO: DADDY pushing MOMMY in wheelchair with DAUGHTER #1 riding by standing on top of MOMMY's feet on foot pedals (not sitting in MOMMY's lap but being as close to MOMMY as possible). GRANDMA and GRANDPA walk behind. Each person is introspective, "preparing" to see the baby. No one knows what to expect.

CUT TO: group walking into PCICU everyone covered in germ gowns. MOMMY greets nurses with obvious familiarity. DADDY wheels MOMMY to hand-washing station and then wheels MOMMY over to infant ICU bed where BABY is lying. Everyone else washes hands and walks over to stand next to MOMMY.

CUT TO: Baby wearing a diaper and nothing else. She has an IV in her hand, a feeding tube in her nose, and countless other "things" attached to numerous machines. Her body is entirely covered with wires.

The NURSE carefully unplugs a few wires, gently wraps BABY in a blanket, lifts BABY from hospital bed, rearranges wires and puts BABY into MOMMY's arms.

DAUGHTER #1 walks over to investigate new bundle.

> DAUGHTER #1
> That's her?

> MOMMY
> Yes. Would you like to say "hi"?

> DAUGHTER #1
> Okay. Hi. (pause)
> She didn't say hi back. (statement)

> MOMMY
> Well, she's sleeping.

> DAUGHTER #1
> I'm going to sing to her. (proclamation)
> TWINKLE TWINKLE WITTLE STAWR.
> HOW I WONDER WHAT YOU ARWR.
> (loudly) (continues a few times)

CUT TO: Nurse and other adults. Everyone is moved. GRANDMA has tears running down her face. (not unusual, Grandma always has tears running down her face)

CAMERA HOLDS on MOMMY, DAUGHTER #1 and BABY. Other family members join around them, hugging each other and looking at baby.

FADE TO BLACK

My parents flew to Boston to help take care of my older daughter while I was in the hospital recuperating and our youngest daughter was in the PCICU at the children's hospital. Unfortunately, my c-section ended up being scheduled during what those in the acting biz call "tech week." That means, in addition to everything else we were going through, my husband was in the final week of directing and producing the winter show at the school where he was teaching. He was balancing a very demanding schedule with a family that was falling apart. He was *stressed*.

Since he couldn't be home to take care of the three-year-old, and I couldn't be home to take care of the three-year-old, the grandparents stepped in. I don't think I can express clearly what a sacrifice that was for them. My parents, particularly my dad, are not big travelers. They really enjoy the comforts of home. They do not like flying, they are not used to riding trains, and for sure, they are not used to walking everywhere on concrete sidewalks.

Add to that the task of staying in a small apartment with a family that includes a three-year-old, *without* the privacy of a guest room and everything suddenly became "uncomfortable" for all of us. Nothing about this screams "vacation."

My husband brought my parents and my oldest daughter to the hospital to see me the day after our baby daughter was born. The New England area had been hit with yet another dose of winter, and my parents had just experienced their first snow storm/cold weather/public transportation adventure. It's not easy to walk five blocks in the snow to a train, take a train four stops, and then walk another six to seven blocks to a hospital while tugging along a three-year-old. My husband and I were used to it, but out-of-owners didn't stand a chance.

I was happy to see familiar faces and impressed everyone had "weathered" the trip. I appreciated their willingness to make this trek, through the storm, uphill both ways, over the mountains, okay, okay, not really. I was just happy they came. I knew it was important for my parents to see for themselves that their daughter was okay... and to meet their grandchild. It was equally important for me to see my oldest daughter. That mommy thing, you just can't turn it off. My older daughter also needed to see that mommy was still... well, mommy. We just all needed to see each other. There is reassurance in the face-to-face.

My older daughter did her best to act like she was on some kind of family fun day, but I could tell she was burdened by our situation. She had only seen my parents a total of four times in her entire life and I noticed the current relationship between them was... strained.

My sweet, overly-intelligent, normally independent daughter looked at me with her gorgeous big brown eyes and asked a very awkward question.

"Mommy, when will you be home?"

She has never been known for her ability to embrace change. All this upheaval was tough for her to embrace. I may not have been the best mother in the world while dealing with my second pregnancy, but sadly, I was the most stable thing in her life. In my absence, she was forced to be comfortable with two people who were supposed to be as familiar as family, but were in reality strangers.

It was not an easy task to take my daughter to visit my side of the family. For one thing, we lived up north, and they all lived in the south. Even before my injury, this trip was exhausting. In fact, every trip to my hometown was uncannily similar to the movie *Planes, Trains and Automobiles*. First, we had to lug our suitcases to the train. Then, take train #1 to the downtown connection hub.

Then, take train #2 to the stop closest to the airport. Then, take a shuttle from the train stop to the airport terminal. Then, walk through the airport to the gate. Then, sit and wait to board the plane. Then, board the plane for a three hour flight. Then, land at the closest airport to my parent's home. Then, either be picked up by a relative or rent a car for another two to three hour car trip (remember this whole time we are carrying luggage, entertaining a toddler and recovering from a separated pelvis). Finally, "you have arrived at your destination." It was a little grueling, but we did it. Family was important enough to us to make it happen. We just couldn't do it more than once or twice a year. Hence, the reason my daughter's grandparents were strangers.

I hugged my daughter tight and told her I would see her soon. She walked out with my parents, stuck in an impossible situation she couldn't escape. Unfortunately, all I could do was let her go. I understood in theory, it was a good thing for them to go home. Their situation would only improve with forced fellowship.

Still... a funny thing happened on the trip back to the train. My three-year-old fell asleep *while* she was walking. No, I'm not kidding. She literally *fell asleep*.

According to my mom and dad, her little legs were still moving, so they assumed she was awake. When they spoke to her, she didn't respond with her normal level of gregariousness. She didn't respond at all. Concerned, they looked down at her and realized her chin was resting fully on her chest, her eyes were closed and she was breathing deeply. She was sound asleep. If my parents hadn't been holding tightly to her hands she would have fallen face first into the snow. Stress can do funny things to everyone, even three-year-olds.

She wasn't the only one. Back at the hospital, I was struggling with a new form of panic. When it came time for my husband to leave, I went a little crazy on the inside.

He did his husbandly duty. He asked me if there was anything

I needed. He asked if I needed him to stay a little while, but then, almost in the same breath, he filled me in on his crazy schedule. He was under great pressure to keep his job, provide for his family, and in general keep the train moving *forward*. I could tell he wanted to do the right thing and "be there" for his wife, but I could also tell he was really hoping I would tell him I was fine so he could go. It took me a long time to realize this wasn't cruel on his part. It was his way of surviving. So, I did what I always did. I pretended it was okay for him to leave, because I couldn't stand to admit I needed him to stay.

Out loud I said, "Okay, see you later."

On the inside I said, *Please don't go. Please. I don't want to be alone.*

I didn't want to have to say it. I wanted for him to want to stay with me without me having to beg.

Please, please, don't make me beg.

CHAPTER FIFTEEN

A MUDDLED MESS

As with many of my memories about this time in my life, things are a muddled mess. I know certain things happened, because I have photos that prove these events to me, but I don't necessarily *remember* them.

I know I went back and forth from my room at the hospital to the PCICU at the children's hospital, because I have seen a photo of me riding in a wheelchair being pushed across the connector bridge by my husband. We were accompanied by my parents and my three-year-old, so I know it happened soon after my youngest daughter's birth, maybe even on that day everyone came to visit. We must have taken multiple trips across the pedestrian connection bridge, because it is one of the few things my older daughter talks about when she is asked about her visits to the hospital. She remembers the bridge even if I don't.

I don't remember exactly when this happened, but according to the baby calendar I somehow managed to keep, four days after my baby daughter was born, she was moved from the PCICU and transferred into a temporary patient room. Her tiny body didn't fit into the vast expanse of the room designed to accommodate much larger children. It did, however, accommodate a mommy, a daddy, two grandparents and three-year-old with room to spare. Solidarity in numbers.

On the same day, I was also "checked out" of my room in postpartum recovery. For the next two days, I stayed with my daughter in this room as much as I could, going home only to sleep. No, I don't have any idea how I stayed at the hospital so much while I was recovering from a c-section. I just did.

I remember her bed had green sheets. I remember she was wrapped like a burrito in a white blanket with pink and blue stripes. I remember it bothered me that the sheets and the blanket didn't match. I remember the bed was elevated to promote better breathing and that somehow my daughter didn't slide down the mattress. She was stuck to the bed like she was attached with Velcro.

I remember after the first day we shared our room with another little girl and her mother. They too were waiting in the purgatory of the unknown. I remember looking into the eyes of that other mother and seeing a mirror image of myself in her soul. We were part of the same club, but we smiled and pretended we weren't. She could get through the day without the need for a wheelchair so, yeah, I was a little bit jealous. It was a ridiculous thing to be, but... inner two-year-old BRAT strikes again.

I remember the Boston area schools and business community participated in something called "Winter Break," and because my daughter was born the Friday before this break that the hospital was almost entirely empty (hence the party in the delivery room earlier).

I was fascinated by the "quietness" of such a large hospital. I appreciated this calm, soft version of a normally frantic environment. I had no idea what a blessing this was at the time, but of course now that I look back, I can see that this calm, quiet existence was just what I needed. It was definitely the calm before the storm.

I know I put on the "germ gown" and held my newborn, wires and all, in the PCICU because again there is a photo of me sitting in a wheelchair wearing a germ gown holding my newborn. I do remember the day my three-year-old sang *Twinkle Twinkle Little Star* to her new baby sister. There are some things you just don't forget.

There are other things for which I don't need photos to remind me they happened. For example, I remember vividly the moment when my baby girl not only ripped the feeding tube out of her nose, but also grasped and pulled out the IV in her arm. Babies with these types of heart conditions often have trouble eating. The effort required to drink and digest food is too much stress on their bodies. That's why they usually need a feeding tube. Not true for our little bundle of joy. When she ripped out her feeding tube for the fourth time, the nurse decided to try to feed her with a bottle. She drank the whole thing.

I remember on one of the days my husband was taking me from home to the hospital to see our daughter, we got confused and ended up on the "wrong" side of the PCICU. We weren't allowed to enter through the door that was located right in front of us. No, we were going to have to walk all the way back to the elevator... take the elevator back down to the lobby... walk around to the other set of elevators... take those elevators back to the PCICU floor... walk back to the other side of the PCICU... okay, okay I see you get it.

I remember collapsing into a chair in defeat, because I had already walked farther than someone with a separated pelvis/ c-section was ever supposed to. I was beyond done. I remember feeling unrelenting love for my husband who said,

"No. We won't be doing any of that. First, you are going to get a wheel chair for my wife. Second, you are going to walk us through to our daughter."

My knight in shining armor. He might as well have ridden up to the doors of the PCICU on a white horse.

When the nurse proclaimed, "None shall pass!" he might as well have responded by pointing his sword at her chest and proclaiming,

"You shall assist this lady in her time of need or face the consequences of thy actions!"

Since this is not usually something I appreciate, let me just appreciate it now. *This* was exactly what I needed. I had no idea how desperate I was for him to intervene. He chose to step in even though normally he would have been criticized for his efforts. *How does this guy still love me?* He must have been pretty "insistent" because the nurse flew into action...

"Oh a c-section? Oh a daughter with a heart condition? Oh, of course, of course, come right this way."

I remember she added, "Why didn't you say something to begin with?"

And I also remember thinking, *Really?!? That's what you want to say to me in this moment? Really?!?*

Why if I wasn't stuck here in this wheel chair with a major injury... I would... probably... do nothing. Who are we kidding? I would do nothing.

And of course, I don't need any photos to remember the day the doctor came to tell me it was time for our baby girl to go to surgery. I remember that day with perfect clarity.

Back to the movie.

OPEN: INTERIOR/HOSPITAL ROOM
BOSTON CHILDREN'S HOSPITAL/EARLY MORNING

TITLE: Four Days Later

CAMERA HOLDS on MOMMY sitting next to hospital

bed in rocking chair holding BABY and humming softly. BABY is swaddled in blanket. MOMMY quietly enjoying time with BABY.

Wires connect BABY to multiple machines. Machines make appropriate beeping noises.

CUT TO: DOCTOR as he walks into the room and stands next to MOMMY

> DOCTOR
> So how are we doing?

> MOMMY
> (smiles)
> OK. I guess.

DADDY walks in with a cup of coffee and crosses room to stand next to DOCTOR and MOMMY

> DOCTOR
> We just got her test results. Her heart function has started to decline and we are concerned about the fluid on her lungs. I think we need to get her into surgery.

> MOMMY
> When?

> DOCTOR
> Today. Now.

                    DADDY
                 Really? Now?
           (grabs MOMMY's hand)

                    DOCTOR
           Yes. We will walk you down to
             surgery in a few hours.

DOCTOR leaves.

CAMERA HOLDS on MOMMY and DADDY left in
shock. CAMERA pulls back - room feels big,
overwhelming.

MOMMY and DADDY get smaller and smaller.

FADE TO BLACK

CHAPTER SIXTEEN

GOOD JOB BABY GIRL

Our daughter was only six days old when our cardiologist announced the time had come for surgery. Again, we were forced to listen to a jumbled mess of medical jargon while signing a giant stack of paperwork. Somehow, even while taking high doses of pain meds, I was not only supposed to listen, I was supposed to understand it all. Basically, I was not allowed to sue if somehow something went wrong in the middle of all this stuff I didn't even remotely understand. Got it.

"First we are going to repair her VSD," the doctor said.

Oh, yeah. I forgot to mention our daughter had other issues besides a missing pulmonary artery and pulmonary valve. Just add it to the pile. It was all more than I wanted to know.

"We will be taking a… blah… blah… blah… and implanting a blah… blah… blah… then we will be detaching a… blah… blah… blah and then finally the surgery will be complete."

I must confess I don't remember all of the details of this conversation. Sorry. In this instance, the details aren't really important. It's just a bunch of medical jargon anyway.

"Oh. So it's like plumbing," says my husband, with an attempt to inject humor into the stress.

"Yeah. Sure," the doc says with absolutely no laughter. "It's like plumbing."

So much for lightening the mood.

Soon after this conversation, I remember standing in the hallway that led to the pediatric surgical wing. It was a mere matter of hours between "we will be taking your daughter to surgery" and the actual taking of her. I remember standing next to my husband in a brightly lit, white hallway while holding my seven-day-old daughter in my arms. I remember looking down at her and thinking to myself, *No way. There is no way I'm handing this child over to those people. No way, no way, no way, no way....*

Back to the movie.

OPEN: INTERIOR/BOSTON HOSPITAL/HALLWAY

CAMERA HOLDS on MOMMY and DADDY standing in front of sign that says "Pediatric Surgery." MOMMY holding BABY. DADDY stands with arms around MOMMY. Two young DOCTORS stand nearby waiting to take BABY to surgery.

MOMMY

(crying)

I don't think I can do this.

DADDY

(with emotion)

Me either.

MOMMY and DADDY cry over and hug BABY murmuring "We love yous" and other reassurances.

DOCTORS motion that it's time to let them take
the BABY.

MOMMY won't let go. She clings to the baby,
wetting the baby's face with her tears.

DADDY makes small motion towards helping MOMMY
hand over BABY.

                    MOMMY
                  (whispers)
              Not yet… not yet…

CAMERA HOLDS on MOMMY - hugs baby close almost
"blocking" the doctors from taking her.

                    MOMMY
        (with great emotion, through tears)
        OK, baby girl... this is it. All you have
        to do is take a nice long nap while the
              doctors do all the work. OK?

MOMMY makes small motion toward letting go. In
one swift move the DOCTORS seize their moment,
swoop in, grab BABY, and walk quickly down hall
toward the double doors of surgical wing.

CUT TO: MOMMY and DADDY - left standing in hallway
with empty hands and obviously deflated spirits.

CAMERA pulls back from couple and continues
down hallway away from MOMMY and DADDY (from
POV of BABY as if BABY was looking back at her

parents and seeing them fade away).

Emphasize smallness of two parents standing lonely in a large, colorless hallway.

VOICE-OVER/MOMMY
(whisper)
Ouch

FADE TO BLACK

I was standing in that bright, sterile hallway when for the first time in a long time, I let my tears flow appropriately in the moment they were supposed to flow. Unfortunately, once the water works started, I really and truly could not turn them off. That's how come I was wailing, like only my inner two-year-old could wail, when it came time to hand over my baby to the surgical team.

I knew I *had* to do the unthinkable. I knew I *had* to hand her over to the doctors and trust she would come back to me. I knew it, but I couldn't *do* it. I was sobbing uncontrollably and my heart was breaking, and yet, I had no choice. I still had to let go of my little girl and give her away to... strangers.

The emptiness that consumed me after they took her away felt like a freight train. With shaky legs and a heavy heart, I turned and wobbled toward the waiting room. My husband was next to me, helping me walk, but I wouldn't let him in to the darkness around my soul. I wouldn't let anybody in. The weight of my sadness was stifling, but I still couldn't share my grief.

After I had collected myself as much as I could, we walked to the special waiting room made for parents with children in heart surgery. We sat in stilted silence in a room with a bunch of other parents sitting in stilted silence. It was a weird camaraderie. We all smiled at each other with immediate recognition, but no one wanted to compare stories.

I can't speak for the rest of the parents sitting in that room, but I know I didn't have any room left in my spirit to share their grief or even their joy. I have been in other waiting rooms with other cardiac-baby parents, and it has always been the same. I can only assume this is also true of other parents sitting in other waiting rooms across the wide spectrum of childhood illnesses. No one wants to break the stilted silence. No one wants to be "friends." At least, not here in this place.

We knew we were going to be waiting a long time. In a perfect world with every single thing lining up just as it should, our daughter was going to be on the by-pass machine for at least five hours. That adds up to a minimum of an eight-hour surgery. One day's work to fix a six-day-old infant's heart. Crazy.

I don't really remember all of the things we did to fill all of that time, but I'm sure I read a book or at least a magazine. I can almost guarantee that I watched television. At some point, I probably got something to eat. I drank a lot of coffee. Then, I probably read some more, watched some more television, and probably got something else to eat.

I wish I could remember the names of the books I read, or any of the television shows I watched, but I don't. I know that, as I have become more seasoned at sitting in waiting rooms, I have mastered how to enter "the zone." That imaginary place where it was somehow "comfortable" to sit and do "nothing" for a long period of time. Normally, I can't do nothing for so long.

Perhaps, this is where having a separated pelvis comes in handy. I didn't know it, but all that time I spent sitting in recovery was actually training for the marathon of sitting I was going to have to get used to. All that time, I was learning how to quiet my spirit and sit and… wait. Not really the lesson I was looking forward to learning but I suppose, on some level, it was a valuable one.

Throughout the surgery, the nurses kept us updated with a series of texts. It was so… strange… to receive these short quips about the life or death state our daughter. It went a little bit like this…...

ANESTHESIOLOGIST DONE - DAUGHTER ASLEEP

Good. Deep Breath.

ON RESPIRATOR

Okay. They have hooked her up to oxygen. Time to pass the time with lots of TV and yes, let's get some coffee.

GOING ON BY-PASS

Okay now that statement makes me a little more... uncomfortable. I need a distraction. More TV. More coffee.

ON BY-PASS STARTING SURGERY

Okay, now that statement is just wrong. Am I still supposed to be okay with knowing that at this moment the doctors are cutting into my baby girl with a scalpel?

Maybe I should try reading instead. Perhaps a good book will distract me.

SURGERY IN PROGRESS

Am I supposed to still be sitting here like everything is fine? "In Progress" means that they most certainly have their hands (or at least fingers) deep into my baby girl's chest cavity. Time to medicate with more TV and more coffee and something else to read because the first thing is obviously not working.

Five hours, multiple activities and four cups of coffee later we received:

SURGERY STILL IN PROGRESS

Back to TV. Back to Coffee. Back to reading.

Several hours later.

SURGERY COMPLETE

It's done? Already?

FIRST ATTEMPT TO COME OFF BY-PASS

Wait that is not the same as surgery complete.

Wait a minute that means…

WILL LET YOU KNOW WHEN HEART IS BEATING ON ITS OWN

Please, oh, please. Little baby heart. Start beating.

Fifteen very tense minutes later.

HEART IS BEATING

Deep breath.

DOCTOR CLOSING

Wait, that means she's still open???

DOCTOR HAS CLOSED
MOVING TO RECOVERY ROOM

Okay, that's good. Recovery is good.

SURGEON WILL BE OUT SOON TO
TAKE YOU TO SEE YOUR DAUGHTER

Oh, God, please help me. Now I have to see her.

Less than 20 minutes later we were sitting across a table from our pediatric cardiac surgeon. Boston Children's has these conference rooms where a surgeon can meet with the parents of kids in surgery. They are designed to offer the best opportunity for everyone to maintain privacy and to stay calm. They are also very uncomfortable. I remember the chair I was sitting on was not kind to my pelvic injury or my c-section. I think I chose to notice this, because it was easier to complain (even if just to myself) than it was to listen to what the surgeon had to say.

"First of all, she did great and the surgery for now was a success," says the surgeon.

What? What did he say?

I was having a flash back to the muddled lack of focus I had the last time we received "news" about our daughter.

Did he just say the words "great" and "for now" in the same sentence? Was that casual, off-handed assurance without any real promise of solution attached? Hmmm.....

"She did great," the surgeon repeats because he knows we didn't get it the first time around. "We were able to repair blah.... blah.... blah..... medical jargon.... blah... blah... blah.... but ultimately, we can say this initial surgery was a success. I'm going to take you to her now. Follow me."

We stood up and followed him to the PCICU. My husband and the surgeon walked faster than I was able to follow, which left me lagging behind a bit. Normally, that would have made me angry. For once, I was okay with it. This was one time when I didn't want to come in first.

My husband and the surgeon were engaging in some light banter to fill the air and space where happiness should be. It was awkward and I didn't care to join in. As I walked along behind them, I wrestled with exactly how I was feeling. I wrestled with exactly how I thought I *should* be feeling. I wanted to set that crazy level of grief, worry and anxiety aside and feel "good" for a second. After all, my daughter had just survived her first of many heart surgeries... but, I couldn't. I hadn't seen her with my very own eyes... yet. I wasn't sure it would actually make a difference, but it was worth a try.

I focused on putting one foot in front of another. So, I could walk down the hallway. So, I could arrive at the PCICU. So, I could see my very fragile baby girl. There was no way to get ready for that. In the place of tears, I put on my brave face again, because I felt like I was supposed to feel something... else. I was supposed to be relieved, joyful, optimistic, but what I felt was a weird looming cloud of heaviness and doubt.

At some point, we made it to the PCICU and took the slow, hesitant walk over to the hospital bed where my daughter was recovering. I was trying to get there quickly and hold myself back at the same time. I couldn't wait to see for myself that she was still alive, but nothing in me wanted to see a six-day-old infant covered in wires with a giant scar that goes from just below her neck all the way down to just above her belly button. She had barely even begun to live, and already she was overcoming death. I thought I was going to be relieved to see her alive, but I wasn't. I was not relieved, joyful or optimistic. Suddenly, I was pissed. *This is not okay, not even close.*

In an instant, I saw before me the future of our life together. A multitude of images flashed through my brain: more surgeries, more hospital stays, more doctors, more tests, more frustration, more anger. I saw it all before me, and I felt the burn of that anger take over my entire body from the top of my head down to the tip of my toes. I realized I was *always* going to struggle with my emotional distress over the life this little girl had been born into. I was constantly going to want to *fight* for her, and be ferociously *against* everything that was going to happen to her. I was always going to feel this burning anger.

Then I took a second look.

The spirit of this little girl has always brought me back to my senses. I couldn't stay angry, dead and grief stricken, because once I was finally standing next to her, finally looking at her, *really* looking at her, my heart completely melted.

She had a giant tube coming out of her mouth helping her to breathe. Every inch of her skin was covered with gauze and medical tape, and there were wires *everywhere*. It was shocking to see so much "stuff" attached to something so tiny. There was nothing pretty about it, and yet, I was mesmerized by her. She was so incredibly beautiful.

Her eyes were closed and amazingly she looked peaceful. Even with all of that ugly surrounding her, somehow she was resting.

The only place I could touch her was on her fuzzy little head. I was frustrated by that, but it didn't seem quite right to complain.

Good job, baby girl, I whispered as I rubbed my hand gently over her head fuzz. *I'm so proud of you.*

I was forced to face the facts about the two sides of the job before me. Yes, I was going to have to learn to be angry when it was right to be angry, but I was also going to have to be calm when I needed to be calm. I was going to have to learn to give her the room she needed to scream, and the peace she needed to rest. I was going to have to learn to cry when it was okay to cry, but smile and reassure her that everything was going to be okay when she needed me. She had a lot to teach me, I had a lot to learn. It was not a roller coaster I looked forward to riding, but as I gazed down at her and rubbed her soft, fuzzy head, I realized, *how could I possibly resist?*

CHAPTER SEVENTEEN

THIS IDIOT,
THIS ONE RIGHT HERE

OPEN: INTERIOR/TARGET DEPARTMENT STORE
MOMMY on motorized cart.

DAUGHTER #1 standing in front of MOMMY's knees.

CAMERA follows MOMMY on motorized cart.

MUSIC: Pumping, invigorating, with a driving beat. Humorously in direct opposition to activity of MOMMY. She is not "pumped up" but is frantic, desperate. Emphasize "speed" of cart to seem like it's racing down Target aisles like a sports car.

She tries to navigate down aisle but instead is bumping into clothing racks and shelves, pulling clothes down and knocking over signs.

DAUGHTER #1 laughs with glee. GRANDMA and DADDY

walk behind "cleaning up" the destruction.

MOMMY is frantically on a mission. She goes forward and backs up, turns and swoops as if her cart is a fine tuned machine. MOMMY loudly pokes fun at the sound of the cart backing up.

                    MOMMY
              BEEP! BEEP! BEEP!

                  DAUGHTER #1
                (mimics MOMMY)
              BEEP! BEEP! BEEP!

MOMMY continues to crack jokes at her own expense to try to hide her "crazy" and her feelings of embarrassment that she, as a former athlete, is now zooming around on a motorized cart in the middle of a Target. It is a ridiculous scene all the way around.

CAMERA follows family through multiple aisles of the store until MOMMY finally gets to baby section. She stops in front of display of onesies.

CAMERA Pans over vast multitude of choices.

CLOSE UP of MOMMY… thinking… thinking…

                    MOMMY
        Not those… not those… hmmmm…

She rifles through the selection from her seated

perch, reaching high, knocking down other items as she awkwardly tries to find what she needs WITHOUT asking for any help. Finally, finding the ones she needs in the size she needs. She overloads her arms with multi-packs of onesies and, with almost no agility, throws them into her cart.

DADDY quickly removes most of the packs and returns them back to the display, still "covering" for MOMMY's frantic activity.

CAMERA follows MOMMY as she tries to turn around. It takes several attempts to "turn" with the cart going forward a few inches then BEEP… BEEP… BEEPS… as it backs up a few inches.

                    MOMMY
                (maniacally)
              BEEP! BEEP! BEEP!

                  DAUGHTER #1
              (echoes laughing)
              BEEP! BEEP! BEEP!

CUT TO: DADDY shakes his head in disbelief. Obviously, uncomfortable with his wife's choice to turn this situation into a game.

Cart still trying to turn around. Continues for a while.

GRANDMA and DADDY stand back, helpless. DADDY

motions that he might step forward to offer help and then changes his mind and quickly steps back to "safety." MOMMY would not welcome his assistance at this time.

MOMMY finally breaks free and barrels back down the aisle to the check out area, knocking down more items from the shelves. DAUGHTER #1 laughs with glee.

CAMERA HOLDS on back of MOMMY and cart... there she goes...

CUT TO: GRANDMA and DADDY hang their heads and slowly follow along behind picking up things off floor and putting them back onto the shelves as they go.

FADE TO BLACK

So, there I was barreling down the aisles of a Target riding on one of those motorized scooter things that are normally parked at the front of the store. They are there for specific reason. In fact, they are there for a GOOD reason. I just never thought that reason would apply to me.

I can't even begin to explain how it felt to actually NEED one of those cumbersome scooters in order to go shopping. Apparently, one of my "life lessons" included gaining some empathy for those who find themselves physically challenged. That's the only way I can explain how, I, the former athlete, kept ending up in these comical, very un-athletic, situations (in light of this newly obtained empathy, let me just say that I tip my hat to all of those who are permanently physically impaired -

I could never do what you do).

I was not good at driving that "thing." I must have banged into a thousand racks, shelves and/or store displays. I left a wide wake of destruction behind me. I'm not sure it made sense for an extremely emotionally unstable woman who was taking pain medications to even be in a Target store, much less operating "machinery." It felt eerily familiar to my former life with a separated pelvis and a wheelchair. *Will I ever be able to STAND and face the challenges before me? Will I always have to sit?*

How exactly did I end up in a Target while my baby girl was fresh out of surgery? Well, it went a little like this....

We had come home from the hospital the day before. Our baby had been pronounced "stable." She was going to stay sedated in the PCICU for another 24 hours, so there wasn't much we could do other than stand next to the bed and stare at her. As much as I wanted to do that, I had actually allowed myself to go home and try to sleep. I did my best to rest, but I did not succeed. I'm the queen of making earth shattering realizations... right before I fall asleep. This is a trait that my husband kindly tolerates, but secretly abhors. He cannot understand why his normally reticent and introverted wife becomes wildly chatty at exactly the very moment he wants to sleep.

Unfortunately for everyone involved, my moment of pre-sleep clarity had revealed we didn't have the right kind of onesies. We had acquired a large number of onesies from various sources, hand-me-downs, gifts, etc. They were adorable. I couldn't use any of them. None of them were going to work for an infant who had just had heart surgery. *How could I have been so stupid?*

It was going to be impossible to pull a onesie over the head of our daughter and then somehow maneuver it around all of the wires, medical tape and giant "owies" to then snap it at the bottom over her diaper. Not to mention we shouldn't cover up her wound, because every two hours a nurse or a doctor was coming by to check her stitches, take her vitals, etc., etc. It would be a lot of work to take that very impractical onesie off and on, off and on and off and on *over and over*. What we needed were the boring, white, hospital style onesies that wrap in front like a robe and snap on the side. We needed loose, soft material that wouldn't pull and tug on her multiple layers of medical tape, piles of wires, and sensitive skin. We needed to think less about how "cute" those other onesies looked and be more practical. More function, less flare.

We had completely planned it out all wrong. My fractured little soul obsessed over my failure to solve the onesie problem until it officially became a crisis (at least according to the voices inside my head).

My great moment of just-before-sleep "wisdom" led to my overzealous need to go to Target, where, of course, I ended up wildly banging and beeping on a motorized scooter. I should have been anywhere else other than there. ANYWHERE. But, there I was anyway, acting out in a very-unlike-me kind of way. Again.

Since there was no way I was going on a ride on the crazy train all by myself, I made everyone else in my immediate vicinity come with me. Everyone included my three-year-old, my mom and my husband. My dad had gone home, but my mom was able to stay behind for a few more days. One big happy family, right? You would think I had learned that lesson the first time at the pediatrician's office in New York. Sadly, I did not. *Sigh*.

Of course, I could have sent my husband out on this mission. He could have easily purchased the kind of onesies we needed, all by himself. I could have sent my mom, or a friend. Even my three-year-old could have handled this simple task. I should have let it go, but I couldn't. *I* was going to go to Target and *I* was going to pick out ugly, plain, white wrap-around, snap onesies and *I* wasn't going to let anything stop me. Get out of my way. Maniacal Mommy is out for onesies. Watch out.

Soon after, I was sitting in the car we had borrowed for our little outing. *Thank you sweet friends who loan cars to desperate psychotic mommies. I so totally love you.* Our little band of merry shoppers had stowed away our purchases into the trunk. My mom had buckled my three-year-old into her seat. My husband had secured me into mine, and we were about to pull out of the parking lot when my husband's phone rang. I knew it was the hospital long before my husband even had a chance to push the accept button. I knew that was why I had been so frantic all morning. I was in a hurry, because I had a feeling... this wasn't going to be a good day.

"Okay... yes... okay... okay... yes, we will be right there," my husband said.

My husband is a fantastic actor. He can pretend to be almost anything on stage. He is very convincing. By contrast, he is a very honest man in real life. What you see is what you get. I could tell he was trying to stay calm, be strong, and not send his crazy wife over the edge forever, but it was too late. I had already read his honest face. I was already spiraling.

I will forever remember the seconds after he hung up as the time I was drowning in quicksand. I didn't even know what was wrong yet, but I knew I was going to never forgive myself.

What was I doing at Target?!?

What kind of idiot, who should be home recovering from her own surgery by the way, spends a morning shopping at Target when she should have been sitting next to her newborn in the hospital?!?

I know. This idiot. This one right here.

Back to the movie.

OPEN: EXTERIOR/CHILDREN'S HOSPITAL BOSTON

CAMERA follows small four-door sedan holding MOMMY and DADDY as they hastily pull up in front of lobby doors.

> DADDY
> Should we pay for the valet?

> MOMMY
> (while unbuckling)
> Definitely.

They exit car, check in with the parking attendant, hand over keys and enter hospital.

CUT TO: NEXT SCENE
INTERIOR/PCICU

CAMERA HOLDS on double doors. They open and MOMMY and DADDY enter frantically looking for the nurse in charge of their daughter's care.

A NURSE from across the room catches their eye and motions them over to the bedside of their daughter.

MOMMY and DADDY walk over to hospital bed and look anxiously at the nurse.

> NURSE
> The doctor is on his way.

CUT TO: new set of wires and leads coming from newborn's head. MOMMY looks at nurse with a question (unspoken) on her face.

                    NURSE
        (understanding MOMMY's confusion)
        She is connected to an EEG machine.

                    MOMMY
            (looks frantically at DADDY)
        How am I supposed to touch her?
        I can't touch her... (shaky)

DADDY grabs MOMMY's hand and places it on BABY'S cheek. MOMMY smiles and gently rubs newborn's cheek with her knuckle. Momentarily relieved.

DOCTOR enters.

                    DOCTOR
            We have her test results.
        Let's sit down so we can talk.

FADE TO BLACK

Our daughter was experiencing something called post-op seizures. She had been on the by-pass machine for longer than her little body, and particularly her brain, could handle. She was in aftershock, so to speak.

After my husband and I rushed to the hospital and "raced" to her recovery room, we once again found ourselves standing next to our newborn daughter and listening to a doctor explain a very complicated medical situation to a couple of brain dead parents. *Again,* I did not hear what the doctor was saying. Really, I heard nothing. Not even my normal muffled mess I reserve for doctors when I want to tune out something I can't stand to process. I was totally focused on my daughter, and silently, inwardly begging for her forgiveness.

I should have been here. O, sweet baby girl, I should have been here, I whispered.

An EEG machine had been hooked up to her, so her head was completely covered in leads and wires. Her cute, little fuzzy head used to be the only place I could touch her, and now, I could no longer do that. I tried a few times to hold her, bond with her, just touch her in some way, but I failed miserably. I couldn't get to her. She was blocked by all of the technology keeping her alive. I was forced to touch a knuckle to her cheek and gently rub an area about as big as a dime.

Yep, I was burning with anger all over again.

The doctors tasked me to stand next to my daughter's bed and let them know when she started to seize again. Apparently, the idea was to get the kind of data they needed to decide whether these seizures would pass, or if they needed to start a medication to stop them.

It was good to be given a task. I was desperate for something to do. Even if that thing was something I was going to do anyway. I wasn't going to leave my daughter's bedside any time soon, so I was relieved my job was to stand next to the bed and stare at her.

"Here she goes," I said. "She is starting to seize."

"Thanks, Mom," The nurse says as if I just conquered the world.

Thank God for her. She made me feel like I was truly participating, even though of course, I wasn't. All I was doing was standing helplessly next to my daughter and watching as her eyes rolled into the back of her head and her body jerked and twitched in a very unnatural way.

I thought deciding to give birth to this beautiful creature was difficult. I thought handing my daughter over to the anesthesiologist was hard. I thought seeing her for the first time with a giant scar on her chest was beyond comprehension. I didn't know it yet, but this was one of the most defining moments in my story. This moment attacked me in a new and frightening way. I was unprepared for it. It attacked me at the very instant I thought my baby girl was going to be "fine."

Even though I was able to pretend to keep it together at first, when the doctor told me they were going to give my sweet baby a medication to stop the seizures, I lost my mind. I do not know why the idea of dosing my baby with this medication was the final straw for me, but it was. Again, I followed my irrational pattern of emotional irregularity. I didn't cry from the guilt and the feeling of failure that came when I was at a Target instead of a hospital. I held that in. Instead, I became a basket case when the doctors took the only SANE course of action available. The medication wasn't one of many solutions, it was the only solution. Somehow, I had convinced myself my daughter didn't need it. *Oh, no, here comes the verbal diarrhea...*

As the room began to spin. I remember feeling like I was in the middle of a fish bowl. Everyone around me was out of focus. While they could see me, I couldn't clearly see them.

My husband turned to me and said. "It's going to be okay. This is something they HAVE to do."

His reassurance only made me more afraid.

No one was trying to hurt her. They were trying to SAVE her. But that's not what it felt like to me. Thank God for those times when doctors make the right decision even when crazy mothers are irrationally yelling at them.

My daughter survived those post-op seizures, with "imperceptible brain damage," because the doctors did the right thing. The doctors acted quickly, gave my daughter what she NEEDED and ultimately saved her without any intervention from me. *I* did not get to be part of this decision for my daughter. *I* did not get to decide. It was that feeling of helplessness that disturbed me all the way down to my core.

As I look back on this time, I can recognize that this was the moment when my circumstances began to slowly chisel away at my ability to hope. So many things had already knocked me around. I was still dizzy from the punches I had received. Even so, before this moment, I still had a small portion of hope that things would someday get better.

Now I see that adding this struggle to my growing pile of struggles really did register in my brain as "too much." I can't honestly say I'm over it, even now. The tears streaming down my face as I write about this reveal how I really feel. Of course, at the time, I didn't let it show. I turned off another switch in my brain and stuffed some more grief down inside for later. At this moment, I had to be strong. I had to stay calm. I had to be a mother.

After her recovery from all the post-op complications, my daughter was finally transferred to a permanent hospital room where we set up camp for several weeks. Again, I functioned from a place of nebulous fog. I can't remember anything about exactly what happened on a daily basis.

Before these crazy interruptions into my psyche, I had a good memory. I could recount the most minute details. One time in NYC, some friends of ours were having a debate about the exact phrasing of a quote from a movie.

After much deliberation, one of my friends said, "Let's roll the video tape... Betts?"

To which I answered word for word exactly what the character said. That was then.

It is annoying to me now that, as I desperately search my

brain for specific details about exactly what happened, I can see nothing but small glimpses of images.

I remember what the hospital room looked like in theory, but I can't remember what color the walls were. I remember it by how it felt and even more by how it smelled, but I cannot "see" it in my mind.

I remember the sink, because I must have washed my hands a million times. I remember the smell of the soap.

I remember the taste of hospital food, but I couldn't tell you for the life of me what I ate.

I can recall I spent an endless amount of time doing nothing and everything at the same time. I just can't remember exactly what I was doing. I must have passed the time somehow, I just don't have any idea how I did it.

I do remember I changed those open front onesies over and over again. I also remember learning how to swaddle around wires, tapes and scars.

Note: guess who ended up being really good at swaddling even with all those obstacles? My husband! Who knew?

Otherwise, it's all one giant blur of stethoscopes and scrubs. I don't even remember the names of the nurses who tirelessly took care of my baby and sometimes also took care of me. I don't remember the names of the med students who "learned" at the foot of her bed. I don't remember. I try, but I can't.

In an almost anti-climatic way, ten weeks after her birth, my daughter came home to stay. Ten weeks. Even though it may have been a short time by calendar, it felt like an eternity. I can't believe how much my life was interrupted by this extremely short passing of time.

I wanted desperately to trust in this miracle. I wanted to steal back a piece of the hope I had lost, but I was pessimistic about ever getting it back again. I knew intellectually it was possible, but in my heart, I'm afraid I didn't believe it. That strong woman of faith? Part of her was still present, but only part.

Back to the movie.

OPEN: EXTERIOR/BOSTON CITY STREET
CAMERA HOLDS on street in front of apartment where the FAMILY lives. In an eerily similar scenario, a "borrowed" car pulls up to the front of apartment building and MOMMY and DADDY exit the car.

                    MOMMY
            Here we are again...

                    DADDY
        At least this time you can walk.

                    MOMMY
                (with sadness)
                At least.

MOMMY glances at back seat to see sleeping newborn tiny in comparison to size of baby carrier.

MOMMY smiles.

DADDY takes BABY out of baby carrier in backseat of car and hands the tiny bundle to MOMMY. MOMMY starts slow trek over to building steps.

DADDY removes car seat, closes car and follows behind MOMMY.

CUT TO: door of apartment as it opens and DADDY,

MOMMY and BABY walk in to greet DAUGHTER #1 and GRANDMA. Everyone talks over each other with greetings and laughter. They stand together gawking at BABY.

                    VOICE-OVER/MOMMY
          Welcome home, (pause) Ella.

FADE TO BLACK

CHAPTER EIGHTEEN
ZOMBIE PINBALLS

OPEN: INTERIOR/BOSTON APARTMENT/KITCHEN
SCENE set up to look like medical lab.

CLOSE UP shows line of oral syringes. Two hands wearing medical gloves pick up the syringes and begin the process of "pulling meds." Medicine gets sucked into the syringe. Hand flicks the side of the syringe to settle the liquid and then pushes the plunger gently to remove the air bubble.

An out-of-focus face (woman) with a surgical mask examines the syringe to confirm dose correct. Double checks large chart on the wall and checks the syringe one last time. Once she is satisfied the dosage is correct, she places it down on a sterile, metal tray and picks up the next syringe.

As CAMERA pulls back, the SCENE morphs into

the kitchen of FAMILY apartment. The masked lab technician morphs into MOMMY standing at kitchen counter (enhance surprise factor of "civilian" performing a task normally done by a lab technician).

MOMMY finishes the process and then takes six syringes into the living room where she walks up to her infant daughter sitting in a baby seat. BABY is happy, adorable.

MOMMY hesitates at the idea of giving this much medicine to something so small. She takes a deep breath.

                    MOMMY
              (slightly nervous)
          Okay, baby girl. Open Wide.

FADE TO NEXT SCENE

OPEN: INTERIOR/FAMILY APARTMENT/BATHROOM
Scene made to "look like" sterile hospital bathroom. BABY lying on hospital counter on a white hospital towel. An out of focus person wearing a surgical mask and surgical gloves (woman) is dipping a cloth into a pink hospital issued tub of soapy water. She rings out the cloth and moves towards BABY.

SCENE morphs to bathroom in FAMILY apartment. MOMMY kneels next to baby with a bowl of soapy water and a cloth. She rinses the cloth just like the nurse did, rings it out, and holds cloth above BABY. BABY lying on bathroom floor on top of soft, fluffy towel. Medical tape covers the baby's chest from the bottom of her neck to her belly button. Her skin is red and splotchy where other pieces of tape have been removed. She has bruises and marks from arterial lines, IVs, chest tubes, and catheters. Wounds cover her entire body. Yet, she is bright-eyed and smiley. A happy baby.

MOMMY is overwhelmed with how to clean such a fragile body. MOMMY hesitates then takes a deep breath.

MOMMY
(nervous)
Okay, baby girl. Let's get clean.

FADE TO NEXT SCENE

OPEN: INTERIOR/FAMILY APARTMENT/BEDROOM
SCENE set to look like a hospital room. BABY on sterile changing table. Person in surgical mask and medical gloves (woman) finishes changing BABY's diaper and begins to put footed pajamas on BABY. BABY with medical tape, wounds, etc. still uncomfortably showing.

BABY gurgles, happy despite all that.

SCENE morphs into child's bedroom of FAMILY apartment. Woman morphs into MOMMY who looks down dubiously at baby wondering how to put clothes onto such a fragile body. MOMMY hesitates and takes a deep breath.

                    MOMMY
                  (nervous)
       Okay, baby girl. Let's get dressed.

FADE TO BLACK

My daughter came home from the hospital, and we did our best to get back to some version of our previous life. At this point, we would have been happy to return to anything similar to our life "before," which of course was already challenging. I wish I could say I was in the kind of place where I slogged through this mud in a healthy and positive way. I did not. I suppose, on some level it is a testament to my strength, and to my faith, that I even remotely survived at all. Maybe. I was in a pretty dark season, so I'm not sure I was a testament to anything.

When they released us from the hospital, our baby girl was as stable as she could be. That's not the same as actually "stable," or "healthy" or "healed." I have had to slowly and painfully learn the difference. Doctors have an amazing ability to work within the nuances of words. As a parent, I have often misinterpreted what those words actually mean in the day to day struggle of... life. According to the docs, she was healthy enough to live a life on the "outside." I wasn't so sure. She still seemed pretty fragile to me.

It was difficult to act like things were fine when it felt like our home had been transformed into a medical recovery unit. Yes, of course I'm exaggerating. We didn't really wear medical gloves, or surgical masks, or use sterile medical equipment. It just sort of "felt" that way, because of all the things we DID have to do.

I had to learn a lot of new tricks. Probably, the most difficult of these was learning how to pull meds. I remember going through the process and feeling more like a lab technician instead of a mother. *Sigh*.

At one point, our baby was taking six different medications with doses like .1 ml and .3 ml. She was only ten weeks old so... yikes. Six different forms of meds, six different amounts, six different dosage frequencies. How is it possible that a doctor sends a newborn home to sleep deprived parents and tells them to dose something as important as *Dijoxin*? Or *Lasix*? Sounds crazy... right? It made absolutely no sense to me then, and I'm not sure I can figure it out now.

This is one time where it is a good thing to be a perfectionist. Almost like I could give myself permission to use what would, under other circumstances, be considered a character flaw to my advantage. It was okay to be an over zealous control freak, my daughter's life depended on it.

Even though we had technically been discharged from the hospital, it didn't really feel like we were home. We had an obscene number of doctor's appointments to keep. If I look back on this time with any clarity, it always looks a little like this....

OPEN: INTERIOR/FAMILY APARTMENT

TITLE: Doctor Office Montage

FADE IN: MOMMY places BABY in stroller.

Buckle - SNAP

MOMMY
(to DAUGHTER #1)
C'mon kiddo.

DAUGHTER #1 joins. ALL exit apartment.

Door closes - CLICK

FADE TO BLACK

OPEN: EXTERIOR/TRAIN STOP

MOMMY, DAUGHTER #1, BABY get on train. Train is
elevated. Passengers must step up three stairs
in order to board train (exaggerate how taxing
it is on MOMMY to lift stroller up stairs and
also make sure DAUGHTER #1 boards safely).

Train Doors Close - FWAMP

FADE TO BLACK

OPEN: EXTERIOR/TRAIN STOP

Train Doors Open - FWAMP

MOMMY, DAUGHTER #1, BABY exit train. MOMMY
carries stroller down train steps then turns to
make sure DAUGHTER #1 exits safely.

FADE TO BLACK

OPEN: INTERIOR/PEDIATRICIAN'S OFFICE

Elevator doors open - DING

ENTER doctor's office filled with stereotypical cute and fluffy decor. We read a sign on wall.

SIGN: "Brookline Pediatrics"

MOMMY places BABY on examination table.

Paper on table - KRINKLE

                    PEDIATRICIAN
            (walks in, shakes MOMMY's hand)
                Hi, I'm Doctor Klein.

Pediatrician pulls out a shot. MOMMY holds BABY still. Shot goes in to baby's arm.

BABY cries.

                      MOMMY
               It's okay baby girl,
               it will be over soon.

                   DAUGHTER #1
                 Can we go yet?

                      MOMMY
            (looks toward other daughter)
               Soon, sweet girl, soon.

FADE TO BLACK

OPEN: BACK TO INTERIOR/APARTMENT (different day)

MOMMY places BABY in stroller.

Buckle - SNAP

                         MOMMY
                      C'mon kiddo.

DAUGHTER #1 joins. ALL exit apartment.

Door closes - CLICK

FADE TO BLACK

OPEN: EXTERIOR/TRAIN STOP

MOMMY, DAUGHTER #1, BABY get on train.

Train door closes - FWAMP

FADE TO BLACK

OPEN: EXTERIOR/TRAIN STOP

Train door opens - FWAMP

MOMMY, DAUGHTER #1, BABY exit train.

FADE TO BLACK

OPEN: INTERIOR/BOSTON CHILDREN'S

Elevator doors open - DING

ENTER doctor's office with brightly colored walls but decor is sparse. No soft fluffy animals. The sign on the wall reads

SIGN: "Pediatric Cardiology"

MOMMY places baby on top of examination table.

Paper - KRINKLE

Four members of medical staff walk in.

                    PED CARDIOLOGIST
          (walks to MOMMY and shakes her hand)
            Hi, I'm Dr. Rodriguez. This is our
              Fellow, Dr. Mayer, our Resident,
            Dr. Cohen, and this is Amy (nurse).

From BABY's POV all of the doctor's faces hover over baby.

                         MOMMY
          (pushes her face in - making room)
        It's okay baby girl, it will be over soon.

                      DAUGHTER #1
                    Can we go yet?

                         MOMMY
          (looks toward other daughter)
              Soon, sweet girl, soon.

FADE TO BLACK

OPEN: INTERIOR/APARTMENT (different day)
Same sequence as before with shorter scenes.
Speed up rhythm.

Baby in stroller

Stroller buckle - SNAP

                    MOMMY
                C'mon kiddo.

Door closes - CLICK

Walk up steps to train.
Train door closes - FWAMP
Train door opens - FWAMP
All exit train

Elevator door opens - DING

ENTER doctor's office.

SIGN: "Pediatric Radiology"

MOMMY puts baby on x-ray table.

Paper - KRINKLE

NURSE gently places plastic cover over baby to
hold her in place. BABY cries and looks at MOMMY
in desperation (please make it stop).

                    MOMMY
              (from across room)
   It's okay baby girl, it will be over soon.

MOMMY steps behind wall into "safe zone"

                  DAUGHTER #1
                Can we go yet?

                    MOMMY
   (turns puts arm around older daughter)
            Soon, sweet girl, soon.

FADE TO BLACK

OPEN: INTERIOR/APARTMENT/ENTRYWAY
(different day)(tempo of scene accelerated)

Stroller buckle - SNAP

                    MOMMY
        (off camera) C'mon... (exhausted)

Door closes - CLICK
Board train - FWAMP
Exit train - FWAMP
Elevator doors - DING

ENTER doctor's office.

SIGN: "Pediatric Neurology"

MOMMY places BABY on examination table.

Paper - KRINKLE

> DOCTOR
> Hi, I'm Dr. Blah.
> And this is Dr. Blah Blah.
> (names of doctors losing importance)

MOMMY shakes hands.

Doctors turn to BABY.

Before they even touch her, BABY cries.

> MOMMY
> It's okay baby girl… (deep breath)
> it will be over… soon…

> DAUGHTER #1
> Can we go yet?

> MOMMY
> (with sigh)
> Soon… soon...

FADE TO BLACK

OPEN: INTERIOR/APARTMENT
(different day)(tempo of scene accelerated)

Stroller buckle - SNAP

MOMMY doesn't even call older DAUGHTER, she follows along without being asked.

Door closes - CLICK
Enter train - FWAMP
Exit train - FWAMP
In elevator, BABY sees doctor and starts crying.

                    MOMMY
        Hang in there baby girl. It'll be over…
             (looks off to distance) soon…

Elevator doors - DING

ENTER examination room

SIGN: "Pediatric Gastroenterology"

Paper - KRINKLE

                    DOCTOR
              Hi, I'm doctor…

                    MOMMY
              (cuts him off)
                   Hi.
              (shakes hand)
          What do you say we just
            get this over with?

FADE TO BLACK

For the record, I only remember the name of our pediatrician and our pediatric cardiologist. All those other guys definitely introduced themselves to me, but I have no recollection of what they looked like, let alone their names.

We bounced around between the multiple doctor's offices kind of like zombie pinballs. My oldest daughter was constantly forced to come along with us. She was an amazing big sister. She rarely complained and continued to excel at home, at school and at making friends. If it weren't for the parents of the friends she made at the playground or at school, I wouldn't have had any acquaintances at all. She was a strong, independent, intelligent four-year-old. Thanks to her fortitude, I was able to survive those first few months. If she had needed me as much as other four-year-olds normally need their mothers, I don't think I would have survived.

Everywhere we turned, someone somewhere was giving our baby a check-up. In a weird way, it was kind of reassuring. If there was something wrong, we sure couldn't find it, and it "wasn't for a lack of looking" (to quote a movie that reveals way too much information about how old I am). For the most part, the doctors all tried to assure me she was doing well. They said she was doing great even "for a baby with a major medical condition."

You heard it too, right? That small extra phrase at the end that reminds me "doing great" is not the same as "all healed" or even (God forbid) "normal."

At least, she was excelling at the task of meeting all of her medical "marks." On paper, she was blowing this CHD thing out of the water. She was eating better than she should have been. Miracle. Even though she began her life dangerously under weight, she was growing more than a CHD case "normally" would. Miracle. And even though she had a long complicated first surgery with post-op seizures, she didn't show any signs of developmental delay. Miracle.

The doctors patted my head and sent me on my way with their well wishes, almost pushing me out the door. It was time to put aside all my questions, queries and concerns. I had worn out my welcome.

I did my best to believe them. I really wanted to trust them, but I had lost my ability to completely buy in to the "all is well" philosophy back when I was banging around in a motorized scooter at Target. I no longer trusted that the word "okay" meant what I wanted it to mean.

It's hard to look back and see how all that hard stuff distracted from this dynamo of a baby. She didn't care at all that she had a major medical condition. Even this early in her life, she was full of *brightness* and *joy* and *strength*. She ate, she slept, she giggled, she gurgled, she grew, and she survived. She was beyond a medical miracle. She was magic.

I, on the other hand, was overwhelmed, sad, sore, and exhausted. With no way to take a time out to regroup, I pushed on to embrace this second round of motherhood with my designated uniform.

Out in public, I wore my "I'm okay" mask and most of the time I was still pretty good at convincing everyone around me this was true. I hid behind my resilient children and the abundant optimism of my husband. I let them take all of the attention, so no one would really notice what was going on with me. A darkness was starting to settle over me, and unfortunately, I was too distracted by my circumstances to notice.

CHAPTER NINETEEN
THE PIT

OPEN: INTERIOR BEDROOM

CAMERA HOLDS on MOMMY sleeping
Slow dissolve into dream sequence

MOMMY lying at bottom of mountain where she fell
from cliff. Body distorted and still. It is late
in the evening, dusk. Darkness is falling and it
is becoming hard to see. MOMMY wiggles fingers.
Moans. Gingerly sits up. Shakes head a little
and slowly stands.

She looks up at mountain side with a grimace and
searches her body for new wounds. She stumbles
forward with purposeful intention of walking
away from mountain.

                    VOICE-OVER/MOMMY
                      (mumbling)
            No more… mountain… climbing…

She stumbles through the darkness attempting to make her way... somewhere. There is a blindness to her search.

CUT TO: From MOMMY's POV we look out and see a path barely visible. MOMMY steps forward towards the path but her foot does not land on solid ground. MOMMY's face registers shock then gives sarcastic "here we go again" to camera.

CAMERA HOLDS on darkness as MOMMY plummets down into the bottom of a dark pit.

OFF CAMERA: sound of body hitting the ground - THUMP

CAMERA from top of pit looks down on MOMMY. MOMMY lies in awkward position not even trying to get up.

                    VOICE-OVER/MOMMY
                         Ouch.

FADE TO BLACK

I know I somehow went through the motions of keeping it together during all of this, because people around me keep saying I looked great. I seemed strong. They couldn't believe I was doing so well. I had this loud cheering section around me *all the time* telling me to keep going. I was grateful, of course. It was nice to know people cared.

It was also *suffocating*.

I am certain I was not doing as well as everyone around me

thought I was. I know this, because even a small glimpse back into what I remember about this time sends my whole body, mind and soul into a dizzy panic. I can barely keep myself from wailing with grief.

Somewhere in there, I think I would have loved to hear just one person say, "Hey, you look like a wreck. Need a shoulder to cry on?"

But, I had my mask securely locked in place, and I was following my default setting of keeping everyone at arms length. Why would anyone think I needed them? Answer: they wouldn't.

What happened next is hard for me to talk about. Mostly, because it is the part of my journey where it felt like I fell down into a dark pit *after* I had already fallen from a cliff. I think, up until this point, I had been able to rally back from my grief and pain and at least pretend to be living. Unfortunately, with each new event, it was getting harder and harder to keep up appearances. My edges were starting to fray. My mask was starting to crack. My perfectionism was starting to crumble. It all just kept *hurting*.

If I had drawn a "Progression of Emotional Stability" chart for this time in my life, it probably would have looked a little bit like this....

Top to bottom on the left side, I would have listed "happy with high level of emotional stability" then "content with normal level of emotionally stability" and then "dark with dangerously low level of emotional stability." Along the bottom of the line graph, I would have listed the "events" of my life in chronological order.

The first event listed would have been "moved to NY" so my line would have started at the top of the chart next to "happy with high level of emotional stability." The line would go down *a lot*, almost all the way down to "dangerously low," next to "separated pelvis" but then it would have bounced back up next to "able to walk again." It would have gone down below "normal" again when we moved from NY but then rallied back up once we were settled in Boston. It would have gone up and down erratically next to "found out pregnant again" and plummeted down next to "baby has heart condition." There would have been a small rally next to "baby survives surgery," but then another plummet next to "post-op seizures." It would have hit a plateau just above "dangerously low emotional stability" after our baby girl came home from the hospital to reflect that my growing sadness, guilt and grief had reached a flat existence.

Occasionally, this flat line would have been interrupted with a small blip up next to titles like "older daughter's first day of preschool," "baby says first word," "older daughter throws a 'Bird Day' party," "baby smiles," "spent day at aquarium with friends" and best of all "Daddy's home." Unfortunately, most of the time the line would have stayed down near the bottom next to dangerously low. Mommy was not in a good place.

Back to the movie.

INTERIOR/PEDIATRICIAN'S OFFICE

CAMERA HOLDS on BABY (four months old) wearing only a diaper smiling up at camera.

TITLE: Falling Into the Pit: Part One

From off camera MOMMY talks to PEDIATRICIAN

                          MOMMY
           So this sore at the top of her
           scar doesn't seem to be healing.

                          PEDIATRICIAN
            Yes, I see that. I have a solution
            but you are not going to like it.

                             MOMMY
                      I usually don't.

PEDIATRICIAN picks up scalpel and heads toward
infected sore at top of BABY's scar.

MOMMY's face winces.
BABY screams in pain.

FADE TO BLACK

   I am not sure why this doctor's appointment got so far under
my skin, but it did. I think I was really bothered by the fact that
my baby daughter's scar had finally healed, and yet, there we were
again with another "issue." Sutures that did not dissolve correctly
were not on my radar. Slicing into an infected sore at the top of a
long scar stretching across the chest of a four-month-old baby was
not on my list of fun activities for the day. I was worn down from
all of the extra stuff that kept happening on top of what we were
already dealing with. I needed a time out, a break, but that was
impossible.
   This was supposed to be a simple, fun, gentle day. We had
planned to get this quick check up out of the way, then swing
by a friend's house to drop off our older daughter for a play date.
My husband, my three-year-old, my baby and me, we *all* went
to this appointment (yep, we are "the Keatings," we travel in a
group...).
   At the time, it made sense. My daughter came, because it was
going to be easy to drop her off on the way home. My husband

was there, because by some fluke he was actually home at the same time we had an appointment. It was a rare opportunity for him to participate.

It was a great relief to have him present. Even if, all he did was entertain our three-year-old while I held our baby down so she wouldn't squirm. This was supposed to be one of the easy appointments. It was not supposed to be like *this*.

You would think after all of my extensive experience with things not going as planned, I would have been better prepared. I wasn't. I was so broken in so many places, I didn't have time to prepare for new wounds. The old ones hadn't healed yet. I think that is why a simple out-patient procedure (that my daughter recovered from in a matter of minutes by the way) felt like a gushing open wound.

As we were leaving the doctor's office, we thought it was prudent to call our friends and make sure we were still on for a play date. To be honest, I was hoping they were going to say no. I was kind of ready to head home and collapse. No such luck. Our friends were *happy* to have us come over. *Crap.*

When we arrived at our friend's house, she asked if we wanted to come in for a while. Every ounce of me wanted to say no. I needed space. My husband, on the other hand, said, "Sure!" He is the one in this relationship who thrives in social settings. My lack of ability to voice what I needed left me in that awkward place of joining in or causing a scene. We both know which one I chose.

In we marched with all of our baggage… our baggage that had me off balance, disoriented, and off my game. That's how I missed it. I missed something big.

While we were superficially chatting though our experience at the doctor, my friend let it slip that she was really tired.

"Why?" I said.

"Because of my mom," she said.

"Oh right," I said, "because your mom is sick."

My friend answered me with something… something I didn't quite hear… something that didn't register.

Unintentionally, I moved on to a different topic. I don't remember exactly what topic I changed the conversation to, but I'm betting I moved the conversation back to me and my problems. Unfortunately, the thing I missed, the thing my friend told me without really telling me was that her mother who had been sick for months had "passed away" (her words) *that morning*. She had been up all night dealing with death, and here we were coming over for a play date.

As I look back on that day, *I can't believe* she told us to come over. *I can't believe* she actually invited us *all* into her home. In my defense, she's the one who told us to come. We had even tried to give her an "out." She didn't take it. In hindsight, I understand she, like me, was looking for a distraction. A way to make the pain in her heart a little easier to tolerate.

If I hadn't had so much on my plate I probably would have noticed it was unusual for my friend's husband to be home in the middle of the day. If I had been able to pay attention, I would have also noticed that all three of her boys were home, including the oldest who was already in elementary school. I would like to hope that in an alternate universe, I would have been able to read between the lines. Normally, I'm pretty good at that sort of thing. This time I didn't notice any of those things. I was way too distracted.

While I had glossed over my experience at the pediatrician (probably with a lackluster attempt at humor), my friend had also kept her distance. She had brushed over her painful news in a way that made the information unclear, because the truth of the matter was that both of us had been stretched *beyond* what was manageable. Neither of us had anything left to give. We were just two grieving people trying to survive.

So, I dropped off my oldest daughter so she could play. I complained about our experience at the pediatrician. I drank my friend's water. I ate her grapes. And, I left less than 20 minutes later. I left with NO acknowledgment of her pain. I didn't even hug her.

Later (maybe six months or so), when my brain temporarily came back online for a moment, I discovered there was this little nugget of "information" stuck in the back of my mind. It was something I couldn't quite process. It was in there, but I couldn't quite grab onto it. I knew something, somewhere was... not right... but I couldn't put my finger on what exactly. I pondered it, but I never quite connected the dots.

Then one morning, while I was standing in the middle of our neighborhood playground pushing my younger daughter on the swings, I happened to glance up to see this friend entering the playground with her boys. I saw her face and I replayed that morning on my internal DVD. As I caught small glimpses of what happened that day, suddenly the fog lifted. The pieces of the puzzle fell into place.

I *realized* what she had said without really saying it. Her mom had died *that* day. Her mom had *died* even before we began our trip to the pediatrician's office. And I missed it. I missed it entirely.

Immediately my heart was broken. I couldn't believe what I had done. I had completely ignored her pain, because I was so distracted by my own. Yes, what I was going through was hard, indescribable even. I had plenty of reasons to be distracted from the life happening outside of my situation, but really that's no excuse.

Any friend who heard this story from her point of view might have taken me off the "friend" list permanently. If *I* had heard this story from someone, *I* probably would have stopped being *my* friend. This is how we hurt people. This is how we sever relationships. She could have easily (and with good reason) cut me out of her life completely. Thankfully, she didn't.

I was able to apologize to my friend that morning, while we stood together under the monkey bars watching our children climb. She graciously forgave me for my unintentionally callous behavior. She didn't have to, but she did. She was able to give me something I was in no position to give myself.

I could barely receive her forgiveness. I didn't think I deserved it. My actions were completely accidental, and I knew I couldn't change what I had done, but... *When had I become so dead inside?*

CHAPTER TWENTY

She's Eating, She's Pooping, She's Fine

I know it's hard to believe, but somehow, I moved forward from that bad-day-at-the-pediatrician-totally-ignoring-my-friend's-pain moment and kept going. If we looked at my Emotional Stability chart we would see the line go up to slightly above "dangerously low" and plateau there temporarily. Things started to feel, well not normal really, but marginally better.

Unfortunately, just when I thought I was starting to get the hang of all of this new stuff… things changed, again. By the time our newborn was almost five months old, our sweet baby girl slowly went from "stable" to… an undefinable "not so much."

At first, she was just a little cranky and not acting like herself.

"Probably her teeth," everyone said. "Don't worry."

But I did. I worried.

Then, I noticed that after her naps there would be a puddle of sweat under her head. I called our cardiologist and peppered him with a rapid fire of questions. When I finally paused to catch my breath, he said,

"She's probably just overheated. Dress her in lighter clothing. Don't cover her with a blanket. I'm sure it's nothing. Don't worry."

But I did. I worried.

Slowly, she got worse.

The crankiness increased, the sweat puddle got larger, and occasionally she seemed to have trouble breathing.

Or was that just my over active imagination?

"I'm sure she is fine," the doctors said, "don't worry."

But I did. I worried.

More time passed, she developed more symptoms. They screamed out at me like a flashing warning sign. Something was there... something I couldn't put my finger on... something was wrong...

"Probably just a growth spurt" the pediatrician said. "She's eating. She's pooping. She's fine."

(Translation: Stop worrying crazy mama. You are not a doctor.)

BUT I did. I worried.

After about three months of not sleeping and of second guessing myself, I approached my pediatrician again.

"Please," I said, "it seems like something is WRONG. She just doesn't seem like herself."

"If there is something wrong I can't find it," the pediatrician said, with a patronizing pat on my arm. "You are going to have to let her cry. She has to work it out... on her own (smug smile)."

Is this feeling of hatred toward my doctor normal?

Somehow, I managed to take a deep breath. Somehow, I didn't punch my pediatrician in the face. I should have gotten a gold star. Instead, I went back home, and I worried.

I had done this before, of course, with my first daughter. I was familiar with the all night agony of listening to your baby cry while you are supposed to be teaching them to sleep. I gotta say, I wasn't good at it the first time, and I was pretty sure I wasn't going to be good at it the second time either. My baby girl seemed like she was crying a cry of *pain*, but then, what did I know? I was just her mother. I listened to the doctors. I let her cry, but I continued to worry.

Back to the movie.

INTERIOR/FAMILY APARTMENT/VARIOUS LOCATIONS

TITLE: Falling Into the Pit: Part Two

The BABY is not sleeping montage.

SCENE ONE: Dark Bedroom. MOMMY asleep in bed.

BABY cries.

MOMMY looks over to other side of bed.
DADDY is not home.

VOICE-OVER/MOMMY
Right. Still at rehearsal.

MOMMY crawls out of bed and walks down hallway to BABY's room. Peeks at OLDER SISTER in other bed to make sure she is still sleeping. MOMMY is relieved to see she is. MOMMY walks over to crib. Pats baby gently on belly.

MOMMY
Shhhhh, shhhhh baby girl. You're okay.
Time to sleep. Shhhhh… shhhh…

MOMMY gives BABY pacifier and tucks baby blanket back in around BABY. Satisfied BABY is back to sleep, she exits room.

FADE TO NEXT SCENE

SCENE TWO: Dark Bedroom. MOMMY asleep in bed. BABY cries. MOMMY looks over at other side of bed. DADDY home and asleep. MOMMY too tired to get up. BABY cries again. DADDY wakes up.

                    DADDY
            I'll take it this time.

                    MOMMY
                   Thanks.

DADDY crawls out of bed and stumbles down hallway. Pauses to check on DAUGHTER #1 and then continues to crib. Hands baby pacifier, tucks in blanket around baby, and pats BABY gently on the back. (BABY has grown and now sleeps on belly)

                    DADDY
         Hey, you're okay. Time to sleep…

DADDY exits room.

FADE TO NEXT SCENE

SCENE THREE: Dark Bedroom.
MOMMY asleep in bed.

BABY cries.

MOMMY looks over at other side of bed. DADDY home, but snoring.

                    VOICE-OVER/MOMMY
               Right. Just got home.

MOMMY crawls out of bed and stumbles down
hallway. Pauses to check on DAUGHTER #1 and
continues to crib (BABY bigger and can now pull
herself up to stand on crib bars).

MOMMY hesitates, shakes her head in an attempt
to wake up enough to perform task at hand. She
gently lays BABY down, hands baby pacifier, tucks
in blanket around baby, and pats BABY gently on
back (mechanically)

                        MOMMY
                     (mutters)
     Shhhh… shhhh… baby girl… time to sleep…

Without even wondering if BABY is really asleep,
MOMMY turns and stumbles back to door. CAMERA
follows MOMMY back to bedroom. She crawls back
into bed.

BABY cries.

                        MOMMY
                    (to DADDY)
             Maybe we should move her
             out into the living room.

                        DADDY
                     (sleepy)
            Yeah… might be a good idea…

FADE TO NEXT SCENE

SCENE FOUR: Apartment Living Room.
CAMERA looks up at faces of MOMMY and DADDY
from BABY's POV (inside portable crib). They
look shell-shocked, exhausted.

                    MOMMY
          Think she's going to sleep tonight?

                    DADDY
          I hope so. It's my turn on the couch.

                    MOMMY
                Good luck.

CUT TO: Dark living room.
DADDY asleep on couch.

BABY cries.

                    DADDY
                Groans

FADE TO NEXT SCENE

SCENE FIVE: Dark living room.
MOMMY asleep on couch.

BABY cries.

MOMMY doesn't respond.

BABY's cries become louder, more frantic.

MOMMY moans, rolls over and slowly sits up.

                    MOMMY
          Okay, okay. I'm coming… I'm coming…

MOMMY drags herself off couch and over to portable
crib. BABY standing and crying with desperation.
MOMMY leans heavily on side of crib.

                    MOMMY
          What is it, baby girl? What's wrong?

No answer. MOMMY sighs.

She lays BABY back down, gives her a pacifier,
pats her belly and tucks blanket in around her.

                    MOMMY
              You have to go back to sleep.
               Please, please go to sleep.

MOMMY stumbles back to couch. Plops down.
Closes eyes.

BABY cries.

MOMMY groans but again drags herself back over
to the crib. Goes through process again, tucks
in BABY and stumbles back to couch.

BABY cries with more urgency and more volume.

MOMMY moans and pulls pillow over her head and punches it in frustration. MOMMY again drags herself back over to the crib. Goes through process again, tucks in BABY and stumbles back to couch.

BABY cries turn to desperate screaming.

MOMMY stomps over to crib, picks up BABY and pushes her down onto the bottom of the crib, less gently than she should.

MOMMY
(irrationally, yelling)
Just go to sleep! Go to sleep! Go to sleep!

MOMMY looks down at her hands in shock. Then covers her mouth in disbelief as if the ugly words could be stuffed back in. She backs away from crib disoriented and obviously full of horror from her actions.

MOMMY
(voice breaking as she slumps down to sit on floor next to crib) (more softly, sobbing)
Go to sleep… please… baby girl… please… please… please… go to sleep

BABY still crying.

FADE TO BLACK

After a few months of doing the "baby won't sleep" shuffle, my husband and I were at the end of our collective rope. We had moved our daughter out to the living room in an attempt to let our older daughter get some sleep, and my husband and I were trying to take turns sleeping on the couch.

Unfortunately, because my husband's job was so incredibly demanding, I had been participating the most in the "stay up all night" party. We thought this made sense, after all *theoretically* I was able to take naps during the day when the baby took naps, right?

In case you were wondering, no, I did not get to take naps. I know it's been a while since I mentioned her, but I actually had another daughter who had grown from age three to age four with very little assistance from me. She was an amazingly resilient little person, but occasionally, she still needed her mommy.

I was lying on the couch across the room from the crib when I heard my little bundle of joy start to whimper on that fateful night when I actually yelled at my sweet, fragile, medical miracle. That night when I actually "pushed" her down into her bed much harder than I *ever* intended. I was shocked by my actions. Suddenly, this strong, capable, good in a crisis, thick-skinned mountain-girl perfectionist had screwed up, big time. I had seen merely a glimpse into a dark, dark place and I never wanted to see it again.

We sat there together, my baby daughter and I, and we cried and cried and cried. Even the stoic in me couldn't stop the flood of those tears. With great regret, I tried to soothe my daughter with the best "mommy loves you" voice I could muster, but I did it from across the room so I could keep her safe.

By the time my husband made it home later that night, we had both finally fallen asleep. He had no idea my exhaustion had reached an unmanageable level. That made it easier for me to pretend it never happened. I was still tired, stressed, exhausted and in physical pain, but I had been scared straight. The horror of "what could have been" helped me keep my rage under control… just barely, but under control, nonetheless.

.

CHAPTER TWENTY ONE
BATHTUB SPIRITUALITY, THE SEQUEL

I don't know how, but I managed to plow through those days and weeks with very little sleep. My girls got food to eat and a cozy place to sleep, but I'm not sure they got much else from me. I think I might have "checked out" for a while. It might be interesting to note that sleep deprivation is one of the most successful forms of interrogation used at Guantanamo. However, parents might have a slight edge over spies. At least, we get to drink coffee.

Of course, I understand I'm not the only parent who has ever done the "I'm not sleeping but of course I'm totally fine" dance. Unfortunately, this is not a time when knowing someone else was going through the same thing I was going through helped. The ONLY thing that would have helped was SLEEP. The deadening of my senses continued, but I *still* thought I was doing okay. I *thought* I was surviving. What happened next left little room for discussion. It was obvious I was no longer myself.

Get comfortable, we're going back to the movie.

OPEN: BLACK SCREEN

TITLE: Falling Into the Pit: Part Three

FADE IN: INTERIOR FAMILY APARTMENT BATHROOM

CAMERA shows series of close-ups: Hand turns on faucet of water. Water flows into bath. Hand adds bubble bath. Bare foot steps into bath.

CUT TO: MOMMY resting head against back of tub and closes eyes. After a moment MOMMY sinks into water placing entire head under bubbles. (Still a PG movie so everything is appropriately covered - bubbles in all the right places - Mommy has not lost any of her modesty)

CAMERA (from above) HOLDS on Bubble Bath

MUSIC: Instrumental, melancholy.
Builds to show desperate suspense.

CAMERA moves in closer to bubbles. MOMMY still under water. Suspension builds as more time passes and passes and passes.

Just when we think, where is she? Is she? Is she going to?

                    DEEP VOICE
                  (from Heaven)
                    Sit up!

CUT TO: view from side - as if standing at door to bathroom. Room fills with light and a

paranormal hand reaches down from ceiling and
pulls MOMMY up from water.

MOMMY sits up.

She sputters, coughs and gasps for air. She sobs
in agony but like before she stifles her sobs
so no one outside of the bathroom can hear. Her
body is shaking, she rocks back and forth her
arms wrapped tightly around her chest. Her face
screams in anguish and still she never makes an
outward sound.

FADE TO BLACK

All I had intended to do was take a bath. I just wanted a
moment to *rest*. Man, that warm water felt so good. Boy-o-boy,
did I ever want it to work its magic into my body and soul. I
wanted to try to rejuvenate some of the spirit that used to be me.
Foolishly, I thought a warm bath would solve everything. In total
compliance to this idea, I closed my eyes and surrendered my
whole body to the water.

Being under water only felt good for an instant, because
almost immediately, the dark cloud that had been following me
for months crowded out my peace. Out of nowhere, a thought
occurred to me... *What if I don't sit up?*

Suddenly, there I was thinking no one would miss me if I
just went ahead and gave up. I actually convinced myself everyone
would be okay without me. My husband could find someone else
to marry. My girls could survive without me. My family would
be sad, but they would eventually get over it. My friends would
mourn, but life would go on. The world could easily keep turning
without me. I stayed under the water where it was quiet and

calm, and I felt safe. I was so tired, I just couldn't keep fighting anymore. I was so dead on the inside, I did not care anymore.

What?!? (pause) *WHAT?!?*

Almost immediately, my lungs started to burn and death became something real, not just a concept. At first I didn't care, I thought I was ready to go. Doing this crazy life was too hard. I was done. After a few seconds, I came to my senses.

"Do I really want to die?" I asked myself.

"No!" I screamed back.

Unfortunately, I had waited too long to come to that conclusion. I tried to sit up, I wanted to sit up, but I couldn't. It felt like I was stuck under the weight of a pile of bricks. I physically could not pull myself up from the water. The darkness was too heavy. So, I prepared myself to give up.

I didn't want to. Crazy strong athletic farm girls *don't* give up. We *fight*. In desperation, I whispered, *Help me. Please help me*, just like I had done the last time I was having a bathtub breakdown (after I found out about my daughter's heart condition). I wasn't sure my prayer would be heard. I truly thought this was going to be the end.

I can't easily explain what happened next without it sounding strange. To me, it *felt* like something big and strong reached down (from where exactly I cannot confirm, although as a woman of faith, I do believe it was heaven sent) and with one hand placed a thumb on one side of my rib cage and fingers on the other and lifted me out of the water similar to the way a person palms and lifts a basketball.

Suddenly, I was sitting up again, coughing and gasping for air and of course sobbing…. quietly…

Whether I wanted to or not, I was forced to come to the realization I had almost allowed myself to die. I was also forced to realize I wasn't in that room alone. God had rescued me. Here in a bathtub full of strategically placed bubbles. Here, in the middle of the darkness of suicide. God was here. God saved me.

I know, I know, you could explain what really happened in this moment a number of ways. You could say it all happened in my imagination. That in my fractured, altered state I just "thought" a hand reached down and palmed me like a basketball. Even I could believe maybe I imagined the whole thing... but then again, maybe I didn't.

I don't want to spend too much time trying to make sense of it. Ultimately, it doesn't matter to me *how* I was able to sit up. All I really care about is that I *did*.

While I had not set out to commit suicide in any way, I definitely had allowed the idea that death was better than life to permeate all the way down into the core of my soul. I was unprepared to face exactly what that meant for me long-term. I needed to handle it right away, but I'm sad to say I did not. *Still*, I did not let people in. (I know, I know... it's annoying me too!) In fact, this moment made me feel even more isolated.

I could not accept the fact that I was a woman of faith *and* that I had entertained the idea of suicide. Just like I had blocked everyone who cared about me from having access to my life, my denial had now blocked my God from having full access to my heart. Of course, my faith was always with me, just waiting for me to apply it, but somewhere in the crazy mix of my circumstances, I had become distracted... so very distracted.

Thank God (literally), I had finally made one giant step *forward*. On my Emotional Stability chart, there would be a rally point that goes UP dramatically from "dangerously low." It wouldn't go all the way back up to "normal level of emotional stability," but at least it wasn't stuck down at the bottom anymore. I found I could cling to a new truth. My God was bigger than death. I wasn't exactly ready to start living, not yet, but at least now I knew I didn't want to die.

CHAPTER TWENTY TWO
RESUSCITATION

If I had shared any of this information with anyone, particularly a trained professional, they would have immediately realized something was wrong. They would have identified I needed more than just a hug and a prayer. They would have known it was time to intervene. That would have required I actually admit I had a problem. I didn't and so, of course, no one knew. Not even those closest to me. And definitely not my husband. I was too ashamed of my failures to share.

Experiencing these three very specific "moments" (ignoring my friend's pain, shoving my baby, and almost drowning) did help me pull a piece of myself back into my life. It was like I had gotten resuscitated… like my heart had received three shocks from a defibrillator. My heart was beating again, but I wasn't living. Not really.

Unfortunately, this rally didn't stop me from dragging around a big suitcase full of guilt. It followed along behind me like a destructive security blanket. I felt guilty that I was angry at my sweet baby girl for her inability to sleep. I felt guilty for being angry at my husband for being gone all the time. I felt guilty every time I yelled at my four year old for, well, acting like a four year old. Most of all, I was angry at myself for even allowing the idea of suicide to ever enter my mind. I had no grace for myself. No ability to accept my failures. No forgiveness for me.

Somehow, I thought this "weakness" was better stuffed down and ignored. All that denial made it hard to make even the simplest of decisions. I *should* have hired someone to help me take care of my children, so I could have a break. I *should* have gotten myself into therapy. At the very least, I *should* have called a friend and begged for help. I never *should* have let it get this far. This was not the kind of person I ever wanted to be. I wanted to be a loving, caring mother. An intelligent, wise woman. A decent human being. A woman of faith. *What had happened to me?*

Looking back, I would have done many things very differently. I would have pushed the cardiologists harder. I would have asked for more tests. I definitely would have found a different pediatrician. I would have insisted my husband find a way to be home more. I would have realized no matter how much it hurt, I needed to keep searching for that safe place where I could yell, scream, moan, groan, and *vent*. I would have found a counselor, a therapist, a guru... anything!

Again, I was distracted. I was too busy stumbling around in the bottom of a pit.

However, after my resuscitation, I did manage to gain enough strength to approach our doctors again. I can still see them rolling their eyes at me as I opened my mouth to say, "So I noticed..." I didn't care. I kept pushing them, annoying them, and questioning them. Regardless of how "off" I was, I could not shake the feeling there was something wrong with my baby. Eventually, I managed to convince our pediatric cardiologist to take a closer look. FINALLY, there on the monitor was the evidence the doctors needed. The irregular variations on my daughter's EKG proved

I had been right. Something was wrong.

It was enough to motivate our doctor to send us to the Cardiac Cath Lab for more information. Several hours later, that procedure revealed not only was the conduit in our daughters heart kinked (insert: blocked), but her pulmonary arteries had barely grown and were stenotic (insert: too skinny) and she had an aneurysm (insert: *are you freaking kidding me?!*) located in her heart at the base of the conduit. Immediate heart surgery was the next step.

I tried really hard not to let my inner two-year-old say, *"I was right and you were wrong that's why I can sing this song..."* but I couldn't resist. I was RIGHT. For the past seven months, I had been fighting for my daughter, fighting for my sanity, fighting to get some SLEEP, and all this time I was *right*.

Oh, how sweet that (imaginary) vindication tasted. Oh, how I relished my cocky "in-your-face" (silent) rant to the doctors. Boy-o-boy did I ever bask in my self-righteous (private) gloating. I was right, I was right, I was right! Of course, what I really wish was that I had been wrong.

The choices the doctors made were the right ones. They were trying to intervene as little as possible to give my daughter as much room as possible to heal. They didn't want to sedate her again so soon after her first surgery. They wanted her heart to stabilize, her lungs to grow, and her brain to heal. They didn't really care that we weren't getting any sleep. Sleep was way down on the list of priorities. At least, the doctors had years of training to work from. I had a bachelor's degree in *art*.

However, I had something no one else in this medical equation had. I was the baby's mother. I was forever connected to this child. And, just because I need to say it one more time, *I was right*. I had finally earned the respect of our medical team, because my mother's intuition had trumped medical science. Yay, me.

Now that I'm all the way *over here* and looking back on that time *back then*, I understand there were a variety of ways this could have gone. I mean really, we were all *guessing*. The fact that my daughter survived at all is nothing short of a miracle. And, these doctors weren't dummies. Not even close. These docs were the best of the best at the #1 hospital in the nation. If they didn't know what to do, no one did.

I don't think I cried at all when they wheeled my daughter down the hall to her second heart surgery. I know. It sounds weird to me too, but it's true. I was eerily calm. It almost felt like the doctors owed us this one, because she was still under warranty. Like they were giving us a free upgrade to fix the bugs. Somehow, I had figured out *this time* she was going to be fine.

This surgery went more quickly. Before I even had a chance to drink too much coffee, I found myself standing beside her hospital bed. Her tiny body had a long, red, fresh scar. Her intubation tube, IV, arterial lines, chest tubes, and pacing wires made it difficult to find a place to touch her. *Again*, I had to settle for rubbing her cheek with my knuckle between the wires.

Oh my sweet baby girl, I'm so proud of you, I heard myself gasp in relief for a second time.

This time, however, my relief was guarded. I had learned my lesson that day at Target. This roller coaster ride was far from over.

This was the moment… the moment where it dawned on me her condition was *permanent*. I knew this information already, of course, but somehow this time it became real. I finally understood these kinds of moments would *never* end. I understood that for the rest of my life, I would continue to find myself standing beside her hospital bed *not holding her*.

Inside this overwhelmingly mind-numbing realization, it was hard for me to find hope. It was hard for me to find a way to look forward to the life before me.

Maybe I had the whole my-God-is-bigger-than-death thing down, but I wasn't so sure He was bigger than the pain of actually *living*.

INSTANT REPLAY

MOMMY gives snide "here we go again" look to the camera before we watch her fall into the pit.

Off camera, body hits the ground - THUMP.

                    VOICE-OVER/MOMMY
                        Ouch

FADE TO BLACK

CHAPTER TWENTY TWO
GOD TALKS TO ME THROUGH TV

OPEN: INTERIOR/FAMILY APARTMENT/LIVING ROOM

CAMERA HOLDS on MOMMY sitting on couch holding BABY (about 14 months old).

BABY asleep.

MOMMY watching TV while holding BABY. Reflection of television plays across her face, otherwise the room is dark.

IN BACKGROUND (off camera) sound of television show. Show tells a version of the "A Man Fell Into a Hole" story.

MOMMY mindlessly watches show - rocking BABY - passing the time until BABY falls asleep.

OFF CAMERA TV show continues.

CAMERA stays with MOMMY.

                    SHOW
    This guy is walking down the street and he
      falls into a hole. The wall is so steep
                he can't get out...

(muffles into background - hear in small
snippets)

MOMMY pushes forward to edge of couch suddenly
"awake" and paying close attention

                    SHOW
      ...doctor writes out a prescription
                and moves on...

MOMMY pushes forward again. The colors from the
television continue to play across MOMMY'S face.

                    SHOW
      A priest writes down a prayer...
                and moves on.

MOMMY crosses room to stand directly in front
of TV. She kneels down to get a closer look... to
be "part" of the scene... to hear better (still
holding baby).

                    SHOW
      Then a friend comes by and jumps
                down in the hole...

MOMMY moves closer

                    SHOW
     ... idiot, now we're both stuck in here ...

MOMMY moves closer

                    SHOW
     ...but I've been down here before and I
              know the way out...

MOMMY places hand on TV screen in reverence -
almost as if she is praying.

                VOICE-OVER/MOMMY
                    (whisper)
        Someone who knows the way out...

FADE TO BLACK

   Yes, there is truth in television. A late night re-run may have been the only way my exhausted brain could connect the dots. The only way to get through to a stubborn TV junkie like me is to actually use the TV. God does work in mysterious ways.

   I didn't know how to talk about what I was going through, but the idea of finding that person who had been here before made sense to me. I wanted to connect with that person who knew the way out. I would have done almost anything to find them.

   Occasionally, I would try to put myself out there, kick the tires so to speak. I almost treated it like a game. I almost *relished* the shock value from the emotional baggage on which I was sitting. Like I had received a badge that I could pull out occasionally to identify myself. *"Betts Keating,* (flash badge), *Emotional Basket Case."* I couldn't wait to see how someone would react.

That's when I would become a stereotypical New Yorker. With my over inflated attitude, I pointed my finger in people's faces and said, "You think you wanna help? Do ya?"

To which that poor person would run away in fear.

I can't say I blame them. I was not a pleasant person to be around for a long time. I was closed off, cold and cranky with a big barrel of angry boiling under the surface just waiting to blow. I did not make it easy to reach out to me. I did not make it easy to love me.

There were a lot of really great people, sweet family and friends, who did their best to encourage me. My college friends, my *sisters*, tried to stay in touch, but even they couldn't reach me. People prayed for me, sang over me, and quoted scripture at me. They tried their best to draw me out of my pain, but it was no good. Their words of encouragement fell on deaf ears. No one had the answers I needed.

In reality, what I wanted, what I *needed*, was to look into someone else's eyes and see recognition, or even better, acceptance. I wanted empathy, not sympathy.

I didn't intend for my words to sound so negative, heavy, and bitter. I didn't intend to alienate the people who loved me and wanted to help, but I did. And, I couldn't figure out how to make it better.

The few responses I did receive felt like shallow platitudes in the face of what I was fighting against. I did not want to hear "what doesn't kill us makes us stronger," or "when life hands you lemons, you make lemonade." I knew for sure I didn't want to drink any drink made from my basket of lemons, no matter how much sugar was added.

I was tired of being told I needed to buck-up, rise above, keep my eyes ahead, think positive thoughts, someday this too will pass, and God never gives us more than we can handle. Those statements HURT, because I wasn't bucking up. I wasn't rising above. I could barely open my eyes. I was definitely not thinking positive thoughts, and NONE of it was passing. It was staying and growing and getting worse at every turn. God definitely gave me more than I could handle, and I was not succeeding at the task before me. Every time someone tried to tell me to "stay strong," it just made me feel like a failure for being so weak.

No one meant to hurt me. No one meant to pile onto my burden, but they couldn't help it. It happened anyway. Every time I tried to let someone in, every time I tried to open up, I would end up feeling brushed off, set aside, and patronized. It was draining, and it hurt my feelings much more than I ever want to think about. "How are you?" became a very painful question. I had no idea how to answer it.

Now, of course, I realize it was unfair for me to expect so much from the people in my life. It certainly wasn't their fault they weren't trained in psychiatry. They did the best they could, but it didn't ease my loneliness. No matter how hard I looked, I never found that person who had been *here* before. No one I spoke to knew the way out.

So I used my sense of humor and my very well established mask to survive. I bobbed and weaved. I deflected. I closed down. I buried my pain down deep. I did not speak the truth. I lied.

What I wanted to hear, what I *needed* to hear, was not what anyone was able to say. I wanted to hear:

"Wow. This STINKS. I can see why you are a broken mess. I can't even *begin* to understand what you are going through. Do you mind if I just sit here and listen while you vent? I promise I won't preach, or judge, or advise, or try to change how you feel about what you are going through. I promise I won't leave even when what you have to say becomes overwhelmingly uncomfortable. I promise I won't leave until the light starts to shine again." And if at all possible, "I've been here before. I know the way out."

Yes, please.

CHAPTER TWENTY THREE

IT'S NOT OVER YET

OPEN: Black screen

TITLE: Back in the Pit

FADE IN: Moonlight shows MOMMY lying on ground in bottom of pit. She slowly, painfully pulls herself up to sitting. She looks around, takes an assessment of her situation and begins to move into action. She starts climbing.

She climbs up a few steps and falls. Climbs and falls. Climbs and falls. Some rocks from up above fall into the pit and hit her on the way down.

One last time she tries to climb but again she slips and falls. She cries out in pain on the way down and lands with a thud on the bottom of the pit.

```
            VOICE-OVER/MOMMY
                 (sobbing)
                 Ouch.
```

FADE TO BLACK

Once again, things seemed to settle down after my daughter survived her second heart surgery. I was able to take a few breaths. Short, frantic breaths, but at least I was breathing.

I took this momentary lull in drama to mean our time on the chopping block was over. I repeated this pattern in the valley after every large event. I tried desperately to convince myself that I was done with the hard stuff. I kept hoping that if I could just get some distance from even one of these large life lessons, then somehow I could gain some perspective. THEN, I could go about the business of healing.

Unfortunately, I never could quite make it out of the pit. Every time I tried to gain some ground, to get to a place where I could reach up and grab a hand for assistance, I would get smacked down again. Like all good overcoming adversity stories, my battle back to healing got worse long before it got better.

If we took another look at the Emotional Stability Chart, we would notice that, in addition to all of the big things pounding down on top of us, there were other, smaller blips that were also creating havoc. Because they rested in the shadows of all the big rises and falls, they mostly went unnoticed and sometimes were practically ignored. Because this kind of stuff stayed over on the side, in the shadows, they always hit us like a huge ugly surprise. We were never prepared... for anything

These things would have had titles like "grandmother dies" and "grandfather dies" and "other grandmother dies."

Sadly, I lost both of my maternal grandparents and my paternal grandmother in the same year I was trying to figure out how to keep my baby daughter alive. It was strange to live so precariously between life and death. I couldn't seem to reconcile how grateful I was to have both of my beautiful girls alive and with me, while at the same time, be so incredibly sad about these great losses. I was very close to all three of these delightful people. They had poured themselves into my life. They were part of my roots.

I attended all three of these funerals, I shed some tears, but I don't really remember being there. I don't think I really was. They definitely deserved more of a send-off than I was able to give.

The chart also would have had titles like "husband's father admitted to permanent care facility" and "mother-in-law's health declines."

My husband's parents, who were older and approximately the same age as my grandparents, were also rapidly declining in their health. Due to their age, we should have been more prepared for this season in their lives, but like I said before, we weren't.

On the chart, we would have also seen multiple blips with titles like "medical bill" and "another medical bill" and "more medical bills" and again "even more medical bills." Across the bottom of the entire chart would have been a bar that exclaimed in large red letters "still broke."

There is no way to predict or even remotely explain the kind of debt required to survive a major medical situation (or two or three). Even with insurance, there is no way to keep the avalanche of financial stress at bay. We were broke. Truly and utterly broke.

Then, at the very end of an already overly burdensome list was the title that really punched us in the gut… "husband loses job."

It was only a few short weeks after our daughter's second surgery when we received the news that my husband's teaching contract would not be renewed. The phrase "not be renewed" is a really nice way of saying "you're fired." The hardest part of this truth was my husband had done his best to do all of the extra things required of him to keep this job. He had sacrificed greatly for them. We had *all* sacrificed greatly. All those times my husband was out *working* instead of being home with us when we so desperately needed him ended up being a giant waste of time. It all added up to a whole lot of *nothing*.

It was painful, it was frustrating, it was incredibly disappointing, and it didn't matter one little bit. No matter how much it hurt, we didn't have a choice. It was time to find another job.

Back to the movie.

OPEN: INTERIOR/FAMILY APARTMENT/KITCHEN

TITLE: March

CAMERA HOLDS on DADDY at kitchen table with a stack of papers and envelopes in front of him. He organizes a packet of application materials, sticks them into a manila envelope, and adds it to a large pile of sealed envelopes (with energy and a smile).

CLIPS WITH SOUND
LICK, SEAL, STAMP, add to stack - PLAHMP
REPEAT - PLAHMP, PLAHMP, PLAHMP

CUT TO: DADDY walks down hallway toward apartment door. From DADDY's point of view we watch while DADDY gives high-fives to MOMMY, DAUGHTER #1, and BABY (as if he is exiting the locker room at a sporting event). SLAP, SLAP, SLAP

DADDY opens door, turns and says…

                    DADDY
                Wish me luck!

              MOMMY/DAUGHTER #1
                Good Luck!

                    BABY
                  (delayed)
                Guud wuck…

CUT TO: DADDY drops off large stack of envelopes
at Post Office.

Stack of envelopes land in mail bin - FWUMP

DADDY nods and gestures "thanks" to postal
worker. He exits PO with a bouncy, happy stroll.
He is very optimistic.

FADE TO NEXT SCENE

OPEN: UNIVERSITY PROFESSOR'S OFFICE
DADDY sitting at his desk reading letters
(rejection).

DADDY CRUMPLES letter and tosses into trash can.
Paper hits bottom of can - THWAMP.

REPEAT: CRUMPLE THWAMP, CRUMPLE THWAMP

DADDY grabs his bag and heads for home.

CUT TO: DADDY walks in to family apartment.
Two DAUGHTERS run to the door.

LITTLE FEET - PAT, PAT, PAT

DAUGHTERS jump into DADDY's arms with happy
exclamations.

MOMMY and DADDY make eye contact over the heads
of their children.

                    MOMMY
                  Anything?

                    DADDY
            (still sounding hopeful)
                  Not yet.

FADE TO NEXT SCENE

OPEN: INTERIOR/FAMILY APARTMENT/KITCHEN

TITLE: April

DADDY at kitchen table again with another stack
of resumes.

CLIPS WITH SOUND (slightly slower)
LICK, SEAL, STAMP, add to stack - PLAHMP.
REPEAT: PLAHMP, PLAHMP, PLAHMP

DADDY walks down hallway toward apartment door
giving high-fives to MOMMY, DAUGHTER #1 and BABY.

SLAP, SLAP, SLAP

> DADDY
> (softer with less enthusiasm)
> Wish me luck.

> MOMMY/DAUGHTER #1
> Good Luck.
> (MOMMY smiles sympathetic smile)

> BABY
> Bye, bye, Daddy...

CUT TO: DADDY drops off another large stack of envelopes at the Post Office. Envelopes land in large bin - FWUMP.

DADDY smiles and thanks postal worker with a nod. Walks out of PO with a less jaunty step.

CUT TO: DADDY in his office.
Reading letters (rejection).

DADDY CRUMPLES letter and tosses
into trash can - THWAMP.

REPEAT: CRUMPLE THWAMP, CRUMPLE THWAMP

Discouraged, slowly grabs his bag and heads for home.

CUT TO: DADDY walks into family apartment.

DAUGHTERS run to the door

LITTLE FEET - PAT, PAT, PAT

DAUGHTERS jump into DADDY's arms with happy
exclamations.

MOMMY and DADDY make eye contact over the heads
of their children.

> MOMMY
> Anything?

> DADDY
> (still sounding hopeful)
> Not yet.

FADE TO NEXT SCENE

OPEN: INTERIOR/FAMILY APARTMENT/KITCHEN

TITLE: May

CLIPS WITH SOUND (slower, less energy)
LICK, SEAL, STAMP, add to stack - PLAHMP

REPEAT - PLAHMP, PLAHMP, PLAHMP

With effort, DADDY gathers stack of envelopes
and walks down hallway of family apartment and
gives half-hearted high-fives to family.
SLAP, SLAP, SLAP (slow, low energy)

DADDY doesn't ask for luck. FAMILY doesn't
say goodbye

CUT TO: DADDY drops another large stack of
envelopes off at post office. Envelopes land in
large bin - FWUMP

DADDY smiles a sheepish grin to postal worker
(with recognition - same person behind desk
every time)

CUT TO: DADDY in his office. Single envelope in
his hand. Another rejection. Phone rings.

                    DADDY
              Hello? Yes, hi.
                 (hopeful)
              Yes. Yes. Okay.
                (rejection)
           Well, thanks for calling.

Hangs up phone. Drops head into hands in defeat
and softly weeps. Feeling of failure heavy in
room. He throws single letter in trash - THWAMP
(heavy)

CUT TO: DADDY walks into family apartment

DAUGHTERS run to him

LITTLE FEET - PAT, PAT, PAT
DAUGHTERS jump into DADDY's arms with
enthusiastic glee.

DADDY responds with forced enthusiasm.

MOMMY and DADDY make eye contact over the heads of their children. MOMMY doesn't even have to ask, she knows there's no news. She smiles with all the encouragement she can muster.

FADE TO BLACK

We were so optimistic… at first. After all, my husband's credentials from a top-rated drama department at a top-rated university were how he got his current job in the first place. We took on this challenge with energy, or at least valiant effort. Unfortunately, possessing great credentials does not always mean you will find a job quickly. My husband sent out 50 (count them 50!) applications. He sent them out to every school that was even remotely offering a job in his field. At this point, we really had no idea where we would end up. We were willing to try anything, anywhere. *It'll be okay… we'll be fine…*

In February, we still hadn't heard back from any prospects, not even for an interview. In March, nothing. In April, he was one of two finalists three different times, and each time, they hired the "other" person. Nothing like a little humility thrown in on top of a lot of stress, right?

None of my feeble attempts to find work reaped any rewards either. Things were… becoming… uncomfortable…

Still we waited.

There were no job prospects in May or June. And finally, no job prospects in July. Since most colleges would begin classes again in August, we assumed it was time to throw in the towel. We had no job, no prospects for a job, and our lease was up on our apartment. We had a six-year-old who needed to start school and a two-year-old who needed constant medical care.

No, really, we're fine.

We were in the process of implementing Plan B (deciding which set of parents we would be moving in with) when we finally got a phone call. A couple of days later my husband was flown out for an interview. We didn't hear anything about this employment opportunity for three weeks. Three very long weeks.

Back to the movie.

OPEN: EXTERIOR NEIGHBORHOOD/CITY PARK/EVENING
CAMERA HOLDS on large outdoor movie screen.

WORDS ON SCREEN: The End.

MUSIC plays as credits roll.

CAMERA moves to FAMILY packing up belongings.

DADDY swings BABY up onto his shoulders.
MOMMY grabs DAUGHTER #1 by the hand.
FAMILY leaves park to walk home.

Cell phone rings.

DADDY answers.

                    DADDY
                Hello? (pause)
        This is Thomas. Yes. Yes. Okay.
      When? Ummm… that's pretty quick.
        I have to pack up my family…
          Okay. Yes. Okay. Thank you.

Hangs up phone. Turns to face MOMMY.

DADDY
I got a job.

DAUGHTER #1
Yay, Daddy!

BABY SISTER
(delayed)
Yay!

MOMMY
Congratulations! Where?

DADDY makes a face that is something between a smile and grimace and says with obvious trepidation.

DADDY
South Carolina?

MOMMY grimaces too but tries to smile through it.

DAUGHTER #1
Where's South Carolina?

FADE TO BLACK

Finally on August 17th, my husband was offered a position as an Assistant Professor of Theater at a small college in a suburb of Charleston, SC. My husband was to start his new position on August 22nd. We needed to arrive in Charleston by August 21st.

In case you missed it, that only gave us four days to say

goodbye to our life in Boston. Four days to say goodbye to friends. Four days to pack up an entire apartment. Four days to organize all of our daughter's medical records. Four days to find a place to live. Four days. Ripping off a bandage doesn't even begin to cover it.

Of course, this was good news. Of course, we were "glad" Daddy had gotten a new job. Of course... *except*. *Except*, it meant we had to move again. *Except*, we were already exhausted. *Except*, we were still broke. *Except*, this new bump in the road heaped more stress, more pain and more grief onto our already fractured souls. We had no time to think. We had no time to process. Goodbye, city. Goodbye, Northeast. Hello, Charleston.

No, really, we're fine... fine... fine....

I kept saying it. I desperately wanted it to be true.

Four days is not enough time to get anything done. It just isn't. We kept our packing to a minimum for this trip, because my husband was going to have to come back to Boston and arrange to have all of our other things sent down at a later time. We were unable to find a moving company on such short notice. We didn't have a forwarding address anyway. Our landlord agreed to let us leave our boxes behind for two weeks while we figured out... something...

It was challenging to decide what we would need. Suddenly, I was desperately sorting through our "stuff" and figuring out what was essential and what was just eye candy. It was time to make another list. This over-achieving organizer needed to check off some boxes.

Packing List:

Our older daughter would be starting school.

Clothes for school. Check.

Our younger daughter would need new doctors.

Medical forms and doctor contacts to transfer all medical info. Check.

My husband would be starting a new job.

Clothes for work. Check.

We would need some dishes, and forks, and spoons.

Kitchen supplies. Check.

We would need a computer so we could search

for a place to live.

Computer. Check.

We would need things for the girls to do.

Toys. Check. DVDs. Check.

TV, we will be watching a lot of TV.

TV. Check.

Bible? Sure, I'll bring it. I'm just not sure I can promise to actually read it. And yes, and we should probably bring our toothbrushes.

Finally, we managed to pull together some belongings. We over-stuffed the back of a rented SUV, we waved goodbye to our current residence, and we headed south. I know this *could* have felt like a good thing. I know some would have seen this as a great opportunity. The low country is paradise to most people. We would be closer to some of our family. We would have the chance to be closer to my husband's parents. It would be kid friendly. It would be *warm*. I just couldn't decide if we were heading back to the land of our roots or if we were just heading backwards.

I forced myself to "do" all the things someone "should" do in this kind of situation. I forced myself to say goodbye to friends. I forced myself to pack. I forced myself to search for places to live. I forced myself to pray. I forced myself to believe. Unfortunately, in the depths of my darkest corners, I lost another piece of myself. I lost another piece of my strength... I lost what was left of my hope.

I found myself muttering under my breath a lot during this time. I wasn't always praying. I definitely wasn't counting my blessings. I'm afraid I was mastering the fine art of grumbling. I tried to stay positive. I tried to speak truth into my broken spirit, but it came out all wrong. It sounded weak, even to me. I had denied myself the right to my actual feelings for so long, I no longer could decipher the truth from the lies.

I tried to convince myself that, compared to a separated pelvis and a child with a heart condition, getting a new job and moving should be a piece of cake. It wasn't. Moving 900 miles from an area best described as southern Canada to the southern coast of South Carolina *wasn't* easy, no matter how much I tried to convince myself. I underestimated the stress involved in packing up a small two bedroom apartment. I underestimated how much I was going to miss living in the city. I underestimated how long it was going to take to drive two small children such a great distance. I underestimated how much this was all going to *hurt*.

Stress, grief, pain, strain, *weight*... it settled around us constantly, everywhere we looked, *all the time*. I needed to pay attention to all of these life changing events, but I had no room left to process them. I gave them a mere nod compared to the grief I should have felt. My inner two-year-old was oddly quiet. She had nothing left to say.

Back to the movie.

OPEN: EXTERIOR/BOSTON

ON STREET OUTSIDE FAMILY APARTMENT

In a montage of quick clips, we see MOMMY and

DADDY are making trips up and down the stairs and back and forth from the building to the car packing a large amount of belongings into the rear storage area.

Exaggerate how "full" the back of the car is. There is not an inch to spare, and yet MOMMY keeps finding places to stuff more in.

Finally the car is packed.

DADDY closes back door (with effort) and MOMMY and DADDY head back into the building a final time.

CUT TO: MOMMY, DADDY, DAUGHTER #1, BABY standing together on street looking at building. Family raises arms and waves goodbye to their home.

MOMMY
Goodbye, Boston.

DADDY, DAUGHTER #1
Bye, Boston!

BABY
Bye... bye...

VOICE-OVER/MOMMY
(whisper)
Bye...

FAMILY climbs into car.

CAMERA pulls back to view scene from above. We see car navigate the city streets and drive away.

FADE TO BLACK

CHAPTER TWENTY FOUR

HOW MUCH GRACE IS ENOUGH?

Before I continue on with more of the story that was hard, let me take a brief time-out to talk about some of the things that happened that were good. There were several very sweet moments of grace during the drudgery of our move.

A friend came over and helped pack up my kitchen. Grace.

When our church found out there would be a lapse in our medical coverage that would have created MAJOR issues for our daughter's healthcare needs, they covered our insurance payments for two months. Grace.

Dear friends came by to say goodbye, give us hugs and tell us how much they were going to miss us. Grace.

Two friends in particular actually had tears in their eyes when they told us goodbye. I remember teasing them about it, while at the same time feeling so empty I couldn't shed my own tears in return. It was endearing to me that they were able to weed through the muck to love us that much. They did that, even though we were broken. They loved us, even though I was a stoic basket case. Grace.

On the drive down, some friends let us spend the night in

their house, in their beds, even though they were on vacation. Grace.

An acquaintance from my hometown (the son of one of my mom's friends), offered to let us use their house in Charleston while we tried to find a place to live. Grace.

When we arrived in Charleston, my mom met us and helped me with the kids, so I could find a place to live. Grace.

A friend of mine who grew up in Charleston talked me through the neighborhoods of the area and helped me figure out where to look for a place to live. Grace.

I wanted all of this grace to be enough. I wanted the things we had to be more than the things we needed. I wanted all the things we had to be enough. I really wanted to count my blessings. I did not. I didn't even come close to following my faith.

I was very angry at my God. My God, who had breathed love into my life time and time again. My God, who had opened my eyes to the love of my husband, had brought to me my beautiful little girls, and had helped me survive the birth of those daughters, had walked with me through it all, had given me so many things that were good... but had left me here with more to bear. I was mad at Him, because none of this grace outweighed the load we were carrying. None of it repaired my broken body. None of it restored my broken soul. None of it healed my daughter's heart. None of it made my husband's transition to his new job easier. None of it FIXED anything.

It was hard to see all of these blessings and still feel so very far behind. It was hard to receive all of those blessings and still be so sad and so very angry. It made even these incredibly sweet blessings feel like sour burdens. I was supposed to soak up and appreciate and celebrate these good things, but all I wanted to do was scream at the top of my lungs.

INSTANT REPLAY: BACK TO THE PIT

MOMMY
(from the bottom of the pit screams)
HEEEEELLLLLLP!

The screams fade to a yell which fade to whisper,
and then to a muffled sob.

MOMMY
Help me. Please help me.

FADE TO BLACK

CHAPTER TWENTY FIVE
BOXES AND BUGS

We took our time on the drive down south, procrastinating as much as we could. None of us really wanted to do this thing we had to do. But no matter what we tried, we could not stop the inevitable. I wish I could say we did this crazy thing, this move to South Carolina, and the skies cleared, the planets aligned, the earth turned on its axis, the birds began to sing, and all was right in the world. I, too, love those kinds of stories. They are so much more comfortable to tell than the other kinds of stories. Everyone loves a happy ending. Unfortunately, moving to South Carolina did not help our situation take a turn for the good. In fact it actually got worse... again.

When we finally arrived in Charleston, all four of us felt like we had been warped into an alternate universe. Everything about our new home was completely different from what we considered familiar.

First of all, it was HOT. Not just regular hot, but steamy, soupy, dripping with sweat, tropical hot. Our bodies had forgotten our roots. We were northerners now. We did hard winters and snow and concrete, NOT palm trees and hot sunshine and sand.

I realize this new home would have been considered perfect to almost anyone else on the planet. In so many ways, it was. In so many ways, it also wasn't.

OPEN: EXTERIOR/DUPLEX TOWNHOUSE/SC
SUV pulls into driveway.

GRANDMA steps out of doorway and with obvious pleasure welcomes the weary travelers to the south.

                    GRANDMA
               (southern accent)
          I'm so glad you are here!

                    MOMMY
                 (tiredly)
             Yeah, me too.

Group enters into small two-story condo. Daughters run to each room to inspect everything.

                    MOMMY
          This is a nice place.
          How long can we stay?

                    GRANDMA
     We have to be out by the weekend.

                    MOMMY
                    OK.

VOICE-OVER/MOMMY
(with shock, whisper)
Five days.

MOMMY and DADDY unpack boxes and belongings.
GRANDMA entertains the kids.

FADE TO NEXT SCENE

My husband left the next day to begin his new job. He not only started a semester of school with no preparation, but he was immediately thrown into directing his school's fall performance. A show he had to cast, direct, build, promote, and strike with very little assistance. I say that only to express the weight of his level of busyness.

He didn't mean to be gone all of the time, but unfortunately, he was rarely home. He could barely stay awake enough to drive himself home at the end of a demanding day. He could barely even think. I don't really remember much about how I was feeling. I don't think it mattered. Feelings had no place in our day to day survival. I cannot speak for my husband, but I was completely numb, functioning on fumes alone.

The first obstacle before us was finding a place to live. It was a long, tedious, confusing process. I couldn't seem to get my brain to function. I couldn't keep track of neighborhoods, or the names of the streets, or the names of the people offering the rentals. We drove for hours, we covered every neighborhood in the greater Charleston area. We found nothing.

After four days of looking, we settled on an apartment complex that had an available two-bedroom. At that point, we didn't care where we landed as long as we had a place to *be*. We should have been more choosy. We also should have done more homework. Living in an urban environment made us forget how those kinds of things work. We ended up waiting for three days until we were "approved." We didn't have three days. We had zero. Our stay at our friends' condo was over. We had nowhere else to go, so we booked a room at a hotel.

OPEN: EXTERIOR/FRIEND'S CONDO

MOMMY and DADDY pack up boxes and belongings into SUV.

                    DADDY
        As soon as we find a place to live
        I'll return this for something cheaper.

                    MOMMY
                     OK
             (doesn't really care)

FAMILY piles into SUV.
GRANDMA follows in mini-van.

CUT TO: arrival at hotel. ALL get out to go to check-in.

At front desk GRANDMA pulls out credit card.

                    MOMMY
                 Thanks, Mom.
             We'll pay you back.

GRANDMA smiles and squeezes her daughter's hand.

FADE TO NEXT SCENE

Staying in a hotel, with a pool, on the coast of South Carolina is normally a vacation. Staying in a hotel you can't afford, with all of the belongings you could stand to pack, while trying to feed and care for two young children, in a new town, while your husband goes to work, is not. I may have spent my life being comfortable with my pillowcase full of "tangs," but the rest of my family required a more permanent habitat.

OPEN: EXTERIOR/HOTEL

MOMMY and DADDY pack car with boxes and belongings.

FAMILY piles into rental SUV.

CUT TO: SUV pulls into parking lot of apartment complex. FAMILY climbs out and walks into empty apartment.

                        DADDY
          (with over-zealous enthusiasm)
               Here we are!

DAUGHTERS run around from room to room to investigate everything.

                        MOMMY
               What's that smell?

                        DADDY
          Is that… cigarette smoke?

FADE TO NEXT SCENE

Finally, we were given the green light, and we were able to move into an apartment. Based on the outward appearance of the apartment complex, we thought we would be safe taking the apartment we had only looked at once. The complex was very nice, the apartment was not. The former tenant of this particular apartment happened to be a tobacco abuser. Every inch of the place reeked of cigarette smoke. This was especially problematic for us, since we had a toddler with a permanent medical condition that involved breathing. Mommy was so not happy. Thankfully, our daughter once again proved her resilience with little to no permanent damage. I'm not so sure I can say the same about me.

It took two months for another apartment to open up. It took about a year for our belongings to stop smelling like second-hand smoke. We should have left that apartment right away. We should have asked for our money back. We couldn't. We had nowhere else to go. We were stuck.

OPEN: INTERIOR/EXTERIOR NEW APARTMENT

MOMMY and DADDY unpack boxes and belongings. Chatting while they do so.

CAMERA moves down to ground.

CLOSE UP reveals an army of roaches, ants, spiders and worms hiding in the grass armed and ready for the war cry.

From the bug's POV, we see MOMMY and DADDY's feet as they enter the apartment. Light leaks out onto the concrete sidewalk. Before the door closes, the HEAD BUG counts down… 3, 2, 1…

CHARGE! Thousands of bugs enter the apartment
and scurry to their hiding places.

MOMMY and DADDY are completely clueless.

                    DAUGHTER #1
                 Mommy, I see bugs.

                     MOMMY
                  (brush off)
                 mmm...hmmm...

FADE TO NEXT SCENE

Apparently, bugs don't mind the smell of cigarette smoke. In
fact, I'm inclined to believe they love it. In South Carolina, the
war against bugs is constant. If you don't stay on top of it, you
are pretty much doomed. We thought once we were settled in,
the bugs would go back to living with us, but in a more out of
sight kind of way. No such luck.

Many an ant scuttled across the floor in our living room.
Cockroaches climbed across our kitchen counter, scuttled across
our dishes every time we opened a cabinet door, and yes, visited
us in our beds while we tried to sleep. I found a giant yellow
banana spider on top of the air mattress one night. I found a
fat worm in my daughter's bed (it had fallen from the air vent).
I nearly puked when I poured a bowl of cereal and a giant
roach fell out of the box and into my bowl. I was afraid to sleep,
afraid to eat, afraid to keep my eyes open, afraid to keep my eyes
closed. I became obsessed with destroying every bug I saw in a
viciously violent form of justice. I was determined to WIN this
battle. Particularly, because I was losing so many of the other
battles I was fighting.

The day after we moved in to the yucky apartment, I was left alone to defend our existence against overwhelming smells and disgusting bugs. My husband, again, had to leave to go back to Boston to pack up the rest of our stuff and arrange for a moving company. It would be nice, at this point, to be able to say that at least our moving company was able to keep their end of the bargain and delivered the rest of our stuff in record time. They didn't. The rest of our belongings did not arrive for another three weeks.

It was nice to have our furniture again and to be able to sleep on a something that was not an air mattress, but because we were waiting to leave our lovely smoke filled, bug infested abode as quickly as possible, there was no need to unpack anything else. I was surrounded by boxes and bugs.

OPEN: INTERIOR/FAMILY APARTMENT/EVENING

MOMMY and DADDY sitting on stools at kitchen bar. Living room full of boxes.

MOMMY places phone down on kitchen counter

                    MOMMY
          The new apartment is ready.

                    DADDY
          Great. Maybe this time
          we can actually unpack.

                    MOMMY
               Maybe...

FADE TO NEXT SCENE

OPEN: EXTERIOR/FAMILY APARTMENT/EARLY MORNING

MOMMY and DADDY are organizing boxes into their daughter's red wagon in order to pull them through the complex to the other apartment.

A car and a truck drive up and park next to them. MOMMY's older brother, his wife, their young son and MOMMY's sister climb out.

Car doors, close - CLICK, CLICK, CLICK

MOMMY's mouth falls open in shock.

                    MOMMY
             What's going on?

                 OLDER BROTHER
              The cavalry is here!

                    MOMMY
                   Why...?

                 OLDER BROTHER
         (bends over to pick up a box)
            We heard you needed to move.

                    MOMMY
              (with emotion)
                I forgot...

                 OLDER BROTHER
                You forgot?

MOMMY
I forgot what it is like
to live close to family.

OLDER BROTHER
Happy to remind you.

FADE TO NEXT SCENE

Close is a relative term by the way. My brother, his family, and my sister had actually driven four hours to help us move. Yes, that is closer than the twenty hours they would have had to drive to visit us in Boston, but, four hours is still a long drive just to carry some boxes. With their help, we were able to move in a matter of hours. At the end of that long day, we ate food, we laughed and we collapsed in exhaustion.

OPEN: INTERIOR/NEW FAMILY APARTMENT
EARLY MORNING

FAMILY and EXTENDED FAMILY slowly wake. Everyone is sore and tired from the move and from sleeping on air mattresses, couches, and the floor.

Slowly the five adults gather in the kitchen greeting each other and chatting about breakfast.

BABY SISTER runs in and MOMMY scoops her up for a hug. MOMMY looks at BABY SISTER's arm.

MOMMY
(panic)
What are all of these red dots from?!?

DADDY

I don't know. Maybe heat rash?

(walks over to take a look)

OLDER BROTHER joins in.

OLDER BROTHER

Ummmm... I think you have fleas.

MOMMY/DADDY

(together)

FLEAS?!?!?

FADE TO BLACK

Something that started out to be so good, once again ended up so bad. As a mother, I felt like a complete failure. Why couldn't I find a decent place for my children to lay their heads? Why must I have this extra burden on top of my current load? *Why? Why? WHY?*

Not only did our carpets have to be replaced, but we had to be treated for fleas *twice* before they finally went away. That's twice we were displaced from our apartment to be "bombed." Twice, I vacuumed every inch of the apartment, every single day, for 14 days. That's another month we waited to unpack. I know, I know... I was supposed to stay positive. But, I couldn't help but think I was being punished in some way. That somehow the entire universe had conspired against me. Fleas? Really?? We didn't even have a dog.

Unfortunately, our living situation was only part of our problem. We were facing other obstacles as well.

We didn't own a car (city dwellers) so somewhere between moving from a condo, to a hotel, to an apartment, to another apartment we were supposed to go car shopping. We didn't. We kept the overpriced SUV for longer than we should have. Another financial "no-no" that we didn't have time to figure out how to avoid. At some point, the financial distress outweighed the emotional stress, and we realized we needed to send the gas guzzling mammoth back to where it came from.

Thankfully, a friend was able to loan us their car for a couple of weeks, while we continued to look for a more permanent form of transportation. Believe me when I say, I do not look back on this act of generosity lightly. Someone loaned us their *car*. Again, at the time, I did not have the ability to be grateful. There were too many other things to worry about.

My husband and I bought our first car in 10 years in September. It was a nice enough car. A small, four door economy, non-gas-guzzling "smart buy." Our second car was purchased in October. It was also a nice enough car - a used 1991 Volvo that had over 200,000 miles on the odometer. We didn't care. We did it. We purchased two vehicles. Shouldn't I have been more excited about the whole thing? No. I felt like I had a noose around my neck. This new mode of transportation did not make sense to my city-dwelling brain. All I could think was, so long walking everywhere. So long trains. Here come car lines and drive-thru windows and *traffic*. Sigh.

Somewhere else in the middle of all those moves, I managed to register my oldest daughter for school. We were late figuring out this part of the equation. We missed registration, orientation, meet the teacher day, fee day, all of it. School down south started long before we arrived from up north. We didn't have a permanent address so I wasn't sure how to turn in a proof of residency. In light of that, I had opted to keep my daughter with me until we had a place to live. My first foray into the bureaucracy of registering a child for a new elementary school in a new town didn't go so well.

OPEN: NEXT SCENE
INTERIOR/ELEMENTARY SCHOOL/FRONT OFFICE

MOMMY stands at desk waiting to speak to the
person behind the desk who is on the phone.

MOMMY tries to be patient but is failing. She opens
her mouth to speak, but the woman behind the desk
holds up her finger in the number one position.
MOMMY closes her mouth and continues to wait.
Finally woman hangs up phone.

                    WOMAN
                (unfriendly)
                Can I help you?

                    MOMMY
            (trying to stay polite)
        Yes, I need to register my daughter
                for first grade.

                    WOMAN
                  (frowns)
        Well, we started school two weeks ago.

                    MOMMY
        Yes, I know. I apologize. We just moved
        here from Boston. School doesn't start
                there until after Labor Day.
        I assumed that was true here as well.

                    WOMAN
        Well, we started school two weeks ago.

MOMMY
(trying to stay calm)
Yes, I know. Again, we just moved here.
Yesterday we finally moved into an apartment.
We have a permanent address now. May I please
register my daughter?

WOMAN
(with obvious disdain)
Fill these out.

MOMMY
Thank you.

MOMMY sits down to fill out forms.
After a short time returns to desk.

MOMMY
So I don't have an electric bill
or a copy of our rental agreement I'll…

WOMAN
(interrupts)
Everyone else got those in two weeks
ago, (pause) when we started school.
(looks over her glasses with eyes
that give the kind of look that lets
you know you are in trouble)

MOMMY
(takes a deep breath)
Yes, I know. WE. JUST. MOVED. HERE.

As soon as I have the rest of the
paperwork I will drop it off.

I will have my daughter
here on Monday to begin classes. Please
have the principal call me if there
is anything else.

MOMMY turns to leave.

                    WOMAN
I'll tell her, but she is going to wonder
why you didn't turn everything in when
school started, (pause) two weeks ago.

MOMMY realizes the futility of a response, sighs
one last time and walks out.

FADE TO BLACK

Somewhere in there, we also managed to find a new medical
team for our baby girl. This conversation, I was prepared for.
I made sure I spoke up about how this was going to go from the
beginning.

OPEN: PEDIATRIC CARDIOLOGY CLINIC

BABY getting check-up. At the end of examination,
MOMMY makes her declaration.

                    MOMMY
             (defensive, assertive)
You need to understand that when I

say something is wrong with my daughter,
you need to believe me. In order for me
to trust you, you are going to have to
trust me. Got it????

DOCTOR
Of course, Mrs. Keating.

MOMMY:
Nope, not good enough.
Don't patronize me.
Look me in the eye and tell me
we are going to work as a team.

DOCTOR
We will make a great team.

DOCTOR and MOMMY stare at each other
(uncomfortable). MOMMY searches for the truth.
DOCTOR looks back with quiet confidence. Finally,
MOMMY nods her approval.

MOMMY
Okay then. See you in three months.

FADE TO BLACK

My sweet baby daughter had managed to make it through
our move to a new town with no new major medical issues. The
miraculous was still at work in the life of this little girl.

Unfortunately, we still had to make the rounds to all of the
doctor's offices. We had to meet everyone, everyone had to give
her a check-up. The cardiologist needed an echo, the pediatrician

needed a blood test, the gastroenterologist needed a stool sample, etc. etc. I found that even though we were in a new town, the level of exhaustion that accompanies multiple doctor visits was exactly the same. In some ways, that's a sad state of affairs. In some ways, it was comforting. At least in this regard, I was in the middle of something familiar.

Inevitably, even though I didn't want to, I found a way to settle. I found a way to unpack for what I hoped would be a final time. I found a way to get my daughter to school everyday. I found a way to establish a new schedule.

I didn't like living in the south again. I didn't like our apartment that smelled like smoke. I didn't like our "other" apartment infested with fleas. I hated *all* of the bugs. I didn't like how I couldn't walk outside without my entire body becoming drenched with sweat. I didn't like that I couldn't walk *anywhere*, because there were no sidewalks. I had to drive to a park to go for a walk. Annoying.

Relying on a car for transportation made me feel stripped of my independence all over again. Actually, this last move had left me feeling stripped of everything. I felt vulnerable, naked, and raw. I no longer had the strength to rely on my ability to be a chameleon. Unlike New York and Boston, I was so miserable in this new place that I no longer cared if I blended. There was nothing left of that girl who found herself in NYC. She was gone for good. I hadn't heard anything from my inner-two-year old for months. I barely heard and rarely listened to the reassuring voice of my faith. I still lived far away from my family. I did not have any friends. I felt more than lonely, I felt alone.

At least, our apartment complex had a pool. If we were going to survive in this new, steamy, hot, bug-infested, confusing place, at the very least, we were going to have to learn how to swim.

CHAPTER TWENTY SIX
THE FINAL DESCENT

Unfortunately, even though we had settled in… sort of… the whirlwind did not stop. We kept having all of these other "things" that interrupted our attempts at something normal. My Emotional Stability Chart looked like the study of a chevron pattern in that first year. I was up and down so much I can't even begin to explain how my brain functioned. I have no idea.

In October, after our belongings arrived but before we moved into the second apartment, my sister got married. I, of course, dropped everything to be there. This was my sister. The one who gave up a year of her life, moved to New York, and took care of me and my firstborn. She deserved for me to be at her wedding. She deserved for me to have my crap together so she could have her special day. I wish I could say I achieved this goal with great accomplishment. Again, I didn't. She definitely deserved way more than I could give. I'm thankful she has forgiven me for my inability to be "available" when she needed me to be. *Baby Sister = 1,000 points. Me = 1 point (for effort only).*

In November, the barrage continued. We were in my husband's hometown for the day, checking on his ailing parents. We had promised our girls a trip to the mall as a peace offering for their good behavior during what was a stressful and emotional visit. It was not easy to see two such vibrant people deteriorate before our eyes.

On our way to the mall, we were t-boned at an intersection. Our light was green, their light was red. The elderly man who hit us swore his foot was on the brake. It wasn't. When he slammed his foot to the floor in an attempt to stop his car, he actually accelerated into the front passenger side of our car. The front passenger side was where I was sitting.

As a reflex, I had placed my hand on the door, because I somehow thought I could stop the on-coming car from actually hitting me. I couldn't. At the same time, I had turned my head slightly in order to make sure my youngest daughter, the one who had survived two heart surgeries, was going to be okay. I thought if I could see her, I could save her.

She got jostled around a little, but did not get hurt. Thank God. In fact, everyone walked away from that horrific moment without injury. Everyone, except for me. Because I had done exactly all of the things that you shouldn't do when a car is about to crash into you, I ended up with another serious injury. My shoulder, my collar bone and my neck were... smashed. Yes, it hurt. It hurt a lot. *Is it weird when your shoulder makes a weird popping sound every time you turn your neck? Because, I am thinking it might be...*

The officer who arrived on the scene took one look at us and with great pity asked,

"Is that a new car?"

To which I replied (with nasty attitude), "Not anymore."

I wasn't crying after the accident, even though my shoulder was killing me. Nope, once again I chose to stay stoic. But, belligerent, sarcastic, smart-mouthed, bratty, two-year-old girl showed up in full color. She had been biding her time, waiting for the perfect moment to speak up. She had the audacity to be rude to the police officer, who was being nothing but helpful. I am so not a fan of her.

Two days after this accident, my husband went out of town to perform in a show in New York. He had made plans to be in this show months before, when we still lived in Boston. He had looked forward to this opportunity with great anticipation. There is nothing better to him than an opportunity to be on stage. It makes his whole spirit come alive.

I understood that backing out of this project would have caused him major disappointment, not to mention stress for the director, but that didn't make it easier for me to let him go. Just like at the hospital after the birth of my second child, he asked me if I needed him to stay. How could I possibly say yes? I should have, but I didn't. *I* wanted him to *choose* to stay home without me having to ask. He REALLY wanted to go. I'm sure you can guess what happened. I did not speak up and he went anyway.

Unfortunately, this left me at home alone with two small children and the inability to move my arm. It felt eerily repetitive of all the other times I had a child who needed care *and* a serious injury that kept me from caring for them. It left me helpless with massive responsibilities… again.

I didn't realize it at the time, but this was the moment I stopped trusting my husband. Somewhere along the way, I had come to the conclusion he was going to keep "leaving" just when I needed him most.

I was hurt by his choice to go to NY when I needed him so desperately to stay home. It wasn't his fault, not entirely. He married the bull-fighting, mountain-born, athletic, farm girl. The girl who could handle anything. Since I was so good at pretending, he had no idea the choices he was making were pushing me away.

Did I choose to deal with that pot of boiling bitterness? You guessed it. No, I did not. Rather than talk about it, I retreated further from him and nursed my wounds in private while stewing in a big bowl of resentment and anger. No, this is not the same place where the unconditional love I promised I would give to him *forever* exists. This is some place... else...

He returned home in January and immediately jumped back into teaching and directing. He was spending every day from eight in the morning until midnight or later teaching and then directing, producing and building a show. Most weekends, he traveled back and forth to his childhood home to care for his parents as best he could. Even if I could have spoken up about my situation, I seriously doubt he could have heard me. Again, not entirely his fault.

My husband didn't intend to make me feel abandoned. He was working desperately to keep the train moving forward. He wanted to take care of us. He needed to provide for his family. It was what he could do. He was busy desperately making sure he produced a good show, took care of his parents, and kept his job. There was no room left on his plate either.

That didn't stop me from dumping unrealistic expectations on his shoulders. It didn't stop me from passive aggressively shooting piercing arrows of frustration, anger and sometimes even hate in his direction. It wasn't fair. It wasn't even remotely *nice*. But, it was all I had to give. Since he couldn't keep up with my long lists of things I needed, I built a nice big wall between me and my greatest love. I held a nasty grudge, and I let the distance between us grow, and grow, and grow.

The distance stayed between us even as my father-in-law passed away a few short weeks later in March, *grief,* right before the opening of my husband's show, *stress*. No, I don't know how we kept going. I really don't. I know for sure I wasn't moving forward to anywhere good. I kept trying to figure out how to get out of the pit. I did not succeed.

In May, just when I thought we were going to begin the process of getting out of the muck, I suffered my final blow.

My husband had survived directing his show, even while he grieved for his father, and was almost finished with his first year of classes.

I had recovered as much as I could from the car accident.

Our oldest daughter had survived first grade (even though she missed the first two weeks).

Our baby girl was still medically stable, even with all of the disruption to her living conditions.

The fleas had been conquered.

The bugs were in a temporary state of surrender.

We were finally making peace with our new home. It had been a long, grueling year, but finally, it was almost summer.

I was looking forward to summer with my girls. My girls, who deserved more than anything to have something *simple* to enjoy without anything *extra* thrown in. We all needed a little of that. I envisioned warm summer days at the beach and the pool. I saw glimpses of a summer *vacation.*

I thought I was going to be able to begin the process of climbing out of the pit. I thought I was going to be able to start putting it all behind me. Unfortunately, I was not at rock bottom. Not yet.

I wanted to find a way to get back to the person I used to be. I mean when the world is falling down all around you, you should return to what you know. *Right?* It made sense at the time.

In my desperate attempt to find something familiar, I decided to play volleyball at a local pick-up game. Athletics was something I understood. No matter what town I lived in, the sports I had played my entire life stayed the same. After all, some of our favorite friends from NYC are the friends we met in Central Park playing volleyball, so why not? It seemed like a great place to start.

Yes, I was still delusional. Yes, I actually thought that even with a banged up shoulder, a c-section and a separated pelvis, I could still play the sport of my youth. If only I could have seen into the future, I never would have gone.

Thirty minutes into the game, which wasn't even close to intense, and a few seconds *after* the play was over, I stepped forward to walk off of the court and... snap. I ruptured my Achilles tendon.

I was enough of an athlete to know immediately what that sound meant. It meant automatic bed rest, and surgery, and an eight week recovery time before I could even begin to walk again. It meant weeks of rehab, more doctor's offices, more medical bills and spending more money we did not have. It also meant I was finally, physically, out of the game. I had been benched and this time, I knew I wouldn't be coming back.

I crawled my way over to the sidelines, and I asked someone to get my husband from the next room. He had stepped out in an effort to entertain our two young children while Mommy took her turn on the court. I took some solace in the fact that my children didn't see me crumple to the floor.

When he walked up to me, all I could say as tears leaked out of my eyes was, "I'm sorry. I'm sorry. I'm so sorry."

I felt nothing but guilt for adding this burden to our already overwhelming situation.

I remember I called my sister soon after my Achilles rupture to tell her what happened, and I couldn't even speak. In a broken, incomprehensible form of communication, I sobbed loudly and uncontrollably into the phone, oblivious to any form of decency, decorum or etiquette. I was so completely and utterly defeated. All I had wanted was a summer vacation. What I received instead was *another* trip to the hospital, *another* surgery, *another* medical bill.

OPEN: BACK TO THE PIT

                    MOMMY
      (from the bottom of the pit screams)
              HEEEEELLLLLLP!

The screams fade to a yell which fade to whisper
and then to a muffled sob.

MOMMY collapses on the ground in defeat.

                    MOMMY
                 (whisper)
        Help me. Please help me.

FADE TO BLACK

CHAPTER TWENTY SEVEN

TIME TO CLIMB THE LADDER

OPEN: Black Screen

TITLE: Still In The Pit

CAMERA from above looks down into the pit. MOMMY is sitting on the ground drawing in the dirt with her finger. All around her are mounds of dirt representing objects like a table, a stool, etc. It is obvious MOMMY has been busy at work making a "home" for herself in the bottom of the pit. MOMMY is no longer screaming for help. She is calmly drawing in the dirt.

The scene is interrupted by a noise off camera. FOOTSTEPS - someone is approaching.

From above we see the back of a man's head enter the frame as he looks down at MOMMY.

                    STRANGER
                    Hello?

MOMMY (startled) looks up in disbelief. Thinking
she is dreaming she ignores the stranger.

                    STRANGER
                (repeats, louder)
                    Hello?

                    MOMMY
        (looks up again tentative, full of doubt)
                    Yes…?

                    STRANGER
        You look like you could use some help.

                    MOMMY
                I'm okay. Thanks.
        (goes back to looking at the dirt)

                    STRANGER
        You don't look okay. You look stuck.

                    MOMMY
            I am stuck, but I'm fine.
        I'll find a way out, eventually.

                    STRANGER
                Are you sure?

                    MOMMY
            Don't I look sure?

                    STRANGER
             No you don't.

UNCOMFORTABLE PAUSE

                    STRANGER
          I've got a ladder up here.
          I could help you get out.

                    MOMMY
            I don't need a ladder.

                    STRANGER
              I think you do.

                    MOMMY
               No, I don't.

                    STRANGER
                Yes, you do.

                    MOMMY
               No, I don't.

                    STRANGER
                YES. You do.

STRANGER throws ladder down into pit with force.
Ladder makes a loud clang as it lands next to
MOMMY. MOMMY looks at it with confusion and
doubt, and still doesn't move. After a moment
she asks...

> MOMMY
> Okay, say I use your ladder
> and I climb up there. What then?

> STRANGER
> How about we find out? I mean anything
> is better than being stuck down there
> in a dark pit, right?

MOMMY shrugs. She's not sure this is true.
After a moment of consideration...

> MOMMY
> Okay. (pause) Okay.

With no other alternatives she stands and begins
to climb the ladder.

FADE TO BLACK

Up to this point, I had screwed up the healing process in a gloriously fantastic way. I had held in my anger, stuffed down my grief, and denied, denied, denied my emotions for so long I was a mere shell of the person I used to be. Some of that emotional numbness, I *had* to embrace in order to survive. Some of it, I held on to because I had become comfortable in my pain. It was familiar. It was safe.

No one around me could recognize how dangerously close all those mistakes were pushing me toward a total and complete breakdown. Thankfully, my primary care physician did.

He wasn't supposed to be diagnosing my mental state. I was in his office for a simple follow-up after the surgery to repair my Achilles tendon rupture. All I needed him to do was sign a little piece of paper confirming my injury, so we could keep our healthcare credit with my husband's employer. Frankly, I'm surprised that I could pass a physical exam, but I did. Even after surgery, my numbers miraculously looked okay. On paper, I should have been on my way to rehabilitation.

Thankfully, this doctor was the first person to look past the facade. He looked down into my pit with his friendly face and his curly brown hair and he said, "Excuse me, but you don't look so good."

It surprised me that this was the person who was willing to reach down into my pit. He was not who I was expecting. He was outside my circle of friends. He was not a member of my family. He did not go to my church. He was a complete stranger. Maybe, that is exactly why he was the most qualified.

He gave me two choices: Get myself on an anti-depressant and start therapy right away *or* get checked into a hospital for an extended stay immediately. Neither of those "suggestions" sounded like anything I even remotely wanted to do.

I wasn't ready to move forward when my doctor threw the ladder into my pit. I still had my mask firmly in place and my heart appropriately guarded. While he was laying out for me all the reasons why I needed to act immediately, I sat there and pretended that I had it all together. The more I resisted the harder he pushed. He kept insisting. I kept resisting.

I couldn't help but see my situation once more through the lens of a camera. In my mind, the whole thing morphed into a poorly made-for-TV movie about PTSD. The kind with the lighting that's slightly "off," and the acting that is painful to watch, and the camera that seems to be constantly stuck in a too-close close-up. I tried to shake the image, but no matter how hard I tried, I couldn't separate myself from this awful after school special.

As is true in all terrible made-for-TV specials, after much

deliberation, there was a change in the background music. In a series of rapid flashbacks, I saw my behavior over the past few months. With new clarity, I realized there were small glimpses into this final breakdown, warnings that should have let me know this was coming. Until this moment, I had ignored them.

For example, I had a panic attack at yoga. That's right. You heard me. I had a panic attack at *yoga*. I mean really, *who does that?*

I collapsed onto the floor of my kitchen, because my daughters had both asked for something to drink - *at the same time.* I slid down the cabinet and plopped onto the kitchen floor and sobbed uncontrollably over the overwhelming burden of pouring milk simultaneously into two separate cups. I didn't even check for roaches first.

I had a meltdown in a pediatrician's office, because I couldn't fill out a medical form. I couldn't remember my husband's birth date or social security number. I was crying uncontrollably while the poor desk clerk kept saying, "It's okay. You can call us with that info later. Ma'am it's okay. Really, it's okay…." as she glanced nervously at her fellow employee. I'm pretty sure I was one phone call away from a straight jacket.

A new acquaintance asked "How long have you lived here?" and rather than try to explain how horrible our South Carolina experience had been, I said, "Not long." And then, I would cry.

On the playground, fellow parents asked, "So, what do you do?" Rather than try to explain that I hadn't been able to work since I had separated my pelvis and given birth to a medical miracle, I would say, "Oh, I'm working from home right now *(liar, liar pants on fire)*." And then, I would cry.

My husband picked up extra work to help us financially which meant he was gone from our home even more than he was *already* gone from our home. Rather than thank him for all of his hard work, I would yell at him for being gone all the time.

And then, I would cry.

All this crying was very out of character for a stoic like me. I didn't care. I couldn't stop.

It wasn't until I was sitting in the middle of my own personal flashback that I finally saw the truth clearly. There was no room left for argument. Finally, I got it through my thick skull that the woman starring in that horrible after school special, that woman on the examination table pretending that everything was fine when it was so NOT, was me. I was the psychotic woman who had been through the trauma, but still believed she was untouched by her circumstances. I was the one who needed the medical intervention. It was me. Me. ME. UGH!

According to my doctor, my response to my long laundry list of issues (insert: all that obnoxious crying) was completely "normal." Delayed and mishandled, but normal none the less.

I was uncomfortable with this realization. Somehow, I thought I was different. Somehow, I thought that grieving, overly-emotional-basket-case thing, that's for everyone else. Not me. But, I couldn't hide it any longer. It leaked through my edges even when I thought I was sufficiently sealed.

It took a while, but my doctor's unrelenting gentle insistence finally broke through. Eight years after my pelvis separation, five years after our move from New York City, two years after the birth of my baby daughter, one year after moving to South Carolina, six months after our car accident and three weeks after rupturing my Achilles tendon, I finally realized it was time. Time to do something right about my emotional state.

Since I was at the bottom, I had nowhere to go but up. It was time to start climbing the ladder. I only had one good leg, but it was time to start climbing anyway.

CHAPTER TWENTY EIGHT

GIVE THE MONSTER
UNDER YOUR BED A NAME

OPEN: INTERIOR/THERAPIST'S OFFICE

MOMMY sitting on couch. Her left foot is propped beside her encased in a large black boot. A pair of crutches leans against the arm of the couch.

A THERAPIST sits in chair facing MOMMY.

THERAPIST and MOMMY stare at each other (awkward).

> THERAPIST
> Okay, let's begin. How about you
> tell me how you ended up here?

> MOMMY
> Ummm...

Slowly MOMMY begins to weep. Then the weep becomes a cry. Then the cry becomes an unholy wail. And MOMMY finally faces the full weight of her grief.

FADE TO BLACK

My first step forward towards healing was making a commitment to attend therapy. A trip to a hospital where I would be cared for by complete strangers who were well trained in ways to help me heal was tempting, but I opted for the therapy instead. I couldn't figure out how to let go of my life enough to check out completely. I couldn't dump the care of our children onto my husband. He was never home, how was he ever going to do drop-off, or pick-up, or homework? Who was going to make *(okay, okay "heat up")* dinner? Who was going to take the girls to all the doctors' appointments? Or to the dentist?

My mom wasn't available for an extended stay this time around. My sister was married and had her own life to live. My friends from college had their own families to raise. I didn't have those kinds of friends in South Carolina, at least not yet. Besides, another trip to a hospital was too much for my spirit to handle.

I'm sure my husband could have figured it out. In fact, he probably would have welcomed the opportunity to have something concrete to do, but I wasn't ready to let it all go. Not yet. You can't make an over-achieving, athletic, farm-girl, control freak give up everything all at once. We're not designed to go cold turkey.

It is kind of ironic, but having an injury that forces you to sit down in order to heal coincides nicely with doctor mandated therapy. As long as I was going to be forced to sit, I might as well get some work done.

It took weeks for me to finally let go and let the therapy work. I had been so guarded for so long I had lost my ability to "share." I am not sure I ever knew how in the first place. Part of my particular form of healing involved learning how to speak in a way that was honest and open about what was really going on. This was a brand new form of communication for me.

When the flood gates finally opened, what came out was a long, agonizing, trauma-induced wail. It was loud. It was uncomfortable. It was painful. But, that's what I did. I wailed. And wailed. And wailed. For weeks and weeks, that was all therapy was for me, a place to wail.

When I finally came face to face with the truth of my sadness, I gave it a name. Grief. Just like those childhood monsters under the bed, once I gave it a name, it no longer had power over me.

My second step forward on the path to healing was agreeing to take medication. This one was really, *really* hard to accept. I was so proud of myself for being relatively medicine free. I was healthy, I drank water, I ate well. I was strong. I was grounded. I was a woman of faith. I was not the kind of person who was supposed to need medication in order to function. I was supposed to be strong enough without it. I once faced down a bull for Pete's sake!

Back to the movie.

OPEN: INTERIOR/THERAPIST'S OFFICE

MOMMY still on couch. Therapist still in chair across from MOMMY. MOMMY wipes her eyes and nose. She looks like she has had a marathon cry.

THERAPIST
I think you need to think
seriously about taking some medication.
I think you're depressed.

                    MOMMY
                  No, I'm not.

                   THERAPIST
                 Yes, you are.

                    MOMMY
                  No, I'm not.

PAUSE

Flashback to that day in my doctor's office when I was sitting on the examination table, sobbing uncontrollably *while* arguing that I didn't need medications to balance my emotional state. Pot? Kettle? Yeah, we are both black.

UNPAUSE

                   THERAPIST:
                 YES, you are.

MOMMY lowers head and wrings her hands. Shakes her head, "no."

                   THERAPIST
         You've been through too much at once.

MOMMY shakes head "no."

                   THERAPIST
         It's too much for your brain to handle.

MOMMY shakes head "no."

THERAPIST

You need help. Let me help you.

MOMMY starts crying again.

FADE TO BLACK

I am happy to say that eventually I gave in to the truth of my situation. I learned to say the word grief out loud. I learned to say the word depression. Admitting something was wrong really was the first step.

I'm one of the lucky ones. The therapy and the medicine did what they were designed to do. They gave me the break my body needed. They gave me my way out. Amazingly, once I started feeling better, I was eventually able to wean myself from both of these things. I finally healed enough that I no longer needed them to function. Still, even with all of that behind me, I am uncomfortable admitting I needed them at all.

There is something to be learned from that. In my Christian world view, distorted or not, I did not feel I had the freedom to have this kind of brokenness. I did not feel I had the freedom to raise the white flag, or call for medical intervention. Every time I tried to fight my way back and failed, I felt like I must not be "Christian" enough. That my faith must not be strong enough. I felt ashamed for having a very real problem that had no immediate solution.

I prayed. I poured my heart out to God. I begged Him to move on my behalf. I wanted for the prayer to be enough to solve my problems. I wanted God to wave his magic wand and poof make it all better. When He didn't answer my prayers *exactly* the way I wanted for Him to answer my prayers, I pouted like a big fat baby.

With the very end of my fingertips, I clung to the truth that

God was still God. I hoped that somehow He was still part of the whole crazy scenario. I read Scripture to confirm it. I played music to beat it into my brain. But, could I honestly say I believed God still *loved* me? Say it and *mean* it? No, I could not. Deep down inside I was in agony, because I felt like the God I had loved my whole life had abandoned me.

Of course, deep down inside, I also knew that God did love me. He had proven Himself to me more than I had ever deserved. But, I couldn't find a way to reconcile that truth with the way the things in my life had gone down. The puzzle pieces did not fit. How could I possibly be this broken and still be a woman of faith? It didn't make sense. It didn't seem possible.

But, it was more than possible, it was irrevocably true. I was broken. Broken in a way that didn't go away quickly. Broken in a way that required real work to fix. Broken, but by the grace of God, still considered a fixer-upper. In other words, not yet condemned.

When I finally stopped wailing, my therapist said something to me that changed everything.

"This situation is terrible," she pronounced. "I am proud of you for surviving as well as you have."

"Proud of me? Really?" I answered. I didn't feel proud of anything.

"Yes, I am proud of you. You are a strong woman. You deserve a medal."

That's when the music swelled and a light from Heaven shined down on me. I didn't realize it, but all this time, this was the only thing I ever needed to hear.

I'm sure she wasn't the first person to say it, but she was the first person I was able to really *hear*. She was outside my current circumstances. She didn't know the person I was before. She didn't know the person I was going to end up becoming. She offered an objective point of view. Sometimes, all you really need is for someone who doesn't know you to listen to your story, commiserate with you on all the yucky bits, and based on the facts alone let you know they are on your side. Even if you have to pay them.

It took me a long time to get to a place where I could hear and understand what I needed to do. I had to unload all of my pain and grief. I had to find a safe place to lay it down. Then I had to make a choice to leave it behind.

This was not new information. I had heard this truth multiple times before. I had spoken this truth to other people multiple times before. I had seen this truth played out in multiple forms on TV, in movies, and in books. Until this moment, I couldn't see how to make this truth a reality in my own version of my movie memoir screenplay novel.

Finally, after all of that wailing, I got it. I couldn't change any of the things that had happened to us. What I could do was change how I was going to choose to live while going through it. I drew a line in the sand. I took another small step forward. I continued to climb the ladder. No turning back.

WE INTERRUPT THIS PROGRAM FOR AN IMPORTANT ANNOUNCEMENT

For a moment, we are going to take a break from the chronological aspect of this story. This next chapter is going to be sort of an insert that covers an uncomfortable topic that deserves its own aside, its own separate section. It is a topic that stayed with us through our entire story. It is a topic that I really hate to discuss. Unfortunately, it's all about the money.

I'm sure you have already ascertained that all of this moving around, living with physical ailments, irregular work patterns and major medical bills adds up to, well, a lot of zeros. When various challenges like these come along, there are more than emotional and physical repercussions. There are major financial ones as well. The level of debt we were thrown into was frustrating, discouraging and downright hair raising.

I struggled with my anger in this area. I battled my resentment. With a heavy feeling of failure, I chastised myself over and over and over again for not being good at basic math. No matter how hard I tried, I could not figure out how to subtract thousands of dollars from zero and still end up in the black. It just wouldn't work out. So I "zoned out" on this part of our story. I dumped this pile of muck onto the over-burdened shoulders of my husband. I had to walk away. I could not handle the grief and pain of our financial distress on top of everything else I was fighting against. And, I hated myself for being so weak.

For a long time, every thing we did, every decision we made was controlled, no *dominated*, by money. In addition every time something "happened" that required money was overwhelming, beyond comprehension and inevitably blown out of proportion. Our daughter needs new shoes? *Impossible.* Ten dollars for that school field trip? *Absolutely not.* Another bill from yet another check up at yet another doctor? *Are you freaking kidding me?!?*

We were what many people called *strapped* but it felt more like being locked in a straight jacket. I didn't like it. I didn't feel good about it. I rarely had a peace about it. I threw massive temper tantrums when I didn't get my way. I spat angry epitaphs at whomever would listen. If you didn't want to know the truth about our situation, it was best not to ask.

Once again, as a woman of faith, I knew I should obediently trust God would show up for us in this painful place. I have to be honest, I did not. We were too proud to ask for help as many times as we actually needed it. We were too proud to be comfortable with the gifts we did receive. On the occasions where we could surrender our pride, the number of times we heard the words, "No, we can't help you," were way more memorable than all the times we heard yes. I hate to admit it, but it is true. The weight of this burden was much heavier than my blessings.

I did not expect God to show up with a big pile of money. Okay, okay, I expected it a *little*. Okay, okay, I wanted it a *lot*. But, just because that is what I *wanted* does not mean that was what *needed* to happen. Sometimes, swallowing the truth really is a bitter pill.

It was very painful to watch people all around us donating money to this cause or that cause, saving something, and helping this or that charity. All around us, people were donating money, big money, to all kinds of things, while we were drowning.

I hated that it mattered to me. I hated that all of that generosity given to someone *else* hurt as much as it did. I felt very self-absorbed and incredibly selfish. Those other things were worthy causes, and most of the time, way more important than our little piece of the pie. Knowing that didn't help. It still hurt. I wanted to be in a "better" place about it, but this kind of pain gave me tunnel vision. Ultimately, what I wanted even more than a big pile of money was to receive a peace about how I *felt*. I wanted the same peace I found in the bathtub. I wanted the faith of my childhood. I needed restoration. I needed relief. I didn't find it.

Again and again and again, every single time we ran out of money by the tenth of the month, I found myself crumpled, crying and beyond comfort. It hurt so much that I couldn't see beyond it. I couldn't find the good in it. I couldn't see the solution from it. I was tired of the constant race against the debt and the below zero balance. I was tired of wanting to be able to go back to work, but not being able to. I was tired of having to ask friends and family over and over and over again for help. I was just flat out fed up. How long was God going to make us wait before He decided to move on our behalf? *How long?*

I need to pause here to recognize some incredible moments of grace in this department. We did have multiple times where people attempted, in the best way they could, to help us financially. It's a long list and there's no way for me to write my "thank you speech" without leaving out someone important. So, let me just say to all of you, thank you. You know who you are, and you know what your generosity meant to us. Those sweet gifts did the hard work of keeping us out of complete and utter destitution. I am forever grateful to each and every one of you. That's why it's so hard to stand here now and sheepishly admit that none of those sweet gifts were *enough*.

I often compared those tiny respites from our financial

distress to the equivalent of putting a band aid on a gunshot wound. Just like in a war, those gifts were necessary to stop the bleeding. They were appropriate action for survival. It's just that... unfortunately... none of those actions actually removed the bullet.

I desperately wanted to be on the other side of the coin (small pun intended). Throughout my life, I had often enjoyed the art of the anonymous gift. I loved meeting people's earthly needs, especially when they least expected it. It was fun! I never even thought twice about it. I never cared about getting a thank you. I never cared about getting earthly accolades (although I did pat myself on my own back a few times). I *thought* this made me okay with money. Obviously, I wasn't. While I didn't take comfort in having lots of money, I did take comfort in my ability to have *enough* money. I really liked being able to pay my bills.

I placed too much significance on my ability to handle "my" money. I *know* I did. I know because of how humiliated I felt when I had to ask for financial help. *Any* financial help. *I* wanted to find a solution to this problem. *I* wanted to do whatever *I* could to solve it. But, I was benched. I was sidelined. My hands were tied. I carried the shame of that failure around with me for years. The failure was stinky. It left me smelly and unpleasant to be around. Yuck.

I would love to say that this issue has been resolved, and God and I have made up. I can't. Our money situation still stinks. Everything about it still hurts. I still have not seen "the bigger picture." I still struggle with why we carried this burden *on top* of all of the other burdens we had to bear. This one, in addition to all of the other ones, felt mean-spirited and petty. Since I know God is not a petty God, I do have to find a way to believe that someday there will be a "reason" for this part of the equation. I also have to find a way to be okay with the fact that I may never know what that reason is. I don't have any answers, at least not yet, but I do have hope that our current situation will be temporary... maybe.

What I do know for sure is that feeling helpless in this area of my life broke me in a way I was unprepared for. The strain it put on our family, the strain it put on our marriage, the strain it put on *everything* was indescribable. It left a big giant scar on my heart and my spirit. Unfortunately, occasionally, it's still bleeding. Maybe someday, I will have more to say on this topic, but for now this part of my story will have to remain "...to be continued."

The silver lining for me is knowing that even as challenging as this part of our story has been, we are surviving it. We are still here. Not out of debt, not even close, but still in the game and still fighting. In the words of my sweet second daughter, we are "more aheader" than we were. Not even remotely close to winning, but not entirely defeated either.

NOW BACK TO OUR REGULARLY
SCHEDULED PROGRAM

CHAPTER TWENTY NINE
I'VE GOT YOUR BACK

OPEN/BLACK SCREEN

TITLE: Healing Montage
MOMMY in a series of short clips.

SCENE ONE: MOMMY at physical therapy. MOMMY is standing on the edge of a platform with her heels hanging off. She does heel raises from flat foot to tippy-toe. PHYSICAL THERAPIST (PT) counting for MOMMY.

>   PT
>   15, 16, come on four more,
>   you need to do 20. That's it…

MOMMY completes reps and steps gingerly down from platform. PT rushes to hand MOMMY crutches. MOMMY collapses onto crutches in exhaustion and relief.

PT

Okay, that was the first set, two more to go.

VOICE-OVER/MOMMY
(internal)
Uuuugggghhh!

SCENE TWO: MOMMY sitting on doctor's table getting a check up.

DOCTOR

Okay, so the low dose of medication we gave you isn't working. We are going to have to add a second medication... blah, blah, blah. You'll need to take one twice a day, blah, blah, blah... You'll need to take the second one three times a day, blah, blah, blah... And we will need to keep you on that third medication for a little while longer. DO NOT mix up your dosages and make sure you take them around the same time every day.

VOICE-OVER/MOMMY
(internal)
Uuuuuugggggghhhh!

SCENE THREE: MOMMY sitting in THERAPIST'S office. THERAPIST hands MOMMY box of tissues.

THERAPIST

Okay, let's try something other than crying today. What do you say to trying

to describe to me what it felt like to
separate your pelvis?

MOMMY opens her mouth to speak and bursts into
tears.

> VOICE-OVER/MOMMY
> (internal)
> Uuuuuugggggghhhh!

SCENE FOUR: MOMMY and DADDY stand in front of
calendar on the front of refrigerator.

> MOMMY
> Any chance you could go with us to the
> cardio appointment next week?

> DADDY
> Probably not.
> (sad, wants to but can't)

> MOMMY
> Any chance you could cover for me with
> the girls so I could get a haircut?

> DADDY
> Probably not until after the show opens.
> (sad, wants to but can't)

> MOMMY
> Do you think you will be home before
> midnight this week?

                    DADDY
                Probably not.
                (defeated)

                    MOMMY
        Okay. See you when we see you…
                (defeated)

                VOICE-OVER/MOMMY
                    (internal)
                Uuuuuuggggghhhh!

SCENE FIVE: MOMMY sitting at table with DADDY
looking at a large pile of medical bills. Both
MOMMY and DADDY stare at the giant pile in
shock. They don't know what to do. There's no
money to pay for any of it.

                    DADDY
                Got any ideas?

MOMMY bursts into tears and says nothing
coherent.

                VOICE-OVER/MOMMY
                    (internal)
                Uuuuuuggggghhhh!

FADE TO BLACK

   Again, I wish I could say once I decided to heal that I moved
forward instantaneously, and in a matter of days everything
was perfect. That's the way it happens in movies, on TV shows,

and in works of fiction. That's not the way it happened for me. Unfortunately, my life didn't stop happening just because I started healing.

Everywhere I turned it seemed I was facing yet another battle to be won, another problem to be solved, and another bill to pay. Like an addict, I returned to the comfort of my pain time and time and time again. Some days, it was just easier to wallow.

When I actually did make progress, it was hard to believe it was substantial, and even more importantly, that it was permanent. The above scenes were what my life felt like. It was as if I was bouncing around from one giant burden to another. No matter how hard I tried, I couldn't seem to catch a break. I rarely felt like I was making any progress.

Physically, I had a lot of work to do. There is no easy way to recover from a ruptured Achilles (in addition to a car accident, a c-section, and a separated pelvis). It takes time. It takes rehab. It takes patience. It takes work. Rushing the process, even a little, essentially means starting over from zero. I couldn't afford to go back to zero. I was desperate for progress.

Being true to that progress meant I had to go against everything that felt natural. Just like the healing process for the separated pelvis, again I was forced to move forward in inches when everything in me wanted to run for miles. I was tired of this being my truth, but something in me believed this would be my last serious injury for a while. I don't know why I thought that, but even if it wasn't true, that thought helped me find an end to my injury-laden tunnel.

One day my rehab therapist took pity on me. He hooked me up to one machine to ice my Achilles while at the same time he put an electro stimulation machine on my shoulder and neck injury while at the same time putting blocks under my hips to relieve the pressure on my injured pelvis. It was pure heaven. Every single place on my body that ached was for a brief moment suspended in the glorious place of relief.

I left physical therapy that day feeling 100 pounds lighter. I stood tall. I walked straight. I looked "ahead" for the first time in ages. I'll never forget it. Progress. Medically assisted progress, but yes, progress.

My marriage suffered greatly from every single aspect of our situation. I know there were times in this story where I made my husband seem like the bad guy. He wasn't. He was and still is a great person. He is a great husband. He is a great father. Did he make some mistakes? Yes. Did he make choices out of selfishness? Yes. Did I? Yes. Is he still making choices based on selfishness? Yes. Am I? Yes. That doesn't make him any less my husband. That doesn't make me any less his wife. It does not change the commitment we made when we said we would marry each other. It doesn't change the fact that we promised to love each other, forever.

Still the damage was done. One partner (me) who survives by staying guarded and retreating further into her pain and one partner (him) who survives by staying busy and constantly being in motion does not a healthy marriage make. I needed to know he would change his schedule to help at home. He needed to know he had the freedom to be gone. He needed to work hard to feel like he was doing all the right things to keep the boat from sinking. I needed him to drop everything and come to my rescue. Unfortunately, I needed him to come to my rescue without me having to ask. Since I was so good at hiding everything that really matters, he was clueless. Lovable, adorable, sweet and kind, but clueless.

Some days, those war wounds are still with us. Some days, they aren't. The one thing I know as truth is that we both want to find our way back to the gregarious boy and the reticent girl who met in an ice cream shop and somehow managed to stay married even when the world gave them plenty of excuses to break up.

We're working on it.

Spiritually, I had a lot of work to do. I had to learn to practice trust when there was no solid ground to stand on. I had to learn to practice faith, even in the dark. I had to learn to practice forgiveness, even though I was furious. I had to learn that burdens and condemnation are not the same thing. I had to learn that feeling misunderstood is not the same as being alone. I had to learn humiliation is not the same as humility.

I didn't like it. It wasn't fun. I did not enjoy the journey. But, my faith did become something *more*, something *better*. I still believe that my God is a God of miracles. I also believe that those miracles don't always look the way I think they should. Some miracles come in unexpected packages. Hopefully, I will remember that for the next time I need to recognize a miracle for what it is and not for what I want it to be.

As a mother, I had a lot of work to do. I needed to repair a lot of damage done to my relationship with both of my girls. I had to earn their trust again. I needed to let them know that they could rely on me, for the small regular stuff as well as the big. For a long time, they would say things that made this clear. Things like, "Mommy, I really need to get some paper for school. Can we go to Staples? Or will that make you cry?" Out of the mouth of babes...

Emotionally, I had a lot of work to do. There was no easy way to recover from all that grief I had stuffed down for years. Again, I was going to make progress in inches. It took a couple of years before I was able to talk about any part of our situation without crying like an idiot. It took another year before I could openly discuss "my feelings." It took another year after that before I really and truly began the process of letting people back into my life.

It was not a simple process to learn how to be vulnerable. I screwed up more than I succeeded. I pushed a lot of people away. I left group settings with a cloud of awkward in my wake. I dumped and ran almost every time I opened my mouth. Too often I brought all conversation to a screeching halt just by revealing small pieces of my situation. No one knew what to do with me. Least of all, me. But, I kept trying. I knew I needed to keep trying.

Then, out of the blue, the most amazing thing happened. One of my college roommates, one of the ladies I mentioned in the preview, moved to the town I was currently living in. That's right, one of my sweetest sisters *moved* to SC and ended up living five minutes from me. There is no way for me to explain why that happened other than to say the man upstairs sent me an angel.

Back to the movie.

OPEN: EXTERIOR/DENSE FOREST
MOMMY stands in middle of clearing in full ninja gear with all of her "senses" on alert. Something is coming.

With loud screams of impending injury, five ninjas charge from behind tree cover to attack.

MOMMY fights them off one by one the best she can but is soon losing ground. She gets in a few jabs, but the battle is too much for her to fight alone.

MOMMY is in trouble.

From OFF CAMERA comes a warrior cry as MOMMY's FRIEND leaps into the middle of the battle. Her presence is so fierce the attacking ninjas pause

to assess the strength of this new warrior.
s
FRIEND looks at MOMMY, winks. She turns to stand
back-to-back with MOMMY facing the enemy ninjas.

The two battle together to fend off the attackers
until one by one they fall. Even five to two the
enemy is no match for this team.

CAMERA pans across enemy ninjas left battered
and bruised on the ground.

CUT TO: MOMMY out of breath and smiling.

                    MOMMY
                 (to FRIEND)
                 Thank you.

                    FRIEND
            Don't worry, I've got your back.

FADE TO BLACK

There is nothing better than a friend who is willing to wear a ninja suit. Thank God she had arrived. She literally jumped into the middle of my battles and started throwing punches.

The first time she gave a right hook to my situation, she spoke for me, when I couldn't form any words. In an effort to connect with people again, I had joined a women's group that met once a week. Once my friend moved to town, I invited her to join me. Guess what? Her life wasn't perfect either. We found we both needed the encouragement.

At this particular meeting, we were supposed to be going

around the table and telling a "brief" version of our backstories. When it was my turn, I faltered. I couldn't seem to put together even the simplest of sentences. I ended up saying something like, "I've had a tough few years, and I will have to tell you all about it some other time."

To which my dear friend interrupted with, "Let me tell you something ladies," she said, with full attitude and a wave of her hand. "This woman has been through hell. I don't know how she is even sitting here."

It was a simple statement, and yet to me, it spoke volumes. She took the attention away from my blubbering. She smoothly moved the conversation forward to something else. That simple act lifted a giant weight off of my shoulders. I didn't have to try so hard to communicate. Suddenly, I had an interpreter.

The second time she stood up for me was in the matter of money. I would call her often and dump the pain of our financial situation all over her sweet soul. She would listen without judgment. She would listen without criticism. Instead, she wept with me. She yelled at God *for* me. She understood how the blessings we were receiving weren't enough and she *cried for me* because she too wished they could be. And when she could, when I really needed it, she put money in my hand. On more than one occasion, and with a check that had way more zeros than I ever deserved. She took action. I didn't even have to ask. She just saw the need and *did* something. More than once. More than she should have. Without ever expecting anything from me.

The third time she fought for me was probably the most important of all. It was also the most painful.

After that first year of living in South Carolina with little to no medical intervention, our baby daughter again went from stable to anything but. She had faced multiple issues in addition to a heart condition. Too many issues. Some days it seemed like this little girl was never going to catch a break. One of the most challenging things about dealing with her particular health issues was the lack of a solution. For the rest of her life, there was always going to be a "next."

After seven years of living with this truth, I thought I had gotten to a place where I could accept that these major medical interventions were a permanent part of our life. I thought I was becoming more comfortable with them. Unfortunately, when it comes to watching your child suffer, there really is no end to the emotional roller coaster. I *thought* I was doing better until I found out I wasn't.

All those extra procedures were temporary stops on the way to the inevitable. In the summer of her seventh year of life, the doctors confirmed the one thing we absolutely did not want to hear. It was time for our baby girl to have her third heart surgery.

INSTANT REPLAY

MOMMY hits the ground SMACK!

REPEAT two, three, four times.
SMACK! SMACK! SMACK!

                    VOICE-OVER/MOMMY
                    Ouch.

When I called my friend to tell her the news, I couldn't even say the words out loud, but somehow she heard what I could barely bring myself to say. I was terrified. All that hard work to regain any sort of a former version of myself flew out the window. I might as well have been back at zero.

Except I wasn't.

Before, I would have suffered through my fear alone. *Before*, I would have wallowed for days in silence. *Before*, I never would have admitted I was facing the kind of fear that paralyzes. *Before*, I never would have admitted I was too exhausted to face down death… again.

This time was different. This time I picked up the phone, and I wailed in the presence of a friend. That's when I knew. Finally, I was moving forward.

My friend actually moved back to her home town about two weeks *before* my daughter's third surgery. We pondered this together, because it seemed a bit strange for God to bring her into my life, have her fight such a good fight, and then take her away right before the "big" moment. She had only just arrived and like a puff of smoke, she was gone again.

It was okay. I was able to let her go. She had done her job. She had donned her ninja suit and delivered a giant roundhouse kick to my loneliness, my grief and my frustration. Because of that, I was going to make it through. I was going to be okay. Besides, she was only a phone call away. Now, I knew that to be true.

I can say without a shadow of doubt that God's timing in the gift of her friendship was perfect. I was in a place where I could receive her friendship into my life. She was in a place where she could be in my life. Thankfully, both of those places were physically the same place.

So many things about my healing process were wrong, awkward, painful and distressing. But, not this. This was exactly right.

CHAPTER THIRTY

WELCOME BACK, OLD FRIEND

We had a long wait between the news that our daughter was going to have heart surgery and the actual surgery part. The doctors wanted to wait as long as possible, which ended up being about six months. With every trip to see the cardiologist, I was on the edge of every nerve in my body. *Would this appointment be the one? The one where the doctors tell us that instead of going home we would be going to the hospital, directly to the hospital, no passing Go and definitely no collecting $200 dollars?*

From experience, I knew the hammer could drop at any moment, and there was no way for me to prepare for it. So, we lived in limbo surrounded by a haze of vagueness going through our daily lives with the inevitable looming in the distance. It will always be my least favorite form of torture.

At least this time around, I did my best to be better at being vulnerable. I worked hard to let people in to my circle of pain. A funny thing happened. People showed up. Maybe not always in the way I needed them to, but in the way they could, they showed up. Sometimes, in ways that were completely unexpected. Probably the best example of this was when a whole bunch of people donated their pennies, so my sweet little girl could go and see a dolphin named Winter.

You may remember the story of Winter. She was a young dolphin who was found caught in a crab trap, and due to her extensive injuries, she ended up losing her tail. She could have died, but a group of marine biologists worked with her and kept her alive. It was an amazing story, and Winter became a star. Her story of great tragedy and triumph was depicted in the movie, *Dolphin Tale*. Our baby girl loved this film from the first moment she saw it.

At first, our youngest just watched the movie over and over... and over and over... and over and over again. She watched it so many times, the rest of us couldn't stand to look at it, except that kind of story is addictive. Even when you are sick of seeing it, you watch it... again.

A few months later she started talking about going to see Winter.

She would say things like, "How cool would it be to see Winter?"

"Really cool." I would answer while I pretended not to hear the request in her voice.

That statement grew to "I wish I could go see Winter."

"That would be nice," I would reply.

Soon, she started saying, "*Can* I go see Winter?"

"Maybe," I would say and try to change the subject.

Finally she insisted, "WHEN are you going to take me to see Winter?!"

"I don't know." I reluctantly replied.

I couldn't make any promises. More than anything, my little girl wanted to see this inspirational story up close. She wanted to do more than know about it. She wanted to see it. Feel it. Experience it. Since I was in no position to help her achieve her dream, I desperately tried to distract her.

"Look, something shiny!" I would say and hope she would eventually change her mind.

It was in the fall right before her third heart surgery that the intensity of this request really started to heat up.

"Can I please go see Winter?"

"How 'bout now?"

"Now?"

"Now?"

I wanted to be able to say yes, because there is nothing like the request of your child to melt your resolve, but I couldn't. We were in no position to take a trip of any kind. We were facing another heart surgery, more medical bills and borderline bankruptcy. Vacations of any kind were out of the question.

It broke my heart to look into the face of this sweet little girl and say, "maybe we can see Winter... someday...," instead of "Let's go!" It was grueling to be strong and sensible and grounded when all I ever wanted to do is give a little girl who was lucky to be alive anything she wanted. Anything.

It was early November before I realized it was time to take action. We had just received the news that our daughter's third heart surgery had been officially scheduled for January. We had two months to get ourselves together.

I had a large absence from school to organize. I had a long absence from my life to arrange. I had to figure out a way for my older daughter to remain present in her life, while I would be absent from mine. I had to figure out how to work around my husband's demanding schedule. I had to figure out just exactly how I was going to make it through... again.

In the middle of all of that busy work, I heard that voice in my spirit whisper, "Now. Take her to see Winter, now."

Yes, it was a very "if you build it they will come," kind of moment. I was supposed to trust that I should do this impossible thing, even though, everything I could see or understand said it was impossible. By now I should realize, impossible is exactly the place where we shine. Finally, that still small voice broke through my fog of hopelessness and showed me a way. A way to make a small miracle like this *happen*.

"Take the gifts I have given you and get to work," my inner voice said.

"What?" I replied. "What???"

No, I didn't understand the message at first either. Yes, I'm slow to catch on. After a couple of days, I finally figured it out.

At that time in our lives, we were using our artistic talents to run a fundraising business selling hair accessories for girls. We started this venture because my older daughter, who was nine at the time, decided she was ready to run her own business. She was that kind of kid. Remember? She was the one spelling the word T-A-X-I before she could walk? The one that needed to multi-task? Yes, that kid. Yes, I was still having trouble keeping up with her.

I was reluctant at first, to make this "business" happen, but finally I joined in with her, because she agreed to use some of the money we made to help pay off medical bills. I thought it was going to be a simple little family fundraiser. Nothing more than a glorified lemonade stand. It ended up being so much more than that to all of us.

It provided me with a much needed artistic outlet. It gave my daughter the opportunity to put her mark on the world. It made my husband feel a little less alone in the financial fight. Overall, it gave us something to DO.

It was a relatively local, somewhat private and manageable business. Just exactly the kind of work this introvert prefers. However, it was time. Time to take our lemonade stand viral.

My oldest daughter and I worked tirelessly over a weekend making, photographing, and listing our items on our online site. Then we turned to social media. Here is part of what our post said:

> *Calling all friends and family. We have a little request. We are trying to make Ella's Christmas wish come true. What we need is a little help with gas money. Check out our store and please consider doing some Christmas shopping here. Thanks.*

I pushed enter and 30 minutes later I got a phone call. I'm not kidding. We got a response from our post 30 minutes later. On the other end of the line was a friend from college, whom I had kept in touch with... sporadically... since graduation. He said one of the sweetest things I have ever heard.

"Betsy," he said, using my slightly annoying nickname very few people are allowed to use, "how much money do you need? I'm writing the check right now."

I said, "Are you kidding? We just need a few people to cover gas money so maybe $20?" *(I still don't get it do I?)*

"No," he said, "How much to pay for *all* of the gas you need? Betsy, (again with the nickname, however from him always a term of endearment), it's just money. Let me help. I want to help."

I could hardly speak I was so moved. This friend of all friends was the first to respond? I couldn't believe it, and I will never forget how that felt. It was like I was in my own version of *It's a Wonderful Life.* Here, for the first time in a long time, someone wanted to pay for ALL of our immediate need, not just part of it.

He was not alone. He was just the first of many who responded to our request. Several people bought items from our store. Someone else stepped up and paid for our hotel room. Someone else paid for all of our meals. Others stepped up and gave us gas cards and more random envelopes filled with cash. On and on and on until finally our *entire* trip was paid for. We didn't have to do anything. It was all *completely* covered.

Back to the movie.

OPEN: INTERIOR/EXTERIOR
CLEARWATER MARINE AQUARIUM
EARLY MORNING

CAMERA HOLDS on FAMILY as they stand together on the platform of large aquarium pool. They are leaning over railing looking down at dolphins. After a few minutes, a dolphin trainer walks up to family. She says hello and then leans down to talk to BABY SISTER.

                         TRAINER
                    Are you ready?

BABY SISTER nods yes.

She nervously takes the hand of the TRAINER and walks with her down the steps to the training platform. BABY SISTER kneels down on a towel next to TRAINER.

TRAINER blows whistle and calls dolphin (WINTER) over to platform. WINTER sticks her head up to TRAINER and makes clicking noises, "hello."

Suddenly TRAINER extends arm across BABY SISTER in order to hold her back from falling into the pool. BABY SISTER is so excited to touch WINTER that she almost falls in. Everyone chuckles.

BABY SISTER looks up at MOMMY and smiles with the kind of smile that fills an entire room.

DADDY puts arm around MOMMY.

MOMMY places an arm around DAUGHTER #1.

FAMILY stands there together and watches as one miracle reaches out to touch another.

FADE TO BLACK

There in that smile that filled my daughter's entire face, that's when I saw it. That thing that I hadn't seen for a long time. That piece of me that I thought I had lost forever. That elusive friend. It still existed. It was staring me in the face. Daring me to deny it was real. I couldn't. I still had it. *Hope.*

We survived that next season of surgery. In many ways, it was the worst one yet. For one thing, our daughter was much older. She understood much more about what was happening to her. She was also no longer my sweet little baby, she was now my child. She had a personality. She had thoughts, feelings and emotions. She had a great sense of humor. She gave giant hugs. Not to mention this time, she could talk. I had grown accustomed to seeing her sweet little face smile at me. I wasn't ready to face the reality that I might lose her... again.

Knowing her so well made it much harder to stand next to her bed and let her go through all of the things she needed to go through. It was much harder to hear her cries of fear and pain. It was much harder to hold her still while doctors poked and prodded, added and removed bandages. The day I held her down and watched her scream in agony while they pulled out her chest tubes was particularly rough.

Her IV had malfunctioned, so the nurse tried to give her the "goofy juice" orally. Unfortunately, she squirted it too far in the back of our daughter's mouth. It all came back *out*. The nurse couldn't dose her again, because she couldn't measure an exact amount. Our daughter had to have her chest tubes removed without any pain medication. That's a day I hope to never repeat. EVER. She will forever be my hero.

Overall, it was harder to convince her she was going to be okay, and harder to convince her that the pain would eventually go away. There will never be a comfortable way to do that. It will always feel impossible.

In a lot of ways, this most recent surgery was the easiest one yet. We let people in this time, and that truly made all the difference.

CHAPTER THIRTY ONE

HOME AGAIN

OPEN: EXTERIOR/BEACH/SC COASTLINE
BLACK SCREEN fades into water.

CAMERA zooms quickly over ocean water in similar fashion to the beginning of the movie. The sun's reflection is blinding.

After a moment, CAMERA looks up to see a large white bridge that looks like the sails of a ship (Cooper River Bridge). CAMERA rises until from above we see the bridge and the harbor. Boats float like toys on a pond. CAMERA pauses for a moment. Then, just like before, the CAMERA slowly falls toward the earth moving along the water until it comes to a shoreline.

CAMERA follows along coast. Waves gently wash up onto a sandy shore. A lone figure stands on the sand. CAMERA eventually closes in on figure.

MOMMY stands alone looking out on the horizon. She brings her hand to her forehead, shading the sun and squints as she looks out at the water.

CUT TO: From MOMMY's POV we see the mashed up versions of her former horizons: mountains that blend into NY that blend into Boston. These "vistas" melt into the ocean and disappear leaving behind a bright blue sky.

CUT TO: MOMMY's bare feet, which are not on a cliff, or on a concrete sidewalk, but instead squishing into the wet sand.

MOMMY looks down at her feet (frowns).

> VOICE-OVER/MOMMY
> (incredulously)
> Home?

FADE TO BLACK

Once again, I'm home.

I finally unpacked my pillowcase of "tangs." I finally got rid of all of the boxes. This is my new home. This place with the palm trees and the sand and the heat. Yep, even here, I found it. Home.

I do not have an attachment to this home in the same way I loved NY. It's not covered with concrete and mortar. It is not bustling, crowded or anonymous. There is no subway. No taxis. It is green, full of trees and vegetation and cars and backyards, with REAL grass.

I know, it's weird to me too. I never thought I would end up here. Yet here I am. Even more amazing, here I'm going to stay for a while, because we bought a house. That's right. You heard me. We bought a house. The financially challenged, wandering gypsies. Us. The Keatings. We bought a house.

It's an interesting phenomenon to have a somewhat permanent address after bouncing around for so long. It's unlike anything I have experienced since I left my tiny, one-stop-light, mountain home years ago. It will take some time for me to get used to it. Sometimes, I still call this house the "apartment."

There are many reasons why I love this house. Of course, I love it for all of the reasons that are external. Things like it's cute, it's in a good neighborhood, it's in a good school district, it's conveniently located are all great. But, really, I love it for the feeling of control we have for the first time in a long time. For once, I can make choices about the place I live.

I get to choose whether or not I want grass or flowers to grow around the large green bush by the front door. I can decide whether or not to paint the trim white. I can decide what colors the walls will be. I could even paint the ceiling black if I want (not that I would). I love telling my kids they can paint their room ANY color they want. When they get tired of that color, they can paint it again and again, as many times as they want, and as many times as I can stand. I didn't know it, but all this time what I really wanted was the freedom to use paint.

I love that it has two *(count them two!)* bathrooms, and three *(three!)* bedrooms. It has a *separate* kitchen. I can't even see the refrigerator from the living room! It has a backyard, and someday, I might even learn how to grow something. It is bright, full of light, cheery and inviting. To us, it might as well be a mansion. I can hardly keep how amazing all this is to myself.

On the other hand, it is hard to admit how we got to this new place. It is hard to discuss the multiple acts of kindness that went into making this miracle happen. It has left me feeling unsettled, discontented and... icky. It's like an endlessly itching mosquito bite that I can never fully scratch. Yet again, it has left me feeling like I somehow failed, because we had to ask for help in order to have it. Even after everything we went through, I still wanted to do it... all by myself.

Maybe, finally, I am learning that nothing comes from selfish ambition alone. Somewhere, in everyone's life, there is an act of generosity. Somewhere there is something that came from someone else. It happens. It's okay to admit it. You would think after all of this time and with all of these moments of insane generosity, I could get it through my thick skull that good gifts are allowed, even here on a broken earth. Even here in my broken heart.

In this instance (getting a house), I was more uncomfortable than normal, because... well... the biggest reason we were able to have this crazy, amazing thing was because my husband's mother... died. That sound that you just heard? That was my confidence deflating like a balloon.

I never thought I needed a house. In fact I never thought I would ever own a home. We had grad school bills, medical bills, and children to raise. A house was never even on my radar. I didn't want the stability or the responsibility.

Sure, I knew this opportunity was rare. Sure, I knew this was an important thing to do for my children. Sure, it was probably even worth it, I guess. I still didn't like it, and I definitely didn't want to call this gift an inheritance. That was putting a positive spin on something sad and painful. I couldn't do that anymore... all of my spin was already spun. Besides, I would have gladly given up our house for a few more years with Grandma Carmen.

Yet, there I was again, about to do the impossible.

I know many of you out there know what it is like to be transient. To float from place to place without being sure of where you would "land" next. When you are young and without children, it can be an adventure. Once you enter into parenthood, reluctantly or not, the burden of providing a stable environment to your children becomes paramount. To anyone who has had a semi-permanent place of residence, this will not make sense to you. It is one of those things you do not realize how important it is until you *don't* have it.

We were lucky. Even with our crazy situation, we were never homeless. We were rootless, constantly in transition, but not homeless. We always ended up with a place to live.

I already mentioned the three adults and one newborn in a one-bedroom apartment in NYC, so I don't need to belabor that point. That was really just the beginning of our housing adventure. From our small place in NYC, we moved to the small two bedroom apartment in Boston, which I have also already mentioned. I also already covered our first two apartments in SC with the smell of smoke and war on bugs. Still, thank God, right? A place to live is by far better than nothing.

From the roach war zone, we were blessed once again with an incredible gift. A pastor and his wife were going to take a mission trip overseas for a period of two years. While they were gone, they were looking for someone to take care of their house. There is no way to explain the luxury we were dropped into. This house was gorgeous. It was clean, smoke-free and BUG free. It was also huge! Everywhere we had ever lived before would fit into the kitchen and family room of this house. It was almost impossible to comprehend. I often said it was like asking for a glass of water and getting a milkshake. It felt so incredibly decadent.

However, when you need water, a milkshake isn't necessarily the best thing to drink. There is a price to pay with luxury. Particularly, luxury that doesn't actually belong to you. Heating, cooling, cleaning all come at a price, a price that was painful and stressful at times to pay. But, it was also one of the biggest steps forward we had received in long time. It was something positive. Something beyond our circumstances. A ray of hope.

That hope bloomed into the hearts of our little family. It grew and it slowly brought change to the wandering spirits of the vagabonds, until finally, we were ready to find a place to settle. It was time to find a place to rest.

Since neither my husband nor I particularly cared about owning a home, we had to be convinced. Okay, okay, cajoled, persuaded, *forced* to think this was a good idea. We did not think owning a home was worth the hassle. Neither one of us cared about having a permanent place to "be." Again, when it's the right thing to do, it's the right thing to do. I say that although even now I still don't believe it.

One of the biggest reasons we even considered the idea of obtaining a home was planted in the heart of our youngest daughter. She was desperate for something permanent in her life. She was desperate for something good and solid that she could rely on. It did not take a rocket scientist to understand why she needed this. The signs were everywhere.

It's true, our youngest daughter survived the move. She also weathered our first couple of years in a new place. She even made it through her first year of preschool. But, it is also true that for the rest of her life, she would always go from some doctor's version of stable to a major medical intervention. It's a never-ending truth for me, but it is an overwhelming constant for her. She had finally grown old enough to understand just enough about her situation to develop a very real fear of death.

This fear was so thick, you could almost feel it. It leaked out of her sweet little body in the strangest of ways. I think, like her mother, she couldn't talk about how she was feeling so she acted it out instead. She was clingy, whiny, full of trepidation, and scared to be out of my sight even for a moment.

She went to a gymnastics class, but I had to stand in the

corner of the room where she could see me at all times.

She swam on swim team, but I had to walk up and down the side of the pool next to her, so anytime she turned her head to breathe she could see me.

Other parents didn't get it. Other parents told me to be tough, to not give in to her "shenanigans." Nobody had any idea how vital it was that she feel safe.

It was exhausting, but I would do it all again in a second. It was a necessary part of walking my daughter through an insanely scary situation. Unfortunately, this made it very difficult to do even the most simple of activities. Things like going to school were practically impossible.

First grade was the worst. She screamed and cried and clung to me EVERY single morning when I dropped her off. The teachers had to physically rip her from me. Not in a "having a little separation anxiety" kind of way, but in a separation-anxiety-multiplied-by-10,000 kind of way. It was a gut wrenchingly difficult, embarrassing, uncomfortable, harsh reality. It broke my heart and my spirit every day.

I could tell she had tolerated all that she could stand. I could tell she was losing her ability to cope. Yes, she had hung on to her joy way better than I had but it was obvious she was falling down a hole and I needed to act quickly to pull her back out. It takes a psychotic breakdown to recognize the beginning of a psychotic breakdown. Since I had been here before, I knew the way out.

It took several months of consistent work before I got to the bottom of her anxiety about school.

"Mommy," she finally admitted to me. "I am just so afraid I might die while I am away from you. I'm scared, Mommy. I don't want to die alone."

Not really the words I wanted to hear from my sweet six-year- old who didn't ask for any of this to be dumped on her plate. Not really the words I wanted to hear from anyone, but she had a point. The truth was, death was not only a possibility for her, but a high probability. Overcoming an irrational fear of death is one thing, trusting in the possibility of life is something else entirely.

I racked my brain for ways to make this better. I searched and searched for ways to help her make sense of all this.

What in the world could I do to make this better for her?

She gave me all the clues I needed, it just took me a while to catch up.

Multiple times while we were living in the house where we were house sitting she would say to me, "Mommy, in the next house where we live can the stuff in the house just be 'our' stuff?"

"Sure, Sweet Pea," I would answer, because I didn't have the strength to explain I couldn't make that promise come true.

"Mommy," she would ask again, "in the next place where we live can I decide what colors the walls in my room will be?"

"Sure, bug," I would answer, because discussing wall colors was not at the top of my list of things to do.

"Mommy, in the next house where we live can we have only our furniture?"

"Sure."

"Mommy, in the next house where we live..."

You get the picture. She's a creature of habit when she is asking for something she wants.

Over and over and over again, she said these things. Most of the time, I ignored her, or blew her off, or down right shut her down because I could not dream with her. I could not hope with her for the impossible. She might as well have been asking for the moon.

That brings us back to the beginning of the chapter and to the subject of home. For the first time in our married life, my husband and I agreed it was time to put down some of our own roots. The only question left was HOW?

The God of the universe might have used my sweet, fragile daughter to open up our hearts to this idea, but it was my mother-in-law who made it physically, earthly possible.

My daughter *always* had a special place in her Grandma Carmen's heart. She never called my baby daughter by her given name only. She always called her, "My heart! My Ella Victorious!"

She was proud of this survivor. She celebrated our baby girl sometimes more than we did. She was removed enough from the hardship to enjoy the party. She would have given anything to this little girl. All I had to do was get out of the way.

What a privilege that in my life I have gotten to be home, twice. What a privilege that my daughter had this piece of stability, before she went through her third heart surgery. What a privilege to be able to say thank you for the gift of the impossible.

Thank you, Grandma Carmen. Thank you for the moon.

CHAPTER THIRTY TWO

CLOSING CREDITS

Those who sow with tears
will reap with songs of joy.

Psalm 126:5 (NIV)

OPEN: SUBURBIA/SOUTH CAROLINA/EVENING

CAMERA HOLDS on exterior of small house. DADDY
pulls up in car and walks up sidewalk to front
door. He is about to insert key into lock when
he glances into window next to door.

From DADDY's POV CAMERA closes in on window and
"looks" inside.

It is a small house but it is cheery, happy,
colorful. MOMMY and two DAUGHTERS are sitting
on the couch watching a movie. For a moment we
peek into their life.

CAMERA HOLDS on their faces while the end of the

movie plays across their skin. When the movie
ends, the mother and the daughters look at each
other with expectation. With glee, all three
jump up and start dancing. There is no sound, we
don't hear any music. That is unnecessary. All
we need to see is the sweet abandon of a mother
and two daughters dancing together.

CAMERA CUTS BACK TO DADDY's face. He smiles.
Enters house to join the party.

> VOICE-OVER/MOMMY
> This is what you do at the
> end of a movie. You dance.

CAMERA pulls back from scene exiting home slowly
as music begins to play.

FADE TO BLACK

Of all the things I have discussed in this book, this is the
moment that matters the most. This is my favorite memory. I
recognize it as an important turning point in my story. This was
when a large piece of my sadness turned to joy.

My daughters and I had just finished watching a movie
together. It was late at night, but we weren't sleepy. We were
loving our movie, our popcorn and our time together. I'm sure
we had stayed up late, just us girls.

We were watching a princess movie. Yes, you heard me. We
were watching a princess movie. Definitely not my first choice,
but it was our baby girl's turn to choose and so, yes, it was a
princess movie.

I am not certain exactly which princess movie was in the

queue, but that's not important. What matters is it was exactly the kind of movie my youngest daughter really loves. The kind of movie that was full of adventure and romance. Her favorite part was always the end when the two main characters fell in love. She was only eight, so it was totally adorable.

Thankfully, I did not feel the need to "set her up" with some version of feminist reality, no matter how much I thought I needed to in a former version of myself. Princesses and I never really got along. Thank goodness not everyone in the world agrees with me. Thank goodness there are those out there who dream with big romantic hearts and emotions. They are the ones reaching out to the heart of my sweet, emotional, dreamy, romantic daughter. After all, there is enough reality in her world. She can dream and hope and escape as much as she wants as far as I'm concerned.

At the end of the movie, the credits were rolling and a song started to play. It was a catchy tune that even I couldn't resist (princess movies really have come a long way). I had watched the end of sappy romance movies with my daughter before. I knew what to expect.

I looked at my youngest and said, "You want to dance to the credits don't you?"

She nodded yes and said, "You too, Mommy. Come on!"

So we danced to the credits like a couple of crazy people. We looked like idiots, but we didn't care. We were having a blast.

My older daughter joined in too, even though, like me, she is not a fan of sappy romance. It didn't matter, the truth is that neither of us were able to resist the spirit of this joyful little girl.

When Daddy came home from work, he jumped in and started dancing too. A party just isn't a party until he arrives.

In that sweet moment, I couldn't help but feel a little bit like we were in the middle of our own movie, and we had gotten to the final scene. All the sadness and the ugliness and the pain and the hardship that was endured during our movie was for one moment behind us. This would be the part of the movie when the audience would be crying and laughing and rejoicing with us, because we represent hope... because we are dancing.

The mother, who barely survived the fight, is dancing.

The little girl who was not supposed to be born, who faces down death every morning she wakes up alive, is dancing.

For one brief moment, the dad drops everything that represents stress, responsibility, and work and starts dancing.

Even the cool older sister refuses to sit and watch... because we are dancing.

In the face of adversity.

In the middle of a storm.

With all of our multiple scars.

We are dancing.

And dancing.

And dancing.

ROLL CREDITS

WHERE ARE THEY NOW?

Behind the Scenes of the Making of the
Movie Memoir Screenplay Novel

In the publishing process, it is often wise to grab a group of willing readers to read your book before it releases. Sometimes, these irreplaceable beta readers give you invaluable suggestions. One of those suggestions was I should write an epilogue. I agree. Sometimes, people need closure.

I wish I could tie a big red bow on this story and call it "over," but that's not how it always works in memoirs. Can I say that things are perfect now? No, I can't. The circumstances around our story haven't changed, but we, the main characters, have. Besides, "perfect" is definitely overrated.

My husband and I are still together. I know for a while there it seemed like we might not make it, but so far so good. I do not know what the future holds for us, but for today we are choosing love.

My youngest daughter is doing great. She has gotten to enjoy a season of health for which we are enormously grateful. Yes, she still wrestles with fear. Yes, she will always have more medical interventions. Yes, she will have more heart surgeries. Even with all of that, she is surviving. She is thriving. We continue to work through her situation one day at a time. Every moment we have with her is precious.

My oldest daughter has also continued to thrive with determination, passion, dedication and independence. All the things that make her strong, and also sometimes annoying, are the character traits that have helped her survive our situation. If she didn't have these qualities, I do not know if she would have weathered our storm as well as she did.

Physically, I am doing the best I can. I wish my body would let me do more. There are days when the weather outside is perfect and the part of me that used to run calls out to me, begging me to "go." Everything in me wants to strap on running shoes and take off. That's when I have to stay strong, resist the urge, and make a choice to protect my body from itself. It's hard, but I know it's the right thing to do.

Some days when I go for a bike ride, my legs will ache from my pelvis down to my toes. I have to stop, take a rest, and remind myself that there was a point in my life where I couldn't move my legs at all, and I remind myself to pedal more gently.

And then there are those days when I am in the pool doing water aerobics with people who are 20 years my senior, *and* I am unable to keep up. I have to laugh at the absurdity of it all. *No, I am not the athlete I used to be*, I remind myself. Then, I go back to flipping my flippers. It's what I can do, and I have to find a way to let that be enough.

Emotionally, I am doing much better. I have been able to receive a lot of healing. I am not beyond it all, not completely, but I am better. I can almost carry on an entire conversation without breaking down into a pile of blubbering mess. *Almost.*

I try to make sure I talk to my husband more openly about what is going on in my head. I *work hard* to talk more openly with friends. I try to do a better job sharing my story. Writing helps. If you have a lot of junk in your life to unload, I suggest you write a book. It's very cathartic.

I have also made progress spiritually. I rediscovered my faith. I just had to take a leap *into* the darkness, and trust that God would meet me there. It was in that new and unknown place that I was finally able to replace some of my grief with joy. It took years and lots of self discipline, but yes, I got there... eventually. I also listened to a lot of music. Music helped me remember there are better things in life than wallowing in grief.

Maintaining this place of joy is not easy. It is constantly a choice I make each morning to embrace or ignore. Making this choice doesn't change my circumstances and it doesn't mean the things I am dealing with suddenly stop hurting. It only means I have an opportunity to choose a better way to "deal." Yep, you guessed it, still a work in progress.

Any other closure you might need, any other questions you may have, can be directed to my social media accounts (BettsKeating-Author, @bettskeating) or to my website: www.bettskeating.com.

All the praise and encouragement you may have about this story, you can discuss continuously amongst yourselves or post in numerous fashions on any and all social media. All criticism you may have about this story you can email to:

bettskeating@iprobablywontreadthissodontwasteyourtime.com.

Thanks for watching.

ACKNOWLEDGMENTS

First, I need to thank my family for their existence, because without them this story would have been incredibly boring. I also need to thank them for being my biggest fans and my most enthusiastic cheerleaders. I cannot count how many times my husband and my daughters said, "Keep going! You can do it!" They were right.

Second, thanks to my extended family, especially my sister. Again and again and again, thank you.

Third, I need to thank the ladies of my critique group for the incomprehensible number of times they read this manuscript and gave me insight. It has been a delight to work with each of you.

Fourth, I would like to thank all of my beta readers. Each of you provided invaluable comments that made my writing better. Thanks for helping me to clarify the details.

Fifth, thank you to the ladies at Relevant Pages Press for believing in this project enough to slap your logo on it and put your reputation behind it.

Sixth, thanks to all of our incredibly generous, sweet friends who gave of your time, your vehicles, your homes and your money to help us. You are irreplaceable.

Seventh, thanks to my friend Penny who kept calling me... and calling me... and calling me...

Eighth, thanks to my friend Laura who will forever, in my mind at least, be wearing a ninja suit.

Finally, thanks to you, reader, for taking the time to read this book. Without you, there really is no point in writing

and... THAT'S A WRAP!

Made in the USA
Columbia, SC
10 June 2019